Christopher Burns [illegible] Cumbria. During recent yea[illegible] e *London Review of Books*, *L*[illegible] *rist* is his first novel.

CHRISTOPHER BURNS

Snakewrist

PALADIN
GRAFTON BOOKS
A Division of the Collins Publishing Group

LONDON GLASGOW
TORONTO SYDNEY AUCKLAND

Paladin
Grafton Books
A Division of the Collins Publishing Group
8 Grafton Street, London W1X 3LA

Published in Paladin Books 1988

First published in Great Britain by
Jonathan Cape Ltd 1986

Some of the material in this book first appeared as a short story, 'Differential Structures', in the *London Review of Books*, 1983

ISBN 0-586-08660-9

Printed and bound in Great Britain by
Collins, Glasgow

Set in Ehrhardt

For June, Paul and Iain

Part One

1

That afternoon, before the captive arrived, everything seemed peaceful by the river. Sophie sat beside the water with Dexter's book closed around her fingers. She had been reading it again, but away from the trees the sun was so hot that she had tilted her head to the light. It was pleasant just to close her eyes, to relax and drift in the warmth. Then there was a sudden clamour.

She stood up, the book still in her hand, and looked up the incline to where the villagers were chattering and whooping. For a short while she stood and wondered what was going on, and whether she would be allowed to take part.

She had befriended many of the villagers; now two of them came leaping and shouting down the hill. They skipped and turned to show how exciting all this was. Their skin was brown and shone with health and their penis sheaths bounced as they ran. They took hold of Sophie's arms and began to coax, pull and push her up the hill.

Sophie felt her heart drop away in panic. In a moment of terrifying doubt, she wondered if they had turned against her. She thought that perhaps her moment had arrived. Martyrdom could be only minutes away.

She did not think there would be a captive. She thought only of her own place in things, of the working out of a plan. Here, thousands of miles from home, in an endless forest among savage Indians, she would meet her fate.

But as she neared the throng, and as she was jostled through the bare limbs and backs, she began to realize that something else was happening. It was not Sophie who was the centre of interest. No; they were merely going to show her something the whole village was proud of – a rare animal, perhaps, an unusual find, or some kind of trophy.

The warrior leader strode within the circle. His face and body were barred with black and red, and a porcupine quill was passed through the flesh between his nostrils. He walked rapidly round his admirers, raising a hand full of spears and shaking them so their shafts rattled furiously. He had extended his lower lip by inserting a wooden plug between lip and gum. His voice was insistent and ranged from guttural to high. Sometimes the men broke into cries of approval or stamped their feet; the women, some with children hanging on them, hissed with admiration.

The captive was a child.

It stood naked in the centre of the circle, its eyes bruised with tears and its face numb with shock. Sophie, unexpectedly faced with the likelihood of someone else's death, was relieved and, immediately, ashamed. She hated herself for her own fear and selfishness.

The warrior claimed the child. He seized the boy by the upper arm and swung him in the air, rattling the spears in his other hand. He strutted past the villagers, bellowing his own pride. The boy's face creased and squealed in terror and pain. It was a high, shivering noise. Sophie, picking up the shock of the detail, saw how the boy's buttocks and legs were stained where he had lost control of his bowels.

It would be safest to let events take their own course. But Sophie was overwhelmed by concern for the child. And she had begun to think that this might not be an accident. He could be her responsibility.

She had difficulty following individual words at this speed and inflexion, but their meaning was clear enough. The warrior let go of the boy. He fell in the dust and lay half-crouched with his limbs shaking. The warrior slapped his chest, stamped, bared his teeth. His face blazed with darkness and pride. *He*, tracker, killer, Toothedjaws, had increased all their honour by this deed. *He*.

This went on for about half an hour. The villagers put up a high, ululating song. The other warriors gave their versions and visions of the raid, re-enacting with extravagantly balletic whirls and leaps how they had broached the enemy, split their skulls, scattered their women, fired their homes. The chieftain told again and again how he had seized the child and carried it through the forest. The gods had applauded him as he ran.

After a while everyone seemed to lose interest. Quite suddenly, as if there were nothing else to say or do, they drifted away. The boy lay curled up in the dust, hunched in on himself. His flanks twitched like those of a speared animal.

Sophie knew what would happen. If he were not recaptured and vengeance taken, then he would grow up as one of them. But in all likelihood he would not live for much longer than a few months. If he fretted, or food was short, or they had to move quickly and he had no family to care for him, then he would be abandoned in the forest. Either that or, without compunction, they would kill him.

She had been trying to appear unconcerned throughout all this ritual, but she had been so tense that her fingers ached where they had gripped Dexter's book. She watched the chieftain turn, the last to go, and walk towards a hut. The spears trembled gently in his fist. Sophie bent and picked up the child.

The boy's head lolled as though he were entranced, in a swoon. He stank of his own insides.

No one stopped Sophie as she carried the boy down the incline. She had to brace herself carefully to avoid slipping. The boy's glossy black hair bounced as she walked.

Sophie returned to where she had been sitting. Dozens of yellow butterflies had settled by the river bank and were feeding there, their long wings trembling slightly in the still air. They rose in a wild dispersing cloud as Sophie placed the boy in the river. The shock of the water seemed to revive him and he managed to stand. He looked at Sophie uncomprehendingly. On top of all the violence and horror and terror here was a new, frightening, demonic creature. He did not even know what sex it was. Its hair and skin were the wrong colour, the colour of painted dust; it smelled wrong; its clothes or costume felt extraordinary and strange. The creature was trussed up in them from toes to neck. Its eyes were made wrongly.

It was completely alien.

Sophie washed the boy by splashing him with water and then

rubbing his skin with wet hands. It was the way she had watched Indian parents do it.

Afterwards she put the boy on the ground where she had been sitting. The boy looked up at her with deep, shocked eyes.

Before his arrival she had been going to eat a fruit. She found it and handed it to him. He took it, recognized it, and wolfed it down noisily as if he had not eaten for days. Juice made his mouth and cheeks glisten.

But his flanks were still quivering with shock so, thinking she had better keep him warm, Sophie took off her tunic and put it over his shoulders. The boy drew in his breath and tried to move away, but she held his shoulders and placed it back on him. After a short while he seemed to accept it.

The boy dropped the stone of the fruit. Then he reached out for the book. Surprised, Sophie handed it to him.

The boy handled it in a strange, unfamiliar way. His fingers spread across it. He brushed the corners, the spine, held it to his nostrils and sniffed loudly. Experimentally, cautiously, he put out his tongue and touched the binding with its tip.

The book opened in his hands, the leaves fanning out with a light whirr. The boy dropped it in surprise. It fell page-down in the dust and the boy drew himself away from it as if it was some strange animal waiting to strike.

'It's a book,' Sophie said. They were the first words she spoke to him.

He looked at her, stunned by it all.

She bent down and picked up the book, dusting the pages and straightening them where the fall had creased them. She didn't know what to do with the boy. She had no experience of children at all.

She opened the book at the title page and frontispiece. There was a photograph of a handsome white man. He stood beside an Indian. The boy peered at this extraordinary vision.

'*Journey to the Interior*,' she said, pointing to the title. Then she pointed to the white man. She felt stupid but didn't know why. No one was there to understand her.

'*By Dexter Parnaby*,' she went on. 'My brother.'

The child looked at her. Nothing she said or did made any sense to him. He was marooned in an alien world.

A cry came from the village. High and drawn out. The boy flinched.

Sophie reached out and took his arm gently. 'It's all right,' she said. She knew he couldn't understand but she hoped that, at some deeper level, her words and the way in which she spoke them would reassure him. 'It's all right. You're with me now. I won't let anything happen to you.'

The boy looked round. Tears started to fill his eyes again.

'You're safe,' she said, '*safe*.'

2

'His sister?'

Sophie nodded and, despite herself, gave a slight smile. She had never courted recognition, but it still pleased her.

'He died,' Toby said, and then felt that he had said something crass and ruined his chances.

'A long time ago.'

'It must have been a terrible tragedy,' he continued, hoping to sound considerate.

Sophie was silent. Toby looked directly at her. She was, he supposed, in her early sixties, but she had retained an angular, English kind of handsomeness. Her face was long, almost equine, and her eyes were sharp and alert. She sat with a pen in one hand looking at the notes she had jotted on the desk pad. Toby's CV lay to one side.

'An accident, wasn't it?'

'The plane must have come down somewhere,' she said, 'he could never have survived. Do you know his book?'

Toby was so pleased with his good fortune that he had to lean forward for a second and angle his face away from her to hide a smirk of self-congratulation. 'Yes,' he admitted, composing himself, 'originally published – what? Early fifties?'

'Fifty-two in England, the following year in New York.'

Almost exactly a year before his interview, Toby had helped a Chilean friend catalogue a diplomat's private library. The library had been full of histories, geographies and reference works on all of South America. It had also contained a number of travel books, many of them in English. Dexter Parnaby's had been among them, in an American edition with a specially written preface for American readers. Toby had whiled away a few idle hours by skipping through parts of it.

'It's out of print now,' he said.

'I still get letters from people who find it in libraries or second-hand bookshops. We have several copies, of course. I always used to carry one with me whenever I went away.'

'Of course,' Toby said. He shifted his weight in the chair and it creaked beneath him.

The interview was being held in a mahogany office. The wood was dark and shiny, as if it had been waxed and polished for several generations of lawyers. Toby was happy in such dark, Victorian surroundings. Many of the people he had studied with had gone on to work in libraries with air conditioning and lights like those in operating theatres; Toby was used to polish, dust, and enclosed wooden spaces that suffocated the light. He could easily imagine Sophie's father, and her grandfather, coming to these offices to sort out the family finances and property. Calendars going back years were fixed to the wall.

A specialist bookseller, hired for the day for his technical knowledge, sniffed loudly. Toby felt intuitively that the man would have loved to get his hands on the Parnaby collection. Unlike Toby, he would see things merely in terms of their monetary value.

'Fashions change, Mr Savage,' Sophie said briskly, 'you will appreciate that as well as anyone.'

'It would be nice to see it back on shelves,' Toby murmured.

'And you will no doubt find that certain items on our shelves have, shall we say, become devalued by the whims of fashion. But the whole collection is varied and, I believe, interesting.'

'Did you say your father started it?'

'He loved books. We all did. Dexter was brought up on adventure stories.'

The bookseller coughed. 'Adventure stories,' he mumbled.

They both looked at him.

'I'd like to ask you something about those,' he said. And he then asked Toby several slowly worded questions about early Marryat editions, the illustrations of the Brock brothers, and the bindings of Greville. They were textbook questions. Toby could answer them all. The bookseller snorted quietly and sank back into his chair.

Toby licked his lips slightly. He had prepared lots of little speeches and anecdotes that could have helped his case. He could have told amusing stories about vandals, bad translations, banned works, lost volumes. He had already mentioned pedigree copies, developments in lettering, and misprints. But he was ready to talk for a great deal longer if need be.

'And the texts themselves,' Sophie said.

'Yes?'

She looked up at him. 'A book is more than covers, pages, print, don't you think?'

He stammered just slightly. 'Yes. You're right. The most famous example being the Bible. The book is more than just a book.'

'Almost an ideal?'

Uncertain, he nodded. 'That's right,' he agreed.

Sophie studied Toby. He did not flinch beneath her gaze. She picked up his application form. 'It says on your CV that you have written a little yourself.'

'In a small way. Just a few articles.'

'But you helped in the research on two books.'

'The first when I was at university.The second was later. A lot of that sort of thing goes on. I got a mention in the acknowledgements, that was all.'

'And your contribution was worth more than that?'

'It was substantial.'

'I see.'

Sophie didn't know whether to believe him or not. It was certain, she felt, that he was crediting himself with more experience than he actually possessed. But she could not blame him for that; he was obviously keen to take on the job.

Sophie took to Toby. It couldn't be called a liking; Toby was not, in Sophie's eyes, a likeable person. But of all the applicants, it was Toby who showed the peculiar kind of ambition that Sophie was looking for. He sat easily in the old leather chair. He wore a dark, conservatively styled jacket. He seemed, physically, to be a very ordinary young man, with nothing special to distinguish him. Of all the applicants, it was Toby who looked the least individual, the most bland. But she was sure that beneath all his confidence there was a level of uncertainty and indecision. She knew he could be led.

And below that there was something else. She could sense it, almost taste it. He wanted to be someone. He wanted to make something of his life. He was metallic with selfishness and moral ambition.

He was just what she wanted.

3

He identified the library. It was at the top of the house, overlooking the square. If he walked around the padlocked garden at the centre of the square he could still see its window through the leaves of the plane trees. The blind was always down.

Toby had been through the square several times, approaching it from different angles, all the time taking sightings on the house as he passed it. He had researched two local histories and the London Pevsner in the same way as he'd searched for Sophie Parnaby in the society columns and *Who's Who*. He had found out a lot about the square, a little about the house, and next to nothing about Sophie Parnaby. Given time, though, he thought, he would track her down through old travel books, histories of exploration, and newspaper files.

And he was eager, but slightly apprehensive, about his first day. At the interview he had formed the impression that very few people were welcome in the house. Society shunned the Parnaby home, or was simply excluded.

Toby was curious about the job and excited by its prospects. But he was, he liked to think, professional in his approach. Now he was being the detached, efficient observer. The man who took note, registered facts. Not much would get by *him*. He thought of himself in the same context as an agent spying out the land, a burglar checking before a break-in. He was, after all, studying the group he would infiltrate.

But he saw remarkably little – a delivery of food or fuel down the servants' steps, a postman sliding letters through the box, and sometimes a youngish girl (a maid, he supposed) coming or going from the servants' entrance. And that was all. Once he hung on to the railings at the other side of the gardens, trying to find a way of being comfortable on the spikes, and observed the house carefully. He thought that he was screened by the leaves, and stood there for half an hour until a small ugly woman with a waddling dachshund unlocked the gate nearest to him, went into the garden, and locked it again, all the time staring suspiciously at him. He couldn't take the chance that she knew Sophie Parnaby, so he walked quickly away. All the time he had been there he had seen nothing move within the house.

Of Sophie Parnaby there was no sign. Although once, out of the corner of his eye, Toby thought he saw her. He was hurrying past on an imaginary task. In case he was beginning to be recognized he had borrowed Lucy's bodywarmer just to make him look slightly different. It fitted him tightly but he did not dare zip it up in case he broke it. He was easing it by wriggling his shoulders when he saw what he thought was a woman looking out of a window. She had edged herself between the glass and the lace curtain. She was looking straight at him. He did not dare stop in case she recognized him and realized that he was spying on her, so he put his head down and walked a little too quickly from the square. Once in the streets around it he felt that he had escaped, but also that he had turned his back on something important.

'I've seen her,' he said to Lucy.

'Who?' Lucy was preparing a salad. Wooden bowls of vegetables stood in front of her.

'None other than – ' Toby said, and brought his half-cupped hands to his lips to blow an imaginary fanfare. 'So*ph*ie *Parnaby*.' He spoke like a ringmaster.

'You didn't call, did you?'

'She was just standing at the window. I was on my way to Dillons and I just – '

'You don't go that way to Dillons, surely?'

'I decided to go that way. On impulse. I needed a walk.'

She sliced a tomato and pulled a face as some of the pulp slithered on to the board.

'I'm pretty sure it must have been her.'

'What was she doing?'

'Nothing.'

'Maybe she was watching you pretending to be there by accident.'

Toby gave a slight, dismissive hiss at the suggestion, although he knew he had not been meant to take it seriously. He picked up a lettuce leaf, folded it as symmetrically as he could, and put it into his mouth. He spoke while he was chewing it. 'If only I'd known beforehand that it would be Dexter Parnaby's sister,' he said, 'I would have had a better advantage.'

'But you did fine. You must have come top of the list.'

Toby considered this. 'Yes,' he agreed, picking up a slice of tomato.

'This is supposed to be eaten in about ten minutes, not now.'

'But you'll forgive me,' he said, and was surprised at the lack of humour in his voice. He had meant to sound lighthearted.

'I usually do. And maybe they didn't want to attract the wrong sort of applicants.'

He looked quizzically at her.

'You know what I mean. Perhaps they wanted a broader, more adaptable person rather than someone who specialized in a very narrow field. They know what the job requires; they should know the kind of person they want to do it.'

'They wanted the real me, you mean?'

'You needn't sneer.'

'I'm not.'

They exchanged glances and when she smiled at him he returned the smile, but when her back was turned and he was certain he couldn't been seen in the mirror, he pulled a face at her.

On the day that the job started Toby was early despite himself. By half an hour. He paced around the side streets with a bladder that always seemed full no matter how many times he emptied it. Nervousness had come unexpectedly, and all his detachment had gone. He felt all the symptoms, and knew that when he had to speak he would trip over his tongue, then say things that were so foolish he would want to disappear by dropping through the floor. He prayed he wouldn't blunder into some priceless ornament, send it crashing to the floor where it would shatter beyond recovery. Or that he wouldn't pick up a book that was unique and priceless and then hold it so that the binding tore, or let it fall so that all the pages would be bent and creased forever.

He was still early, although by only five minutes, when he went up the five steps to the front door. The door was a deep and glossy blue, the letter-box of polished brass. The doorbell was set in the stone lintel. He had the feeling of breathlessness he had always experienced before a speech or a reading; a sense that the voice would weaken and fade, leaving its owner mute and stupid in front of everyone else.

Toby pressed the bell.

He expected to hear it sound deep within the house, made tinny by distance, but he heard nothing.

He wondered if it was out of order. While he considered this he turned and looked round the square, at the parked cars, at the trees ringed by spiked railings. Pigeons strutted between the Volvos and Rovers. The ugly neighbour stood in the centre of the garden with her dog squatting beside her. It was defecating with a furious concentration. Toby tried to appear purposeful and businesslike.

The door opened.

The last thing he would have expected to see was a South American Indian. A maid, perhaps, or even a grave-faced butler. He wouldn't have been surprised by a Filipino or a Hong Kong Chinese. But this?

Not that there was anything wrong with the way the man dressed. He wore dark, sober clothes, with a collar and tie and expensive black shoes. He could have been a business executive about to attend a boardroom meeting. But above the collar and tie the face was copper-brown, the skin smooth and almost shiny. The eyes, which were full and black, had the neutral, slightly angled look Toby had seen in documentaries. They were set above wide cheekbones. If they had been European eyes Toby would have been able to make something of them; as it was they were opaque and oddly intimidating. He could read nothing into them.

'Good morning, sir.'

Toby said nothing. The accent, though heavy, did not obscure the clarity of the words. Toby realized that he had expected the man to be incomprehensible.

'Good morning sir.'

'Ah – good morning,' Toby said in a rush, 'my name's Toby Savage. I'm expected.'

'Yes, sir.' Toby couldn't place the accent at all. He felt there were elements of Portuguese or Spanish in it, but there seemed to be a trace of North American as well.

'I'm going to catalogue the library,' he said, and wondered if he should be explaining himself in this way.

'Please come in.'

Once inside Toby began to feel more at ease. For better or worse, the contract had begun. He was reminded, curiously, of a visit to the dentist's. He had always hated having treatment, and postponed his visits as long as possible, but once he was in the surgery he was content enough to go along with the arrangement.

'I will take your coat.'

Toby hesitated. He was wearing a light anorak because the morning had begun with an unseasonably heavy shower.

'Mr Savage?'

He had ceased to be *sir*. 'Yes. Thanks.' Toby slipped off the anorak, remembering as he did so that the inside sleeve of the right arm was loose as almost all the stitching had parted. He hoped it wouldn't be folded so it showed.

The Indian hung the anorak in a small cloakroom to one side of the door. Toby could see a row of metal pegs, that was all.

'My name is Jorge.'

'Ah. Yes.'

'I shall show you to the library.'

'Yes, fine. But what about Miss Parnaby?'

'Miss Parnaby is not here at the moment. If I can answer any of your questions?'

'Not here?'

Jorge shook his head.

'You mean, not in the house?'

'Not in the country.'

'I see.'

'But you may ask me whatever you wish. I will do my best to help with any problems.'

'Okay. Right.'

Toby felt unsettled by this exchange. Here was another thing he had not expected. Whenever he had thought of the job he had imagined being introduced to it by Sophie Parnaby; had visualized a guided tour of the shelves, being given a history of the collection, handed choice volumes to admire.

'One thing, cataloguer.'

Nor had he expected to be addressed in such a way. And Jorge made a slightly guttural sound on the *l*, turning the word into something strange.

'The library is at the top of the house. When you go to it, when you come from it, you pass other rooms. These rooms are private. Do you understand?'

Normally Toby would have smiled and nodded, as if such things need not even have been mentioned, but Jorge's sense of command made him lower his eyes despite himself.

'You needn't worry,' he said, 'I know my job.'

A long hall stretched out before them, with parquet showing on either side of a strip of dark carpet. At the bottom of the stairs, placed so that everyone going up would see it on the wall, was a photograph of Dexter Parnaby. He stared out of the past, the handsome man of action, with a wide-brimmed hat and bush clothing. There was a leather holster fastened on a belt around his waist and he leaned on the vertical barrel of a rifle. A crucifix was at his neck. It would have hung inside his tunic; he must have taken it out especially for the photograph.

Beside him stood an Indian. The Indian was completely naked but the photographer had placed him so that he stood sideways to the camera, his hand shielding his genitals. The silvering of the print captured the sheen and texture of his flanks. He looked like Parnaby's captive, but Parnaby stared ahead, aloof, composed, unshockable, the faintest trace of a smile on his lips. Such things were a commonplace to him.

'Follow me.'

Toby followed Jorge up the stairs.They were lined with small photographs in frames – portraits, groups, buildings; the family history. He was so busy trying to identify them that it was a while before he noticed that, between the back of his shoe and the bottom of his trouser leg, Jorge's flesh was bare. He could see the Achilles tendon, thick and supple, tense beneath the skin.

At the end of the corridor of the top floor proper there was a large wooden door that had been waxed and polished. He could see the grain running through it. Jorge took a large key from his waistcoat pocket and turned it in the lock.

Toby had expected the door to creak, but it swung quietly and easily on its higes.

'Mr Savage.'

His first impression on stepping into the library was of silence, darkness, and the heavy, gloomy shelves. The room extended from the front of the house to the back. He could make out panels of light at the front windows, which were covered with blinds, and he supposed there to be a further set of windows at the back.

'This is vast,' he said, 'it's going to be a bigger job than I expected.'

The library was long and high-ceilinged. Book upon book hid in the murky light. Immediately in front of the windows were a desk and chair. The wooden floor was on two levels. The desk and chair, which faced down the room, stood on a rectangle of floor that was a step higher than the rest of the library. It was easy to imagine it as a Victorian schoolroom, and perhaps that was what it had been in the past. But now a teacher would look out, not on rows of children, but on the ends of library shelves that led away from him towards the far end of the room.

The door at which they stood opened on the level of the shelves, but just a step or so away was the raised platform. Jorge crossed the floor, stepped up, skirted the desk, opened the blinds. They rasped gently and let in the sunshine. He came back and stood at the desk, holding his palm up like a beggar.

'You see?'

'I didn't expect there to be so many. There are years of collecting here.'

Toby walked down a corridor of books. They lined the shelves with few gaps. As he went he lifted a hand and lightly, gingerly touched their spines. As he walked his touch became heavier.

An identical blind was pulled down over the window at the end of the room. It was the colour of old skin. Toby had to tug at it a couple of times to free it and then raise it. It rolled around its spindle to reveal, through the glass, a small private garden surrounded by high walls of red brick.

He turned and walked back down the centre aisle to Jorge. His footsteps echoed round the shelves. Jorge stood behind the chair with his hands spread across its back.

'Years,' Toby repeated.

Jorge gazed at him impassively.

'I'm sorry, but this is a substantial task. I could be here for quite a while.'

The library was quiet. The books kept their own silence. The only noises were from Toby and Jorge – the slight sounds of weight being shifted, of breathing, of minimal movement.

'Maybe I should have been allowed to see the collection before I started. That would have been the logical way of going about things.'

Jorge pulled back the chair. It squealed against the floorboards.

'Try the seat, Mr Savage. You will have to spend many hours here. It should be comfortable.'

Jorge stood beside the chair, poised as if to ease a diner into his favourite table.Toby took his position and sat down. Jorge pushed the chair gently against the back of his legs.

The chair had a smoothly turned back, but it felt hard, as if it had been designed for someone much heavier. Toby sat forward and put his hands on the desk. The desk top was a sheet of thin green leather. 'You don't find these in many houses any more,' he said.

'So I am told.'

Toby spread his hands on the leather and looked down the avenues of books. They receded like some Renaissance exercise in perspective. But there was something not quite right about the room; some disturbance of the symmetry that he was, as yet, only partly conscious of, but which nevertheless nagged at him. And then he thought that it was merely the variety of the books – all their different sizes, colours and textures. Their irregularity would counter the mathematical precision of the view.

Jorge stood beside him fingers linked. If Toby glanced to one side he could see them in sharp focus. They were strong hands with short, powerful fingers. Fingers that could grip and crush. But the cuffs of his shirt were about an inch too long. They didn't end until about midway between wrist and thumb.

'You like what you see?'

'I'm sure there are lots of interesting volumes on the shelves.'

'You can begin, then.'

'I don't think we discussed what form Miss Parnaby wants the survey to take.'

'Tell me.'

Toby gave him a carefully rehearsed summary of methods of cataloguing, of information and retrieval systems, of the possibilities that were opened if you stored everything in a computer. Jorge listened but did not react. 'And on top of that', Toby went on, 'I need adequate heating. And lighting. This room must get very cold in winter.'

'There are strip lights. And radiators beneath the windows.'

'I hope they're good enough. I'll have to stay in here all the time, and it looks as if I could be here well into next year.'

'We shall see. Now you must inspect the collection. Miss Parnaby has said to me that only you will be able to understand it fully. If you wish to walk downstairs to the basement at about midday we can arrange for you to have something to eat. And now, cataloguer, I will not prevent you from beginning your work.'

When he was alone Toby walked to the end of the library furthest from the door, and immediately understood the failure of perspective. The distance between the shelves was not standard. Between two rows there was a wider gap. He turned round the end of the shelves and saw that, hidden from the desk, there was a wrought-iron spiral staircase. The stairs and the upright were painted black, and the steps were wide enough for one person, no more. The spiral reached the ceiling and stopped.

He climbed them. The noise of his shoes on the metal went funnelling down the shelves. There was a trapdoor cut into the ceiling; he could run his fingers along its edges, see where the brass pivots of hinges protruded through the gap. And there was a keyhole. If he'd been able to unlock the door it would have been easy to push it upwards and step into what he guessed would be an attic, a forgotten storeroom stuffed with household effects.

He returned to the shelves and walked round and round them. Here was the accumulation of half a century's collecting, maybe more. Guides to sciences that were no longer true, testaments to beliefs that had become outdated, biographies of those who had sunk into obscurity, works that had been little known but were now cults or classics or rarity items, books from childhoods that had been wiped away. There were picture books in bright primary colours, war economy books on thin paper and with tiny print, books with tooled spines whose bindings were more valuable than their texts, books with accumulations of dust along the upper edges, books that jutted out awkwardly from their companions or were lost when sandwiched between them, books that looked as if they weighed so much that he was apprehensive about lifting them down, books by authors who were well known and books by people he had never heard of. A universe of books.

He also got to know the shelving. The variations in the wood. Where it had strained under the weight; where it had been chipped; where, in places, a pen had marked it. Sometimes, without really thinking, he tapped or slapped the shelving. It reassured him to hear its solidity.

Toby looked round for a few hours, and in the early afternoon he went down the flights of stairs to the basement of the house. At the back of the building was a large kitchen, just below the level of the garden. The kitchen was modern but glancing round the walls, Toby could see pieces of ducting that were survivals from the turn of the century.

Jorge sat at a wooden table. He had a bowl of chopped food in front of him and a table napkin at one side. He was eating the food with his fingers.

On his left sat a girl, a pleasant-faced, shy creature with large-framed glasses. She looked young; she couldn't have been in work for more than a few years.

'Becky,' Jorge said briefly, nodding at her as he picked up a glistening green stalk and placed it in his mouth.

Toby shook hands and smiled his charming smile. 'Call me Toby,' he said.

Becky seemed flustered by this. He struck up an inconsequential, and in the end rather laboured, conversation about the weather. Jorge sat impassively, not joining in.

'Do you work here all the time,Becky?'

'No, Mr Savage I come in to work. I do, you know, things that I'm told to do. But I live out at Mill Hill.'

'There's a room for Becky here,' Jorge said, 'I think she will have to move. It is more convenient.'

'There are two spare rooms along the corridor,' Becky hesitated, and then said 'Toby', as if she did not really want to use the name. 'Do you want something to eat? Mr George tells me we'll have to look after you while you're here.'

'That's fine, thanks, but it's not really hungry work.'

'Make him something,' Jorge said to her, in a way that Toby thought was surprisingly off hand. 'You know a little more about things now,' he said to Toby.

'Yes. A little more.'

Jorge said nothing. His fingers glistened.

'I'm sure it will be a fascinating collection. There are probably all kinds of things hidden away on the shelves.'

Jorge licked his fingers slowly.

'There's a spiral staircase,' Toby said.

'Yes.'

'It leads to a storeroom, I suppose.'

'Yes.'

Toby smiled. 'I thought the library might be even bigger.'

'But you already think it is very big.'

'Yes, it is. But I wondered if it might be on two levels.'

Jorge shook his head. 'No.'

Toby nodded. 'That's all right, then.' He looked across at Becky, and asked her about Sophie Parnaby. She glanced back at Jorge, as if seeking reassurance. But Jorge just kept looking at Toby.

'She's very nice, really,' she said lamely.

'She's a very famous person, isn't she?'

'Yes,' Becky replied.

'Special, would you say? Unique?'

'Very much so, cataloguer,' Jorge said.

'And, at the moment, Jorge, where is she?'

Jorge waited a moment before answering. 'Abroad,' he said.

By now Lucy had been with Toby for some years. Because she had a regular job, she often supported him during periods when he had not been able to earn much money. She had been happy to do this; it seemed to her that she was fulfilling her part of an unwritten, unspoken bargain. Toby had fascinated her. Never before had she met anyone so bookish and yet, she felt, so approachable. He had told her tall stories about collectors, odd tales about bibliophiles; he had been witty and amusing. And he had a belief in his own capabilities which was infectious, even if it was somewhat unresolved. Lucy came from a background of generalized suspicion about higher culture; to Toby, however, literature and its preservation were his whole life. She was bound to fall for him.

She was even prepared to put up with his moods, which often lasted for days at a time, although when he became so selfish he was a difficult and annoying companion. Lucy taught art at a nearby Comprehensive, and she had pinned up some of her own drawings on the walls of the flat. Toby knew very little about art, so he either extravagantly praised them or kept quiet about them. Once, however, she had made an attempt at writing poetry. He had seized on it and taken it to pieces, only noticing the tears in her eyes when he had finished.

The most recent, and one of the most prolonged, of Toby's bad times had only ended with his appointment to the Parnaby library. Since then he had been more content, and even at times extraordinarily happy. The Parnabys interested him so much that he spoke about them as freely and honestly as he could. Lucy had even stopped examining what he told her; before this, she could tell that he was keeping small secrets from her. Nothing important; just things he obviously did not wish to share with her.

While he was still talking about his first day she leaned over and kissed him on the forehead. 'What's that for?' he asked, surprised.

'Because I love you, and because I haven't seen you so happy for a while. I hope it will last.'

'We'll see, I suppose. There are things about the Parnabys that I find intriguing. Jorge, for instance.'

'The Indian?'

'He doesn't wear socks.'

She laughed.

'It's true,' he said, 'he has bare feet with shoes on. Can you explain that?'

'That's how he came to the door? I wouldn't want people judging *me* on how I answered the door.'

'Ah, but this is different. You would just be yourself. So would I. But he's representing someone.'

'True. But she wasn't there. Possibly his standards slipped.'

Toby settled back in his chair and put his hands behind his head. Lucy could tell he was feeling expansive. 'I don't think so. He doesn't seem the type.' He smiled and added, 'He's a bit of a bastard, really.'

'In what way?'

'Well . . . He's not exactly welcoming, to start off with. He likes to think of himself as quite the little dictator, I should imagine. I wonder how much he knows about the Parnabys?'

'If she left him in charge, then he must know quite a lot.'

Toby nodded. 'They must still have some connections out there. It can't be just a coincidence.' He paused for a few seconds before adding, 'It can't be.'

'Perhaps they wonder about *you*, Toby. About how you'll turn out. What the finished result will be. Where you live and whom you live with.'

'Maybe. You know, I expected to meet her. I was quite surprised when she wasn't there. It was the least I expected.'

'Maybe she had other things to do.'

He looked sharply at her.

'I said *other* things, not *better*,' Lucy remarked. 'You'll meet her again soon. You'll have to.'

'I don't know when she'll be back. He won't be drawn. It could be weeks. Months. I don't even know where she is.'

'Toby, in a few months' time even I will have met her. That's what happens. Everything sorts itself out eventually.'

'You?'

Lucy felt herself shrink. She began to realize that he didn't want her to meet the people he talked about all the time. 'Why – do you think I won't?'

He shrugged. 'Do you especially want to?'

'There's no reason for it, I suppose. It just seemed likely that I would pick you up sometime when you're working there.'

'There would be no need.'

'Oh.'

Toby eased himself down in the chair. 'I don't suppose I would ever develop a social relationship with Sophie Parnaby. Although I could very well have a professional one. She wants me for my technical knowledge, after all.'

Lucy was disappointed. It seemed that he was already deciding to exclude her from one of the most important parts of his life. But then she wondered why even she should expect to have a relationship, even a fleeting one, with people such as the Parnabys.

'You're moving in high circles,' she said wistfully.

'Oh yes,' he answered, half-joking, 'she could be in *Who's Who* if she wanted. Maybe she would list me along with Jorge and Becky as part of the family possessions.'

She took up the jokiness of his comments. 'You'll be in there yourself one of these days.'

'Sometimes I think that could never happen. That the world will never hear of either you or me.'

She couldn't decide if he was now being serious. 'That doesn't sound like you, Toby,' she said breezily, 'unless you're fishing for compliments again.'

'Again?'

She nodded, smiling. He looked puzzled.

'Do I do that?' he asked.

'Not as much as you used to.'

'You're kidding me.'

'It's true. When we first met I thought it was just a form of vanity. You were so self-confident in many ways.'

'You thought I just wanted praise?'

She pursed her lips. 'In a way.'

'I didn't.'

'I found out later what it was. When you were angry and you used to call me a bloody farmer's daughter. You wanted a kind of reassurance, that's all. Don't look so surprised; everyone needs it.'

'You think so?'

'It's one reason why couples stay together.'

'And families?'

'Those as well.'

'You still get support from yours.'

'In lots of ways. Maybe you wouldn't recognize some of them, but I do.'

Toby nodded. Lucy still had strong links with her own parents. And he could tell she harboured a longing for marriage and, especially, children. He imagined her talking this over with her parents at the farm. He knew, too, that she still went to church every few months, although he had always said that he found all form of religious belief to be superstitious nonsense.

None of this was for him. His own parents were both dead now, and the ties with them had always been partial and weak. He had rid himself of the notion that the family was a particularly worthwhile social unit. He recognized that it was possible that he, too, could become a father sometime, but as far as he was concerned that would be in the distant future. And, although it was impossible to decide how, he hoped that it would be in circumstances that were unique.

At the moment he was much more interested in a family that was dying out. After Sophie, the Parnabys would be no more.

He found this simple fact intriguing. And, perhaps because he realized that he also could be the last of a line, it was disturbing as well. After Sophie there would only be the library, unchanged, unaffected, always there with the same perspectives, the same universe of stories, anecdote, speculation, classification.

This was the continuity which thrilled Toby. When he walked among old books he was fascinated by the fact of their survival. And, like all impersonal survivals, the books implied personal extinctions.

4

Toby loved books. He loved their pages, their bindings, the lettering on the spines. He would pick them up, turn them over and around, feel their weight and balance. He knew that there was such a thing as a poorly balanced book. He would heft the volume, run the flat of his hands across the boards, feel the edges and corners with the tips of his fingers. He would tilt the book in the light, seeing how it absorbed the rays. He would open it, holding in his mind some ideal sound – the whisper of the perfectly made volume. What he got was the creak of something not so well made, or the faint sigh of something approaching perfection. Worst of all was the harsh loud crack as glue, hardened by the years, broke along the gummed edges.

He read library plates, inscriptions, title pages, publication dates; he scoured the pages for inserts and annotations. He had found, in other libraries, old postcards, newspaper clippings, funeral cards, leather bookmarks, pressed flowers, love letters, bus tickets, shopping lists. He had come across fragments of other people's lives slipped between the sheets – one word, perhaps, that he could never understand; a mysterious time and place jotted on an otherwise blank piece of paper. In margins he had found carefully scripted references to other books, comment (academic, lexical, incorrect, referential) by unknown hands.

But most of all he loved the texts. In whatever typeface, broken by illustration or not, the slightest brush with the text gave him the feeling of excitement that only print could bring. The sense that, as one opened a book, a whole new world unfolded. Like some physicist's paradox, elements of time and place were folded into the pages.

So it was with the Parnaby library. Attracted by the names of authors, the design of a spine, the smell of paper, he opened volume upon volume. On gastronomy, astronomy, anthropology, biology; on geography and geology, religion and culture; on biography and autobiography; on travel, discovery, search. On world upon world.

He sat at the desk, light spilling from the window at his back. In front of him were the beginnings of his system, at one side a manual of techniques, and, piled at his other hand, a heap of volumes he'd picked from the shelves.

His routine was now so organized that Becky would bring him sandwiches and tea while he worked. Sometimes he would ask her to stay and chat with him. He was still eager to find out more about the household in which he worked.

She was unwilling to talk without being coaxed. And when she knocked it was with a tap that was so light that he scarcely heard it.

Once, when she poured his tea, he said, far more sharply than he'd intended, 'For God's sake don't splash the books.' It made her hand quiver. A fluted wave ran down the liquid.

Once or twice she even joined him. Rather than talk about the Parnabys she told him about her uncle who ran a successful second-hand car business, and about how her mother's health could be better. Toby nodded understandingly all the time.

And gradually he found out that Sophie Parnaby slept in the main bedroom at the back of the house, just under the library; that Becky was closer still to moving in to the bedroom near the kitchen, close to Jorge; that a lawyer visited Sophie, and a man who was, Becky thought, a financial adviser of some kind, and, in particular, members of the church often called. Jorge dealt with them when Miss Parnaby was away.

'Jorge does lots of things,' Toby said.

'You can pronounce his name all right,' she said. 'I make a terrible mess of it. I'm awful at funny pronunciations like that. In the end he just said call me George. It's a lot easier.'

'He comes from South America?'

'Yes. I'm not sure where. Miss Parnaby brought him back, I think. It was all a long time ago. Just after I'd been born.'

'As long ago as that?' Toby said wryly, but she did not notice his tone.

'That's where she is now, I think. Some city out there. She has to go once every couple of years, so George told me. Something about her investments. I don't know where exactly.' She giggled as if all geography were an area of arcane knowledge. 'I only know London. And Dorset. And we went to Majorca twice.'

'She had a very famous brother who got lost out there.'

'Yes. I know. His photographs are on the stairs. And beside her bed. There's a photograph of George there too. As a young boy. He looks really strange in it.'

'You know his book?'

She looked blank.

Toby stood up and walked over to the shelves. There were several copies of *Journey to the Interior* stacked there. He picked one up and opened it in front of her. 'That's him,' he said.

'Is it an old book?'

'Just over thirty years. I think he was trying to find a new route by flying over the jungles. He must have crashed, I suppose. He was never heard of again.'

He held the book out to her. She took it and held it uncomfortably in her hands. 'I knew he'd been killed,' she said, 'people only have photographs round the house like that when someone's died too soon.' She lifted the volume slightly, then lowered it again. Books were a strange territory to her.

'He stood no chance,' Toby said, 'not in that terrain. If you're not killed outright you die very soon afterwards.'

He had expected her to leaf through the book, or at least to show some degree of interest. But she was keen to hand it back to him, and as she did so he realized that she was wary of the printed word.

Toby felt such rejections as insults. He felt not only that he had been dismissed, but that most of the known universe had been deliberately ignored. He grimaced, but did not let Becky see him. It was for his own pleasure and justification.

'When does she come back, Becky?'

'I don't know. Sometime soon, I suppose. But I really don't know.'

He put the book back among the others. 'And she has investments out there? What kind?'

'I really don't know, Toby. I just try and do my job. Their

business is no concern of mine. I can't afford to be nosy and I wouldn't want to be. Jobs are hard to get, you know.'

He smiled. 'Don't I know it,' he said.

'I think they were being charitable even by giving it to me. They're good people.' And, with sudden force, she added, 'They're kind to me.'

He was surprised by the unexpected vigour and did not reply.

'Really kind,' she continued, more subdued and a little sullen.

He gave an innocent's laugh, as if he had been wrongly judged. 'I didn't say they weren't. Did I?'

Lucy and Toby spent the weekend at her parents' farm. It was over three hours from London. Toby dozed against the trembling glass of the train window, and woke with a headache and a dry mouth.

These were still troubling him when they went to bed, and during the night he awoke from a nightmare and found himself clinging to the bedclothes as if he teetered at the edge of a huge, vertiginous, terrifying fall.

'It's only a dream,' Lucy reassured him, 'don't worry, it's only a dream.' And she coaxed him back down beside her and put her arms round him. He was clammy with sweat. In the morning he remembered nothing.

Breakfast was bacon and eggs. The farm kept its own hens – they were always there, strutting across the yard or clucking at the door – but no pigs. The bacon was from the town supermarket. Lucy's mother filled up the car boot twice a week with supermarket goods. Toby got lectures on free-range eggs from Lucy's father. 'Look at them yolks,' he would say, 'you can't get yellow like that from factory birds.' And after this he would recount how, where they lived, it was a common sight until quite recently to see pigs being slaughtered.

'Really,' Toby had said. And the farmer had fixed him with his eye and given him a graphic account of how pigs were butchered, how they could smell death, how you could use every bit of a pig with no waste.

Toby, sensing a kind of challenge, pursed his lips and nodded knowingly.

'Funny things, pigs. Strange habits. They'll eat cinders.'

'Is that so?'

'They say some religions won't eat pork. Think it's unclean meat. Sort of polluted, I suppose.'

'Yes,' Toby said airily, 'I know.'

That had been in the early days. Lucy's parents hadn't wanted to trust him and he was wary of them. Now, after two years with her, they had begun to accept him. He'd grown used to their gruffness and acquisitiveness just as he'd grown used to the stone-flagged floors and the smell of manure and wet hay. He limited his conversation to subjects that he thought were safe. They didn't do him the same favour. He had begun to learn about certain local characters, and had also picked up some generalized knowledge of agricultural policies and production quotas. Once they had talked through one subject with a vigour and persistence that had finally goaded him into protest. 'Look,' he said, 'I really don't know the first thing about it. I'm not qualified to give an opinion. If I did know more about it, I'd probably agree with you.'

The father had said, after a pause, 'The trouble is that half the people who decide these things have never worked a farm. They've picked up their knowledge from reading, that's *their* problem.'

Toby had kept his face straight.

But they had accepted his relationship with Lucy. There had never been any repetition of the awkward scene when they had first visited the farm, and been put in separate rooms. Perhaps this victory was token; Lucy was nervous about making love when she thought her parents could hear. The only time they had tried it had been unsuccessful. She was too tense.

So breakfast this morning was as usual, with her father seated at the table head. He'd already been to see to his cattle, and his shirt-sleeves were rolled back. There was a smell of soap from his arms. Toby wondered what he'd been doing, and was sure it would have been something to blunt more refined appetites. The kitchen was full of thin smoke and the sound of constant sizzling.

Whenever he shook hands with her father, Toby was made aware of how small and well-kept his own hands were. They weren't muscular, made stubby by work, and with nails broken down to the quick.

'You had a bad dream last night,' Lucy said.

Toby could hardly remember any of it. 'Did I?'

'You woke up in a fair old state.' Lucy had begun to re-adopt her parents' accents and way of phrasing. She was like that. Once, when they'd gone to France for a short holiday, she had begun to sound French. When Toby had first met her she was in a circle of people whose accents had made him vaguely envious. It was one of the reasons he had been attracted to her.

'Imagination,' her father said, 'that's the trouble. Too much of that is good for no one.'

Imagination was a strong point with him. It was the cause of a lot of unhappiness, imagination; you could never be satisfied if you had it. It was a debilitating quality, one you had to keep on a tight rein. Women, especially, were prone to being laid low by it.

'Something chasing you in your sleep?' he asked drily.

'I don't think so.'

'They say such things never catch you in dreams. I'm not so sure. You should check yourself for scratches.' It had taken Lucy a long time to persuade Toby that this was a kind of humour – slow, uncomplicated, daring you to find it funny. Toby was never able to respond, although he recognized that, if he did, he would be joining some kind of brotherhood.

Lucy's mother filled their plates with crinkled bacon and runny yellow eggs. 'More breakfast, Toby? Sure? You should take no notice of him, you know. He's as daft as a brush.'

But Toby could think of Lucy's parents only as practical people, and he saw them only in practical terms. They planted vegetables, forked manure, steered ploughs. They worked in fields of snow, in meadows drenched with dew, among stubble that would lance the palm, in thick, clogging mud. They were used to heat, and sleet, and fog. They'd wrung the necks of chickens, tugged calves out of their mothers with ropes, picked blowfly maggots from the backs of sheep, cut the balls off bulls. They had cured hams, pickled onions, made jam; they ate pies and meat and eggs at temperatures that burned the mouth. They thought nothing of eating slabs of cheese, drinking pints of milk or beer, spreading their bread or potatoes with bright wedges of butter. According to all that Toby had read, they should have been in mortal danger, but they seemed healthier than most.

Looking at Lucy it would be possible to believe that she was separated from her parents by an extra generation. Although Lucy found close resemblances to her parents in herself, Toby saw only ghosts of their physiognomies and physiques. They had expected her to be a hairdresser or a nurse; although they had never said, she suspected that they had been disappointed when her interests took her in more abstract directions. But they had not stood in her way. And, because of this, the harshness of physical labour had scarcely touched her. She had fine skin, and thin fingers, and a delicate, high-cheekboned face.

'Tell us more about this new job,Toby,' Lucy's mother said.

It was awkward, but it changed the subject. Toby found it difficult to talk about the Parnabys. They belonged to different worlds. To make it more acceptable he talked in technicalities, made it appear that the task was arcane, specialized, and concerned with a particular form of wealth. Financial wealth.

'There's a lot of money in books,' he remarked.

Afterwards Lucy and Toby took a walk across the fields. The chickens followed them a short way, clucking and examining the grass, and the cows moved out of their way. One lifted its tail and urinated into the grass with the force of water from a summer hosepipe.

'There used to be a pond here,' Lucy said. 'When I was a girl the cows used to drink at it. That didn't stop the frogs. There was always frogspawn in it in summer; you could lift it up in big watery clumps. When the froglets migrated there were thousands of them hopping across the field.'

Now there was just a depression in the ground, although the grass was darker green and longer than on the slight rise around it.

'What happened?'

'It was drained. Most farm ponds have been drained around here. You can get a grant to do it, I think.'

There were three dead elms on top of the hillock. The cows still used them as scratching-posts, but apart from that their use had gone. You could lift the bark away; it came off in flakes the size of a hand. Beneath them were the tracks of the beetle that had caused the elm to die. They curled and spread in their own intricate symmetries.

'You used to have to report them,' Lucy continued, 'nobody bothers any more.'

'Won't that mean that the fungus will spread more quickly?'

Lucy shrugged. 'I think they think the battle's lost, anyway.'

Toby put his hand against the bare trunk. It felt dry and faintly powdery. 'They used to say the elm was an important tree, didn't they?'

'They used it for coffins.'

'Really?'

'I don't know what they'll use now. And for chair seats. It doesn't split when you hammer the legs home. So Dad used to say. I suppose they must have made lots of furniture with it. And barns. I don't know why he doesn't cut these down.'

She took his hand and led him away from the trees. The sun grew warmer and a drowsy bee hummed close by.

'Are you happy?' she asked.

The question caught him off guard. He repeated the word, stalling for time.

'Yes. Happy. You've just started what could be an interesting job. You and I have a stable relationship. It's summer. The sun's shining.'

'Yes. Yes, I suppose I am.'

Lucy glanced behind her. The farmhouse sank out of sight behind the rise.

'Dad will be seeing to the milking machines,' she said, 'Mam will be cleaning up. There's no one else about. The labourers are over in the far fields.'

He nodded. He was thinking of shelves and shelves of books, of suddenly taking down a volume so unique he could feel the power through his hands.

She walked next to him; her bared forearm brushed him. 'Let's make love,' she said.

Toby laughed. 'Here? In the open?'

'It's the best place. Air on your skin, sun warming you, the smell of grass, life going on all round. Come on – we can be quick, can't we?' She took hold of her skirt and smiled at him.

Toby spread his hands. 'I'd feel stupid.'

She put her mouth to ear. 'Let's live, Toby.'

He shrugged. Lucy, clutching her underwear in one hand, lay down on the grass with her legs parted. Toby had difficulty pulling his trousers over his shoes and he stumbled. He sat down beside her on the rise and tugged at the inside-out legs. One shoe came off with the trousers and he retrieved it from the leg and put it back on. His legs looked putty-white in the sunshine. Lucy tilted back her head and laughed.

She had to guide him into her. He put his face to one side and let the grass go out of focus, blur into a green mass smelling of growth and soil. He pushed at her with the toes of his shoes stuck into the earth. His climax, when it came, hardly touched him.

Lucy was still breathing heavily. He lifted his eyes a little, drawn by some disturbance at the edge of his vision. Momentarily confused, he watched the grass all around them begin to boil and glisten with black and gossamer. It seethed, welling up from within itself in a puzzling, spreading frenzy. Startled, almost scared, he lifted himself up on his arms. 'Lucy?'

She twisted her head.

All around them hundreds, thousands of ants had erupted to the surface of the field, the females winged for flight, the males clutching them with their tiny black bodies bent for mating. As Toby and Lucy watched, the ants rose, locked together and rising high into the air. Wherever they turned the sky was full of them. They got up and began to dash them from their clothes. Toby felt the tiny bodies against his fingers as he brushed them away.

'It's marvellous.' Lucy was thrilled. 'Isn't it wonderful?'

But Toby felt humilated by the forces of nature and said nothing.

As they watched, swifts appeared from nowhere and began to swoop through the flying ants, plucking them out of the air. Soon the sky above the field was filled, not only with the rising ants, but with birds scything through them.

To Toby this was a bizarre and disturbing spectacle, but Lucy was transported by it.

'It's *marvellous*.'

'Yes,' he said, 'whatever you say.'

Whenever Jorge went up to the library Toby had left the work in progress stacked on the table. There was a pile of volumes he could start on in the morning, a notebook, several cards, some pens and pencils stuck in a circular holder. Jorge bent over the work, picked up the books, turned the pages, flipped through the cards.

'A trap,' he said.

Sophie bent forward. Sunlight was edging the volumes. Across three of them, fixed by their weight, was a fine hair. It shone like a thin copper wire.

'In this light it is obvious,' Jorge said. He picked up the hair and handed it to her. 'Do not lose it.'

She passed it back to him and picked up one of the volumes. 'He plays at games,' she said.

'It must amuse him.' Jorge watched as she opened the books – Herbert Strang, Captain F. S. Brereton, Charles Gilson. When she opened them he saw that they were presents from her father to Dexter. There were inscriptions written on the flyleaf – her brother's name, etched in black ink by a steel nib, and the greetings: *Happy Birthday, from Father; Happy Xmas, from Father.* And a date in the early 1930s.

'Put them back, Jorge.'

He assembled the stack exactly as it had been. Even the hair was put back in its original place, as taut as when Toby had left it. He wouldn't realize.

'Your opinion?' she asked.

Jorge considered his reply. He paused between each sentence. 'He enjoys his work. He is curious about us. He asks Becky many questions, so many that sometimes she cannot remember them all when she repeats them to me.'

'How curious?'

'I think that maybe he finds you and me even more interesting that the library.'

'You don't think I made a mistake?'

Jorge had to be careful. He did not want his chances ruined and he did not want a postponement. 'I do not think a mistake has been made. But only you can judge.'

Sophie walked down between the shelves. 'God moves in mysterious ways,' she said.

Jorge remained silent.

'We're just like people on the ground who cannot see something which is clear from the air.'

She turned, walked past the spiral staircase, and back up to where Jorge sat at the desk.

'I didn't think that when Dexter died,' she said.

'I know that,' he replied quietly. She had told him so many times.

She gave a little sigh and then asked, 'When do you think I should meet him again?'

'He will be back tomorrow.'

'Does he know I'm back?'

'He must expect that you will return soon. Becky has told him several times that you will not be away much longer.'

She looked down at the cards and books. 'He is very efficient.'

'Yes.'

'All right,' she said, 'tomorrow.'

When she left the library the heels of her shoes smacked sharply on the floor, wood on wood. Jorge took one last look round, walked round the desk again, and then went to the door. He scarcely made a sound. His feet were bare.

5

Toby used the servants' entrance now. It was a bolthole down a flight of stone steps that led into the house at basement level. It was protected by thick railings of wrought-iron and a gate which Jorge padlocked at night. Lichen grew on the steps so quickly that they had regularly to be scrubbed and washed with fungicide; the stairwell was always spotted with damp scabs of green.

The lower door opened directly on to an unfurnished passageway. The kitchen and laundry were to one side, the bedroom and spare rooms to the other. There was also a small bathroom which Toby was expected to use rather than visit one of the two upstairs. Becky had told him that these were 'really big'; he imagined them as palatial.

'Morning, Jorge.'

Toby had begun to affect a pronounced breeziness. He thought that his seeming indifference to Jorge's lack of expression would gradually wear away the Indian's resistance. Until then he would remain monolithically intimidating.

'Mr Toby,' Jorge responded, with an expression that Toby took to be one of distaste.

'Another nice day, mm? But perhaps we're in for an early autumn. London winters will be terrible if you're used to a hot climate.'

Jorge turned away.

Toby clapped his hands and rubbed them together to let Jorge know he was eager to get to work. 'No Becky this morning?'

'She is seeing to upstairs.'

'She's kept busy, isn't she? Does she enjoy working for you, do you think?'

'It is her job to be busy.'

Toby waited to see if Jorge would answer the other question, but when he did not Toby said, 'I'd better get up to the library. Shouldn't you be checking on me? Aren't you curious about how things are going?'

'Tell Miss Parnaby, Toby. She will be most interested.'

'One of these days I'll get the chance, I suppose.'

'You can tell her now.'

Toby was astonished. He knew this would happen sometime, but the day had always receded as he approached it.

Jorge smiled at him. His bared teeth gave his face an oddly predatory look. 'You do understand me, don't you?' he asked quietly.

Toby nodded quickly.

Sophie sat by her window overlooking the square. Once again, Toby was struck by her air of confidence. She was a product of an educated, leisured class; Toby saw it in the way she sat, heard it in the way she spoke. Age had made her handsome; and he could tell she was nobody's fool.

On the wall was a Victorian painting of nudes, their hair streaming in a gale, their flesh as white and unblemished as porcelain. Light was reflected from silver at the far side of the room. Sophie sat with her arms resting on a table.

'You've had breakfast?'

'Yes,' he said. He thought he detected a sense of charity in her voice.

She watched him as his eyes glanced round the room, then up at the painting. 'Do you like it?'

'I recognize its . . . authenticity,' he said. 'As a work of art, I mean.'

'The Victorians had a strange idea of nakedness,' she mused, 'I often find myself looking at it and thinking how impossible the models are. Of course, the whole scene is metaphorical, you realize that, but the figures are so impossibly perfect.'

Toby looked upwards at it. The girls, languourous but innocent, bent their hips and breasts into a storm. It whirled their hair, tore the clouds apart, bent the trees. But they remained smooth-skinned, desirable, divine.

'A metaphor, you say?'

'But of course.' Without warning, she switched the subject. 'And your examination of the library? How are things?'

'They're going well, thanks.'

'Sit down and tell me about it.'

So he told her about the cache of her brother's books, of the Garnett abridgement of Doughty, of the first edition Shackleton, the *Revolt in the Desert* copy, the E. M. Forsters, the early Gollancz softcovers, the Rackham illustrations, the handsomely bound children's books.

'I knew of all of these,' she said when he had finished.

'No doubt there will be more,' Toby replied. 'And there are a lot more individual works that I can't really evaluate yet.'

'Evaluate financially, you mean?'

'I was thinking in terms of their rarity and importance. I could give an estimate of their monetary worth if you wanted me to.'

Sophie shook her head. 'No, no. That isn't the purpose at all.'

Toby became aware that there was someone else in the room. He turned to see Jorge standing quietly by the door. He was positioned so as not to be seen by Toby. As soon as Toby turned he smiled – a strange, unexpected smile – and went out of the room. The door closed with a soft click behind him.

'He looks after me,' Sophie said as if she were explaining everything. 'He's invaluable.'

Toby felt slightly unnerved by this. 'He's very quiet,' he commented.

'He's a long way from where he was born. But he still keeps his talents.'

'For silence?'

'Among other qualities. I found Jorge, you know. Did he tell you that?'

'He tells me very little.'

'Yes, I found him. It was a long time ago but I can remember very clearly. Even the colour of the butterflies by the river.' She sighed. The noise was loud in the room.

Toby cleared his throat.

'We don't even know which tribe he came from. But since then he has come to the West. He has been raised as a Christian. He has worked in the houses of the famous. Interesting, don't you think?'

'Fascinating.'

'I often think someone should write his story some day. It's the kind of event which should be preserved. Although it would, perhaps, be difficult to isolate it from other events which surround it.'

Toby thought she was just filling in time. 'I'm sure,' he said.

They talked a little more about the library. Sophie mentioned certain volumes that she was sure Toby would be interested in – Mackenzie's *Wildlife of the Amazon Basin*, Garner's *Bolivian Travels* . . . and then she said that perhaps he should get back to work. It was like a dismissal.

After he had gone Sophie felt doubt enter her heart. It crept about her and then gripped. As a child, in dreams, she used to imagine herself shackled in a dark stone cell, the cold black river pouring in and sweeping, creeping up her legs, genitals, chest, neck, mouth. She awoke terrified. She realized, of course, that these were Dexter's visions, culled from his extensive reading of adventure stories. He inhabited her mind with his extravagant, ludicrous tales of ordeal, of invincible jungle boys, giant pythons, gallant airmen. Because they came from him they were made, somehow, all the more real. In the Parnaby household it was the eldest boy who had all the authority and promise.

The power of those dreams had stayed with her. If she had reason to fear then it could be measured against the fear of those tortures. If she wanted some idea of what it would be like to be deserted by God then all she had to do was to go back to the times when she woke in the dark, crying, vulnerable, doomed beyond hope.

Now she felt a tremor of that desolation. It was distant but undeniably present, and sinister. Often she could find a darker side to her belief; it was, she felt, her temptation. In return for this she was often euphoric with glee and conviction.

Sophie leaned forward and concentrated her mind. As she moved she felt a sudden dull queasiness, but it passed rapidly, although it left her slightly short of breath. Then she bunched her hands together in a double fist and pressed them so tightly together that her forearms trembled. She leaned forward a little further and the queasiness came back, assuming an odd shape within her for a few seconds before it vanished.

She prayed.

Up in the library Toby still felt her presence. He couldn't quite categorize her. He'd tried, of course – eccentric traveller; grieving sister; society lady; book collector – but she evaded them all.

Toby leaned on the metal ladder. He had become more and more attracted to it because it was so different from the rest of the library. He often found himself holding on to it without thinking, or even sitting on its lower steps. When he climbed on it there was a sharp metallic ring that was curiously satisfying after the noise of his footsteps on the wooden floor.

From outside came the whirr of a small motor. Toby climbed the ladder and peered down into the garden. It was a narrow, restricted view, giving him a sharp angle down on to the lawn. Jorge was cutting it with a mower. He was stripped to the waist. The light was bent and warped by the glass, turning him into a flowing copper and black blob.

Toby returned to the shelves. By now he was so used to the minimal sounds of the room that halfway down he paused. Yet he couldn't pinpoint anything apart from the sounds from outside.

He stood still. He was sure there was something there. If he hadn't known that Jorge was outside he would have suspected him of being present.

Toby stood stock still. It was an odd sensation. The kind people must get when they sense ghosts, he thought. Some temporary imbalance of the senses, he told himself. There couldn't be anyone else in the library. If there had been he would be able to hear a footstep, the rustle of clothes, even their breathing. He examined his own feelings with interest. He had no interest in the supernatural, apart from as a literary device. He didn't believe in tales of divination. And yet here was some kind of demonstration as to why people held such beliefs. An unusual burst of activity in some cluster of neural connections, an unaccustomed dislocation of the senses – that was all it was.

But, like someone superstitious, he took a walk around the shelves just to make sure his rationalism was correct.

There was no one there.

It was five minutes later, when he had returned to work at his desk, and the feeling had dwindled, that he saw a movement out of the corner of his eye. Before he had a chance to focus he had figured out what it must be – it was small, tiny even, and on the floor. A mouse?

But it wasn't.

He walked gingerly up to it.

The frog leapt several inches and landed on the floorboards with a light, almost inaudibly soft thud. Its eyes bevelled around, and he could see the movements of its sides, as it breathed. Its lungs seemed paper-thin and yet the hindquarters were of squashy but substantial flesh. Its head seemed both blunt and fragile, as senseless as a snake's, as crushable as an eggshell.

Toby picked up the frog. It gave one kick, a sudden thrust that surprised him with its strength and smoothness, and then, cradled between his hands, it accepted his warmth and quietened. It felt like a mixture of opposites . . . heavy and light, insubstantial yet tough.

Carrying it cupped in front of him, a priest with an offering, he took it down through the house and out into the garden at the back.

As he passed through the kitchen Becky looked askance at him. He wondered what she was thinking. Toby did not wish anyone to think of him as odd, not even those who were of little interest to him. 'It's a frog,' he told Becky, 'I found it in the library, although God knows how it got up there.'

It was the first time he had been in the garden. It was enclosed by high brick walls covered in ivy. Rosebushes had been planted round the lawn. Jorge stood at the end of a thin white cable which looped across the grass and disappeared into the mower. He stopped and watched as Toby walked past. Toby felt the soft give of the earth beneath his feet. He hardly made any noise as he walked to the wall.

It was important to him not to ask Jorge what to do with the frog. He did not even want to look at him. Toby bent and gently deposited the frog in the shade of a bush. It sat there, gave a slow amphibian quiver, and blinked its bulbous eyes.

'I found it on the library floor,' Toby said, bent over and watching it. 'How would it get up there?'

'At home, frogs climb. And sometimes people call them.'

'Maybe they climb here, as well,' Toby said.

'They climb trees.'

Toby turned to him. Jorge was standing bare-chested, his skin fine-grained and healthy. But his arms were folded across his chest like a Pharaoh's. Each hand covered the top of the other arm. And each wrist carried marks like a snake's trail in sand; as if years ago, the skin had been burned away and had then regrown across the wound.

Their symmetry was so shocking, so disturbing that Toby froze for a second. Just at the moment when he had begun to be embarrassed by his own curiosity Jorge lifted his hands from his arms. Just below the shoulders, at the top of the biceps, were the same extraordinary marks.

This stopped Toby again, and confusion washed over him and he blushed. He thought of making excuses, any excuse no matter how unbelievable, and then he rejected it. He straightened up. 'I'm sorry,' he said.

They stood there in the sunshine looking at each other. Toby thought that Jorge had begun to smile, almost sardonically, but then he turned away, pressed the trigger of the mower, and began cutting the grass again. The mower was not fitted with a box and the small green spears of grass hurled thickly out of the blades in a falling arc.

Toby returned to the library.

The next day Sophie visited him at work. She walked along the shelves picking out certain volumes and saying things like 'I remember this well' and 'I never got round to reading that' and 'This was Dexter's copy'.

Toby walked behind her, adding one or two comments of his own on the state of the collection. He was trying to steer her towards the staircase but she kept away from it.

When she picked up an old Edwardian copy of *Seven Years among the Savages of Bolivia* by Lt-Col D. H. Sympson she asked him what he thought of Jorge.

'He's an interesting man,' Toby said cautiously.

'Do you mean he's interesting as an individual? Or that he's interesting because of where he comes from?'

'Well . . . Both, I suppose.'

'I see. As I said to you the other day, his biography would make intriguing reading. It is, of course, inextricably bound up with mine. As mine is inextricably bound up with Dexter's.'

'You started to tell me about Jorge. You never really finished.'

'I found him by the banks of a river. I was reading Dexter's book. *Journey to the Interior*. His loss was still troubling me greatly. It was the cause of much pain and a lot of doubt. That's when Jorge came into my life. Except, of course, that he wasn't called that. He would not tell us his real name. I was the one who christened him Jorge – the patron saint of my own country.'

'He'd got lost, somehow?'

'The tribes still skirmish. They take captives when they can. My tribe, the tribe I was with, were constantly at war. I don't mean that they engaged in continual battle. Years could pass in which there was no violence at all. The forest is big enough for them both. But at this time there had been a few skirmishes and one, in particular, had ended in the death of one of our warriors. When that happens it sets off a chain of retribution. Of revenge. It becomes socially necessary to inflict damage on the opposing tribe. Pride is at stake – a fierce kind of pride, worth dying for. Jorge was captured during a revenge raid on the enemy. He wasn't the aim of the raiding party. Their purpose was humiliation by whatever means possible. They wanted to crack a few skulls, pollute the camp, make themselves devils in the eyes of their enemies. Jorge was just an incidental. He was there and I suppose he was easily caught. He'd certainly be easier to bring back than a fully grown woman. Possibly they ran with him across their shoulders. They must have been waiting for pursuit, but pursuit never came. The whole war just died out. Quite probably it flared up again a year or so later, but Jorge and I were out of the way by then.'

'You were his saviour.'

'He was only a boy. I had to do something. It's possible that I saved his life. Once they'd captured him they didn't know what to do with him. And I had a certain standing in the tribe. Once or twice I doubted it, and believed they would kill me. But I was wrong. I was important to them. I had medicine. I had contacts with the outside world – tenuous ones, yes, but enough to let me bring things up-river. Knives, hats, mirrors, axes, cloth, food they'd never tasted, colours they'd never seen, all kinds of strange sights and smells and sensations. Jorge became mine.'

Sophie walked back to the desk and sat in the chair looking down the library.

'It sounds barbaric, I know,' she said, 'but you mustn't think of it that way. God has his purposes even if we can't understand what they are. In certain tribes one accumulates honour by giving things away. The greater the gift, the higher the honour.'

'He's not your personal property, is he?'

To her the question was naïve and she smiled. 'Good heavens, no. He's free. As free as you or I.'

I'm not particularly free, Toby wanted to say, but he did not open his mouth.

'I took him down-river. Even though he was a gift to me, I still couldn't be sure that he was safe.'

'Why didn't you take him back to his own people?'

She shook her head. 'You don't understand, Toby. They would have moved by then. Their camp would have been polluted. They would have been impossible to find. Even if I had done, there was no guarantee that they would have taken him back. Tribal people can remember details that go back centuries, but if they don't want to remember, if something is associated with impurity or shame, they can expunge it almost totally. There was only one choice.'

'I see,' Toby said, but he didn't. He put his knuckles to his mouth. He believed that when he did that he looked learned and understanding.

'Further down-river was a colony run by American missionaries. Good men. I knew he would be safe there. He would have the best of both worlds.'

'This explains the barefeet.'

She smiled again, like a mother. 'Yes. Jorge has done a lot of adjusting. To capture, to Christianity, to life in the West. I don't think many people would guess his origins. But he still has a sensitivity to certain Western clothes. His feet can slip into leather shoes with no problem, but they are sensitive to anything else. He gets a rash around the ankles.'

'It seems an extraordinary journey.'

'Jorge's life is in stages. All our lives are. It only seems extraordinary if viewed from his beginnings. Taken from wherever he will end, it will all seem entirely natural and understandable. Predictable, even. Or somehow . . . planned. All our lives are like this.'

'And his arms?'

Sophie looked sharply at him. Toby immediately felt that he had said the wrong thing. But he persisted.

'The marks on his arms. On his wrists and biceps. What are they . . . some kind of tribal marking?'

'Tribal marking.' She repeated the words flatly.

'Yes, Toby continued, with a sense of desperation because he suddenly felt that his own impetuousness could lose him everything, 'you know . . . a mark of belonging. Or maturity.' His voice tailed off.

'You're right, she said. 'In a way.' She looked across at him and went on, 'But I'm keeping you from your work.'

'Not at all.'

'But I *am*.'

Toby took the hint and stood up. 'Right,' he said, 'back to it.'

When he told Lucy about the conversation that evening he said he was aware there were whole areas of the Parnaby story about which he knew nothing.

'Perhaps they don't feel that it's your business,' Lucy suggested.

'Maybe not. But I can't just shut them out. And there are certain things you can't push. Not just yet, anyway. I'll bide my time, I suppose.'

'Whatever you say.'

Toby was increasingly unsettled in his relationship with Lucy. He had cause to be grateful to her – he recognized that. She provided him with a stability which his life had often lacked. In its simplest, most material form this meant that she provided him with the comforts of home – good food, laundry, someone warm to sleep with at night. Toby was quite happy to leave all this to Lucy. He always felt that such elements would swallow up all of his free time if he did not have someone to organize them for him.

More important, however, was her influence on his attitudes. Toby had noticed the change in himself several months ago. He had begun to think of their relationship as stable and comfortable. He was sure that this wouldn't be good for him. Although he had lived a narrow, unadventurous life he was fascinated by the lives of others. And often it seemed that they had achieved eminence only after living through deprivation, trial and ordeal. He was concerned that he was somehow being kept away from a harsher, but in the end more rewarding, existence. Lucy was shielding him too much.

Toby walked round the flat. When they had first started to live together they had thought it was a bargain; a real find. It didn't matter that the bedroom was so small that when the door opened it banged against the side of the bed. Nor that the kitchen smelled of gas and old vegetables no matter how many times they cleaned it. It was their first flat with its own bath. They could luxuriate in the privacy and cleanliness of each other's body, so they never worried about the pipes that banged like hammers, or the tap that had dripped for so long it had marked the enamel with a rusty smear.

Toby looked at the ground outside. It had once been a private garden but the walls were now in ruins, and stalks of rosebay willowherb stuck out from heaps of masonry. Local children had broken bottles across them. There was a noise of heavy footsteps from upstairs. Toby and Lucy didn't know the people in the upper flat, had only spoken to them once or twice in the entrance hall, but they'd heard their records played over and over again.

As he grew used to the Parnaby home, Toby began to find the flat decrepit and constricting. He felt he had lived in it so long it had begun to eat into his resolve, like some unstoppable parasite. Yet only a few months ago this had been *their* place. Their haven. Their retreat from the world.

Lucy came up behind him and put her arms round him. She felt him flinch slightly.

'What's wrong?' she asked.

'You're always doing that.'

'Shouldn't I?'

'If you want.'

'What's on your mind?'

She waited but he did not answer.

'Toby?'

'It's this place, I suppose. It's getting me down.'

She saw him watching the outside corner of one of the window-panes. A tiny spider had stretched a web across it and lay to one side, waiting.

'If you want to, we could afford somewhere else. Should we talk about it?'

Toby shrugged.

'We'll have to, if it's affecting you this much.'

'Later,' he said, 'I can't be bothered. Later.'

Toby was daydreaming about parting.

He was too scared to do it, but he knew it would be easy, and weak, to drift along until their lives became so enmeshed, financially and domestically, that it would be impossible to break away.

He just wished that something would come along and take the responsibility off his shoulders. Because he knew that part of him responded to Lucy's steadiness and comfort, and that, at the last moment, his courage would desert him and he would not want to go.

6

It was Toby who suggested they should visit Rachel. He and Lucy travelled for two hours by train, then caught a bus to the university. It was built of grey concrete boxes, piled on one another like a giant's storeroom. The walls were divided by rectangular geometries of glass. Open walkways and flights of grey concrete steps connected the huge bulks of the buildings. In the centre, outside the bar and the bookshop, was a fountain fed by a stream that ran through concrete guttering. Rounded stones and cobbles were fixed in the cement matrix that had been laid around its perimeter. Every time he saw the stones Toby remembered Lucy pointing out the striations. He'd thought they were just marks in the rock, but she'd told him they were scratches showing how it had been carried along by a glacier in the ice age. From the fountain the water drained away into an artificial tarn.

Rachel and Lucy had once shared a flat. They had never been particularly close, although they had once pretended to be, just to take the edge off their loneliness. Now they had drifted further apart. Toby, however, sought to maintain relationships with Rachel. He thought she was much more interesting than Lucy.

Today Rachel's black frizzy hair was tied back above her neck with a ribbon of brightly coloured cloth. He guessed it was from a far corner of the world; she bought things like that.

They ate a meal at the Arts Centre. The Arts Centre was a large, hangar-like building of metal and glass. It lay on a grassy slope above the tarn and was surrounded by four Henry Moores. Rachel talked in a loud, almost over-confident voice that impressed Toby with its lack of self-doubt.

She had made the customary enquiries as to their health, how they were doing, what they would be doing in the future, and from then on she had talked either about herself or about abstract concepts. She worked over and through the lecture she was due to give later that day. Lucy glanced at Toby occasionally as if to tell him that she thought this was very bad form; but Toby was enthralled.

Rachel's speciality was myth. Her amibition was to live her life among people who lived their myths. There wasn't much time to do it; Christianity and Islam were taking over everything. The kind of cultures she wanted to live with were disappearing fast.

Toby thought he had timed his entry to perfection. 'I know a South American Indian,' he said nonchalantly.

'There are lots of them about,' Rachel said, matter-of-fact. 'We even have one or two here on campus. They're not particularly interesting. They know less about their own cultures than I do. Their governments send them over to study agriculture and engineering.'

Toby was smug. 'Ah, but this one's from the interior.'

'Really? What tribe?'

'I'm sorry, I don't know.'

'Ah.'

Toby tried to redeem himself. 'I'm trying to find out, though.'

'And should I have one guess at his name?'

Toby was perplexed. Despite himself, he looked at Lucy for support.

'You've been doing some research,' Lucy said to Rachel.

'After you phoned me, yes. I wondered if it was the same Parnabys.'

'You know about them?' Toby asked.

'Of *course* I know about them. Do you?'

'I work there, for God's sake.'

Rachel was finishing her salad. She paused before replying. Toby looked round at the other diners sitting at their tables of chrome and black. Light, bright but indirect, flooded the restaurant.

'There aren't many people who know exactly for whom they're working. How many shopfloor workers know about their company's involvement in South Africa?'

'But you know about the Parnabys.'

'It's part of my job. When I heard you were cataloguing their library I looked up some facts of my own. It didn't take long. They confirmed what I'd always thought.'

'Which is?'

'He was a bastard,' Rachel said. 'It was a good day for the world when his plane crashed.'

'Rachel,' Lucy said, 'that's very harsh.'

'Not at all. It's a statement of fact.'

'What do you base that on?' Toby asked. 'His book?'

Rachel screwed up her face in a dismissive gesture.

'He was quite an individual, even if you don't admire him,' Toby said with a little hesitancy.

Rachel leaned back and looked directly at him. It made him uncomfortable. Then she told him her opinion of Dexter Parnaby. She had obviously thought very carefully about what she was going to say. It was an accusation.

'He was an adventurer,' she said, 'nothing more. There were thousands like him. He was untrained, hare-brained, starry-eyed, foolish. He had no respect for the countries he passed through and no concern for their inhabitants. If he'd been born earlier he would have been an imperialist, expanding the empire and staking claims and stealing minerals to his heart's content. He was too late for that boom. But it didn't stop him rampaging across a continent with nothing in his brain but thoughts of plunder and glory. He did damage that is beyond repair. He wounded cultures. He gave them fatal wounds.'

Lucy and Toby sat silent. The skilled ferocity of her attack had surprised them both.

Toby could feel Lucy willing him to defend himself.

'That's a bit one-sided, surely,' he began weakly.

'Toby, you've already confessed, in as many words, that you know nothing about it.'

'I – '

'I *do*. Should I give you the references? Would that help convince you?'

'References just to support your argument?'

'I don't need to argue. He's condemned by his own admirers. He was on some kind of quest but couldn't decide what it was or where he was going. One year it was a new Machu Picchu, next it was to track down some ludicrous tale of a white tribe, then it was Inca gold or the source of a river. He couldn't make up his mind. Just as he couldn't realize that what he was doing was *wrong*. Environmentally, anthropologically, morally. He just walked into cultures that had never seen a white man. He helped make them dependent on medicine and drink and Sheffield steel. He talked to them about God and Christ and sacrifice and resurrection. If he could get them to work for him then he would do. He took the wealth of an area – and I mean human wealth, as well – and squandered it.'

'At least he left something behind him. Even if it was only something you hate.'

'Dexter was only the start. If he had religion then it was in a partial, weak kind of way. But you can't separate him from his sister.'

'Sophie? Sophie's a very quiet sort of person. Not like that at all. You should meet her.'

'I don't need to meet her. I see her name as the prime force in a missionary team that operates in South America. The family's very rich. Rich enough to let two spoiled children use a continent as a playground. Rich enough, too, to pump thousands of pounds a year into an organization whose sole purpose is to bring tribes into the arms of a Christian God.'

Toby had begun to remember what Becky had said about a church. About how church members often visited Sophie.

'I'll tell you who your Indian is, Toby. He's a man raised by missionaries intent on smashing tribal cultures. He was taken to New York and exhibited at a rally. The primitive becomes civilized. The damned becomes saved. God triumphs over the Devil.'

'Rachel,' Lucy interrupted, 'Toby only does a job. That's all. You know how librarians feel about books. They're above politics.'

'In that case, Toby,' Rachel said, 'you should be ashamed of yourself.'

The nearby diners turned and looked at them and then back at their meals. Toby felt uneasy at being in the centre of this circle of interest. It didn't stop Rachel.

'You must have gone into this with your eyes open,' she went on, in a light, offhand tone of voice that did nothing to blunt the attack,

'Lucy always tells me how informed you are. Dealing with apartheid is morally more justifiable than this.'

'Rachel,' Lucy said calmly, 'Toby's a cataloguer, not a moralist. And we all have to work within organizations that we may dislike or find to be morally dubious. We have to do that in order to survive. You do, I do, Toby does.'

'That's right,' he said, ineffectively.

'What surprises me, then, is how detached from the world you can be. You – not anyone else, Toby, *you* – are working with a family which has done more than anyone else this century to destroy tribal life. With guns or with Bibles, it doesn't matter. I believe you *would* find the library very interesting; I'm sure you would.'

He nodded. 'I do.'

'And it's interesting because it's one trace left by a gang of crazed, selfish murderers. People who started, and fostered, and still support financially, the greatest crime of this century – the heartless, massive, wholesale destruction of the Indian.'

What little remained of the meal was spent in a strained, awkward gloom, despite all their attempts to raise inoffensive, anodyne subjects. Rachel left first. It was, she said, to do a final revision on her lecture. Toby and Lucy left the restaurant feeling still bruised by the argument.

The Arts Centre had a collection of primitive and modern paintings and sculpture. Images of ritual, dreamtime, celebration, myth faced those of deprivation, anguish, holocaust, madness. They walked round them silently. Lucy paused in front of a Bacon. Inside the cabinet a face smudged with pain opened its mouth in a silent, agonized gape.

'She's becoming intolerable,' Lucy said quietly.

'She's certainly very agressive,' Toby agreed. He didn't particularly want to talk about Rachel. He felt he had been misjudged by her, and he hated his own inadequate response; but her vigour had fascinated him.

'When I knew her she was wrapped up in Arthurian legends. She would go on and on about images of the Grail. It all seemed rather misty and sentimental to me. Now she's got a lot harder. But she still sees things very simply. No shades of grey for her; it's either black or white.'

Toby moved on. A small goddess made of sandstone looked out at him from a glass case. Direct light illuminated its minimal features. Only the barest of indentations and ridges indicated face, breast, belly, sex.

'You could have defended yourself better,' Lucy said.

'I sometimes find it difficult.'

'You needn't hold back just because she used to be a friend of mine.'

He shook his head. 'I wouldn't.'

After a pause, she asked, 'You could think of arguments against her, couldn't you?'

They moved past a huge near-abstract of green, washing in huge swathes down the canvas. 'Of course I could,' he said. 'To start off with, I could probably have trapped her into admitting that her beliefs were built on outmoded, romanticized ideals of the noble savage, the innocence of primitive societies, things like that.'

'Then you should have done.'

He shrugged. 'As I say, sometimes it's difficult.'

'I think everything is difficult at the moment; don't you agree?'

'Maybe so.'

'You're developing a whole part of your life that doesn't touch me. It's like something in a compartment on its own. You tell me that it's there; you say who's in it. But I really don't have any idea what it's like. I only know that it's important to you.'

'I see,' he said.

They left the Centre by the spiral stairs that led, through glass doors on to an overhead walkway. The sun was high, making the metal handrails hot to the touch.

Toby knew what she was thinking of. Years ago, both of them had been in the same place. Thrown together by chance, they had walked round the campus on a summer night.The lights of studies speckled the dark in tiny panels. A ventilation system murmured quietly, echoing softly round the buildings. Lucy and Toby had their hands in their pockets. Mist was rising, opaque and chill, from the tarn. It condensed in large droplets on any metal. They followed the walkway to the upper level of the Centre and stopped at the locked glass doors. The gallery was empty but for the exhibits, and the nightlights gave it an eerie purity. Toby and Lucy joined hands, and leaned against the doors like swimmers at a barrier, like divers who can never enter the submerged wreck of treasure and gloom and phantom luminescence.

Now, a long time later, the gallery was open, all the contents fully lit, and there was a clear sky above. Nothing was magical at all.

They went down to the water's edge. A procession of moorhens, the young already big, made widening arrows across the water. They sat under a willow. The leaves, which Toby touched with one hand, had a slight crinkle to them. He wondered if they were already beginning to die. He pulled a thick springy branch down, let it go, watched it shudder into stillness.

'It's been a long time,' Lucy said.

'You're going to tell me it seems like yesterday.'

'It was. It does.'

A faint breeze stirred the leaves and rushes around the lake.

'Do you remember? We sat here.The willows were full. You told me that Thomas Hardy could identify kinds of tree just by listening to the sound of the wind in their leaves.'

'Someone once told me that. He was an American working on Victorian novel endings.'

'I thought it was marvellous that you told me that.'

'I never checked to see if what he said was true.'

'But it says something about you.'

'It should have told you that I carry round in my head all sorts of obscure and unverifiable anecdotes. That I'm a compiler and a pigeonholer. A cataloguer.'

They watched the wind on the water, saw the reflections move on it. Lucy pushed back some strands of hair that had blown across her face.

Toby snorted. 'Victorian novel endings! Still, there would be a thesis in it somewhere. And maybe even a book. It must have been nice to know, when you started reading, that everything would be explained at the end, all the characters sorted out.'

He was quite prepared to elaborate on this, but she interrupted him.

'Things aren't right,' she said, 'we both know that.'

Toby said nothing.

'Maybe we're too close to talk about things like this. Maybe we should be apart – lovers divided by a sea or a mountain or a forest. Then we could be more honest with each other. We could be exact in what we wanted to say. Closeness sometimes prevents you from saying things that should be said. We could communicate better if we were apart.'

Toby pulled at a few strands of grass. They were surprisingly tough. He grasped the blades and tugged. One of them cut him. The pain stung sharply and he hissed and yanked his hand away. Blood crossed it in a thin, bright line.

'Are you hurt?'

'It made me jump, that's all.'

He could see that she was looking beyond the trees to where there was a humpbacked wooden footbridge. They had stood there once, alone, breathing in unison, without guilt, saying nothing, with a forest of stars all around them.

'Are you suggesting that we part?' he asked.

'I don't want us to fail, Toby.'

The breeze picked up and made the leaves rustle like sheets being pulled from a bed.

'You should say something to me,' she said.

'Like what?'

'I'm doing my best to stop us drifting away from each other. You should do the same. Words can mean a lot.'

'I . . .'

After a few seconds she encouraged him. 'Yes?'

'Look, you can't really expect me to do this. It's no good. It's too sudden. I didn't expect it.'

'There's nothing to inhibit you. There's just you, me, and what's around us. Do you see those trees over there? They've grown. They hide the footbridge now. I can recall everything that we said when we stood on that footbridge. I could write it all down if I wanted.'

She saw him thinking of his response. 'It doesn't help to know the landscape,' he said after a while. 'It doesn't inspire me, if that's what you mean.'

'But you deal in words. You should be better equipped to use them than most people. You let Rachel run rings round you, and now you can't respond when I ask you to tell me what you feel about us.'

'You want me to be like a poet, Lucy. But I'm not. I deal with things in a clinical, rational way. I don't have your imaginative flair. I'm sorry if I disappoint you.'

Lucy sat and watched the water for a while, weighing up what she should do. She decided. There was no point in lying.

'Until I met you, Toby', she said, 'I was only half-alive.'

He looked away. 'You needn't tell me all this.

'It's necessary. Won't you look at me?'

He shook his head. 'Some words are better left unspoken, Lucy.'

'You were kind, you were gentle, you were interesting. And I know that you thought the same way about me. We hit it off with each other. The whole point about love is that it alters people. Everyone told me you were cold, a little indecisive, someone who drifted from one thing to another – '

'Not me,' he said.

'I think they were right. Maybe others told you things about me – how I was provincial, not very talented. Worst of all, probably, they would say that I was ordinary. But what we had wasn't ordinary. We glowed in each other's presence. We flared.'

'You're pitching this a bit too high, Lucy.'

She wanted to grab him and face him, but he angled himself further away.

'I know you could analyse all this if you wanted. That wouldn't matter. It would prove nothing. Experience is what matters. Emotions. You'll have to face them, Toby. What are you going to do?'

After a minute or so he looked at his watch and said, 'We haven't much time.' He stood up. 'The lecture starts shortly.'

Lucy remained seated.

Toby shifted his weight and wondered what to do.

'Come on,' he said. He had meant to sound dominant, but he was midway between testiness and pleading. Lucy got to her feet and followed him, a short distance behind, as if they were in procession.

On the way back through the buildings Toby began to realize, with a force that made him cold, that he was always postponing moments of truth. That, habitually, he put things off, equivocated, until the momentum around him provided him with its own solution. Although he was eager to tell other people how to live their lives, he was so uncertain of himself that he would avoid making choices whenever he could. His professionalism and his cynicism masked that flaw.

The realization carried a cutting edge. He felt a kind of paralysis at its bite. His own estimation of himself fell sharply at its touch. He was egotistical, selfish, vain. He believed his own emotions, his own reactions to be the only ones of value. He was interested in others only in so far as they supported him, employed him, or praised him. He loved himself.

Lucy sat beside him in the lecture theatre. They did not speak.

Rachel, her hair let free and combed outwards in an Italianate frizz, walked up the aisle towards them just before the start of the lecture. She smiled lightly at them both and handed Toby a piece of paper. Then she returned to the focus of the hall.

Toby sat with it between his hands, imagining that it could contain the details of some assignation. It took him more than a minute to realize that it would be something else.

He unfolded the paper just before the lecture started. He could sense Lucy trying to read it as well, but he angled the paper away from her.

It was, as he expected, a list of references. The earliest was a London *Empire News* of the mid-1950s; the others were all of more recent date – *Current Anthropology*, *Man*, the *Sunday Times*, *Intercienca*, and *Indienité, Ethnocide Indigènisme en Amérique Latine.* He refolded the paper and put it in his pocket just as Rachel began to speak.

'Gilgamesh,' she said. Her voice was authoritative and clear. Toby felt a twinge of admiration, or possibly of jealousy. The audience sat motionless, some with pens poised over open notebooks.

'It is, of course, just about the oldest piece of writing that we have. Substantial writing, anyway. And it exists as both myth and literature. Literature because, to some extent, it is shaped as a literary work. Myth because it still carries the force, the characteristics, the messages that surface and resurface in Genesis, the Gospels, Homer.'

Her eyes moved across Toby. He felt them on him for a split second before they passed on.

He and Lucy were careful not to touch. Their bodies were leaning slightly away from each other. Toby knew he could restore things if he wanted to. All he had to do was touch her hand. But he was too bound up in himself. And even if he had not been, his pride would have refused him any compromise. He sat frozen by disaffection and hurt.

'Consider the oppositions – human and divine; civilized and wild; nature and culture; immortality and death. Consider the catastrophe, the journey, the token brought back from the world of the *other*, like the token brought back from the world of the dead. All typical of myth. You could all contribute examples from Western culture, let alone many others.'

She looked round them all, a tiny smile on her lips as if she dared them to contradict her. Lucy shifted uneasily in her seat. Toby stared ahead but wanted to look angrily at her. She didn't appreciate abstract arguments. She didn't recognize Rachel's ability to marshal facts, organize a theme, shape a perspective. He felt bitter at Lucy and moodily angry at himself. He knew he had the same talent as Rachel. Quite probably he had it in greater measure. It was just that he had not yet had a chance to exercise it fully. He hadn't had *good luck*.

'Take the aspect of the two men, closer than brothers, one civilized, the other wild. Gilgamesh and Enkidu are echoed by David and Jonathan, by John the Baptist and Jesus of Nazareth.'

Toby put his hands up to his mouth. He was wondering how Rachel would have dealt with Sophie Parnaby, what she would draw out of the jungle of books, whether or not she would tell the truth to Sophie about her brother.

He wondered what *he* would do.

Within a few days he was consulting a thick, cumbersome volume of old *Empire News* copies bound together. There, at the date Rachel had quoted, was a two-page article on Dexter Parnaby, complete with grainy photographs of him and Sophie.

There was little mention of her in the article, other than as the *devoted sister* who would *never give up the search for her brother*. It was a laudatory piece on Dexter, presenting him as a man with a mission, an heir to Livingstone and Fawcett, a New Elizabethan. The Indians were a simple people, in need of leadership and protection. Those who knew him loved him as a father. But there were still, in the interior, savages, headhunters, living lives of barbarism and brutality. Who knows, asked the writer, where Dexter Parnaby is now – dead in his crashed plane, perhaps, or captured by the wild savages of the interior? Could it be that at last he has found one of the legendary lost cities of gold that early travellers believed hidden in the jungle? A map, with neither scale nor detail, showed the area of his disappearance. Toby knew enough of the geography to realize it covered thousands and thousands of square miles. The flight of the plane was marked by a thick broken line of black, terminating in an arrow and a question mark. The arrow pierced the words *Unexplored Territory*.

7

Toby was working on a scheme. Jorge knew it. He had gone into the library to find Toby quickly covering up a chart. The chart was handwritten, with inked boxes and straggling lines of print. Later that night Jorge had entered the empty library, but even though he searched for half an hour he still could not find the chart.

'He's taking it to his home,' he said to Sophie.

'He'll be working on it there,' Sophie remarked.

'It looks as if he is trying to get something into an order.'

After a pause, she asked, 'Jorge . . . is he taking the bait?'

'I do not know.'

That night Sophie was ill. The sickness came in waves, leaving her feeling unreal but with an aching head. During the worst of these moments, when her breath was shortening, she felt that death was near. That, for some reason, unfathomable but divine, it had been decided that she should die without ever knowing about the future.

In the morning Toby came into the room while she was sitting staring at the Victorian painting. Toby was full of enthusiasm and confidence, but she saw him hesitate momentarily. She knew that she looked worn and uncharacteristically frail.

'I want to do a book,' he said.

She dared not move.

'On Dexter,' he went on.

Sophie's expression did not change, her eyes did not blink, but she felt her heart begin to race.

Toby cleared his throat. 'His biography.'

'Why?' she asked, as neutrally as she could.

Toby justified his decision. Sophie pretended to listen carefully although she was too excited to follow him closely. There was no official biography, Toby said, no indispensable central volume, no drawing together of all the threads. Scholars would need it. Explorers. Historians. South American politicians. Members of the church.

He knows, she thought.

Toby continued. He talked about Dexter's importance, an importance that would not fully be recognized for another fifty or sixty years; about how such a book would have the ingredients of danger, exotic locations, a mysterious disappearance, courage, the unknown. He talked about sources – newspaper articles, *Journey to the Interior*, other travel books; the necessity of interviewing people who knew him, before it was too late.

'I like to think', he said, 'that in years to come a scholar will reach up and take a book from his shelf, carry it over to his table, open it up. The pages will fall open. And there will be Dexter's world.'

'Yes,' she said.

'So that he'll know what it was like to live in Dexter's time. Know what sort of person he was, how he lived his life, what his contributions were.'

'You think he's worth it?'

'I think he deserves it. So do you,'

For years she had hoped that something like this would happen. She believed in her brother so passionately that it had not been enough simply to appoint someone to write about him. The author must be drawn to his subject. Had to come to the realization that he lived for that reason – to write the biography of a great man.

'You have it all mapped out in your mind,' she said.

'I've drawn up a structure on paper. There would be no point in arguing my case if I hadn't prepared it thoroughly.'

'And you foresee a scholarly work – with footnotes, a bibliography, source references.'

He nodded.

'I expect you would be prepared to tell me that there would be an entry under my name in the index. With page references against *youth, travels, support for brother, search for brother, life after brother.*'

'You're the key to all this. I need your support. I would have tried to persuade you with that argument if I had thought you would respond.'

'And my support would be moral? Or financial?'

'Both. All things like this need a patron.'

'And Dexter needs his book?'

'All kinds of bits and pieces of information about Dexter are slipping away. Friends are dying, documents getting lost. It's important to save what can be saved, organize it, fix it in a medium before it's too late. Make him permanent.'

She smiled at him. 'You're not confusing immortality with a mere arrangement of words?'

'I would guess that, to you, immortality is individual permanence. Maybe memorial would be a better word for what I want to achieve.'

She knew he was patronizing her, but she did not care. The facts of Dexter's life would make him see things clearly. 'I don't think you could have chosen a less attractive word,' she said. 'What is going on now is his memorial. The missions among the Indians. The cross in the jungle.'

'In that case', Toby replied softly, 'he needs more than a memorial. You know, I know, and a few other people know how important a figure Dexter was. But what will happen in a few years' time? What will happen when all the documents are gone?'

'Toby,' she said, 'that is one thing you need not worry about.'

The air was dark and suffocating. It had been trapped under the roof for a long time. Jorge climbed back down the ladder into the library; his footsteps rang. 'There is no light,' he said.

They waited for his return. Toby stepped quickly up the stairway and stood inside the open trapdoor. A skylight had been let into the sloping roof of the house but its glass had been painted a dark green during wartime. The dry paint scored thick opaque lines across the panel of dim light. Toby could just make out the bulky shapes of packing cases and the wooden walls angled together into an inverted V.

He wanted to be first up there. He wanted to be first among the packing cases. He wanted to explore their shapes with his hands, to lever their tops away, hear the dry sound of splintering wood.

He was a treasure seeker; it would be fitting for him to be the first to rediscover all the remains of Dexter Parnaby's life.

When Jorge returned Toby had stepped up into the attic. He did this hesitantly because he could not see the floor. He stood on the inner lip of the attic, arms outstretched, for his senses were strange in this new environment. He felt off balance. If he should fall he would fall towards the light. He knew the steps were dangerous, but he felt easier with them than with the black unseen mystery of the attic floor. Jorge's head thrust up through the rectangle of light from the library and then he climbed in. His figure was bulky but agile. Toby swayed from him, involuntarily stretching himself away. Jorge brushed past him. Toby suddenly felt him as a presence. He could see nothing of Jorge but his shape, and he felt like an animal that brushed past him in the night, like a creature of grace and violence and power. He felt as if Jorge could reach out and wound him at any time – break his arms, throttle him, paralyse him with a blow to the body or neck.

Jorge fitted a bulb.

The light, when it came on, was sharp and harsh and made the eyes ache. Shadows were thrown up the sloping walls. In cross-section the room was an irregular triangle. Toby could stand under the apex and walk its length, but the head-space decreased as the walls sloped down to the floor. At the very edges of the room there was just enough space to lie down. At either end of the room were vertical gable-end walls, against which spears, arrows, blowpipes, unrecognizable pieces of wood and dried vegetation and fur were stacked.

The packing cases lay across the centre of the attic. They were solid chests, made hard-edged and cubical by the light. They looked like blocks from a destroyed temple.

Sophie climbed up into the attic. Toby had to take her hand to help her across the threshold. The contrast of light and dark, of the shadow and the spiral made him momentarily think that someone else was following her on the stair, but the illusion passed as quickly as it had come.

Inside the attic the light burned their faces white and threw behind them shadows deep as ink. They looked like actors at a ritual, all fine detail gone and only the essential facial elements remaining.

Sophie had given Jorge the keys to the chests. He bent under the bulb, hunched, and touched the side of one.

Toby felt that he, too, could touch the chests now. He let his fingers stray to the edge of the nearest one. They had travelled far. He thought that they would be much older than either of the Parnabys, although he could see Dexter's name on one, stencilled in large black letters. The edges and corners of the chests had been dented and smoothed, as if they had been pushed, dragged, ferried, hauled across half a world.

Jorge paused, looking up at Sophie and Toby. He held out the keys. They caught the light like silver and gave faint clinks as Sophie took them from him.

'I had to come to terms with his loss,' she said, in a voice which she projected more than she needed to. She turned the keys over in her hand. 'These have been locked away for over twenty years,' she went on, much more quietly.

The first two keys did not fit. The third turned the lock with a decisive snapping click. The lid folded back.

They looked into a deep well of black. Jorge reached up and swivelled the light and the blackness fell, draining away like a spent flood. Out of it rose the books, piles of thick volumes in red leather. They were not bright but dull, as if they had been handled for a hundred years. Toby felt his heart begin to thump harder. His breath was shallow; he saw potential, promise.

'His words?'

It was Jorge who had spoken. The light across his face created new planes, making him look unfeeling and cruel.

'His journal,' Sophie said.

Toby's mouth was dry.

'He carried each volume with him,' she continued, 'you can see how travel has marked them.'

'Have you read them?' Toby asked.

'Yes.'

'All of them?'

'Except the last. After he vanished I read them over and over. They're very detailed. Where he was and what he was doing on certain times and dates. He made geographical notes, observations, speculations. Little thumbnail sketches. Traveller's tales. Bits and pieces of information and hearsay on wildlife, trails, customs, myths. The last journal was the one he took with him on the flight. I often wonder what the final entry was.'

'But you locked them away.'

'I felt they needed to recover. They needed to have their own silence.' She paused. 'Does that sound insane?'

One of Toby's dreams was such a find. He understood her perfectly. 'No,' he said, 'I know exactly what you mean.'

He reached out and felt the top volume with his fingertips. As soon as he touched it he drew his hand away, as if he had been given a tiny shock. He turned to Jorge, who smiled without humour.

'Not just words,' Jorge said.

Toby shook his head, not following.

'Maybe also power,' Jorge explained.

Sophie moved to the other chests, trying the keys in their locks and opening them one by one. The others followed her, witches moving from spell to spell. The walls made their shadows bulky and absurd.

Jorge picked out a package from one of the chests. It had lain on top of a neatly folded pile of clothes. The air reeked of mothballs.

He stood there holding it. He put it to his nostrils and sniffed, then lowered the package. It was book-sized but heavier than it looked.

'I know what it is,' Sophie said.

They both looked at her.

'Go on,' she urged 'open it.'

The package was of oilskin. Jorge weighed it carefully in his hand. He was standing slightly away from the centre of the room so had to bend his head to one side to avoid brushing the ceiling. He looked injured, crippled. He held the package out to Sophie but she shook her head.

He lifted one end of the wrapping. The object unrolled, awkwardly and with a disturbingly broken rhythm as it turned over and over. He pulled the wrapping away. A revolver lay in his hand. It was black and glinted with oil.

Jorge looked up at them with eyes that were bottomless. The light flattened his broad face.

Sophie reached out tentatively. He held the revolver up to her. She touched it gingerly, experimentally, and withdrew. She looked at her fingertips, which had tiny black smudges of oil on them, and held them up to her nose.

'Is it the one in the photograph?' Toby asked.

'Yes, I think so. There will be some ammunition somewhere.'

'He may have shot a few natives with that.'

Jorge dropped his eyes.

'He was a good military man over things like that. Kept his equipment well.' She smiled thinly.

Jorge wrapped up the revolver and they explored the other cases. Here were remnants of Dexter Parnaby's forgotten life. A couple of dozen boy's books, full of roaring adventure on high seas, endless plains, steamy jungles. He'd written his name in them. In one his address expanded into Europe, the Earth, and then out into the Galaxy.

An empty cigarette case (silver), with a perished elastic holder inside and his name inscribed on the inner surface of the case.

Two spectacle cases, with the glasses inside that he had had to wear as a child. They seemed sad relics now that their owner was long dead.

A bundle of papers relating to his army service; a leather belt; a beret; an empty kitbag, neatly rolled up.

Clothes he'd worn on expeditions, including a tunic with many pockets and buttoned straps across the shoulders. Jorge unfolded this and studied it.

Some old school reports and two school photographs from which a fresh-faced Dexter Parnaby gazed, with ranks of his fellows around him. And, from earlier years, a Red Indian head-dress, made by their mother, with gulls' feathers dyed yellow and red and blue. Sophie could remember it from her own childhood. Her earliest memories of her brother were of him war-whooping down the garden and through their rooms, bearing down on the US Cavalry with his imaginary horse.

A packet of ammunition for the revolver.

Sophie unlocked the last case. They gathered round it. Books again. Toby reached down and picked one up. It had a cover that spoke of fake expense. For a second or two he didn't know what it could be. It wasn't a diary; it was printed. Thinking that perhaps this was a family history, published privately years ago, Toby lifted it to the light and opened it.

He flicked through the pages. In successions of anatomically exact engravings, a couple mated in a series of positions.

'A special collection,' Sophie said. 'You're shocked?'

'Surprised.'

Jorge looked at it but his expression did not alter. He stepped back from the case.

'Pornography,' Sophie said, 'all of it. I'm not ashamed. It's necessary to know certain ways of behaviour.'

'His books?' Toby asked.

'Our father's. He had this room as a private library. I understand it was common for Edwardian gentlemen to have such volumes. After he died the collection was boxed and put up here. Dexter wouldn't add to it. Of course, as a youth, he was curious. We both were.'

'This will be worth a lot of money. An *Aretino's Postures* like this is thought to be rather charming these days. Should I tell you something about it?'

'Dexter had a matter-of-fact approach to such things. All these books were familiar to him. He was years ahead of his time. Today, children all have access to such detail.'

'*Aretino's Postures*', Toby said, hefting the book, 'is the name given to a whole series of privately printed books. All issued for the delight and edification of the nobility, the rich, collectors. Each showed all the combinations of physical love. They were the forerunners of modern sex manuals, except that they were done with a deal more artistry and charm. This is a recent one; you can tell by the engravings. But they go back a long way before that. They'd been going for a while when Casanova mentioned them in his memoirs. This is really good. As a cataloguer, that's my opinion.'

'But as a biographer?'

'As a biographer? Well, it's a fact. Maybe just an incidental one.'

'Dexter was a spiritual person. You must know that. He wanted to escape from the physical. He wanted transcendence.'

Jorge stepped forward and placed his hand into the case. He lifted out a sack. It was of coarse, open-textured material and appeared to be empty apart from two smallish objects that lay in the bottom. Sophie drew in her breath.

'They're here,' she said.

Jorge hesitated.

'Go on,' she said, 'you have as much right as anyone. More, perhaps.'

He placed his hand into the mouth of the sack and reached for its contents. He touched them and his face contracted. A spasm passed over it, making him look momentarily disgusted and frightened. Toby watched this sudden change and he, too, felt afraid. His skin felt tight across his back.

'Tip them out,' Sophie said.

'On to the floor?'

'Yes.'

Jorge appeared undecided. For a brief moment everything was still. The shadows did not move on the walls. The three people stood there in the glare, the ransacked cases all around them. They were like grave robbers, Toby suddenly thought, pillagers, looters of the past.

Jorge up-ended the sack.

The objects came sliding, rolling, tumbling out of the sack. They moved like small turnips with leaves and roots lopped away. But they fell in a black wiry whirl of strands, and when their bouncing had stopped and they rolled to rest on the floor the three of them could see that they were cocooned in coils and nests of hair.

Jorge hissed. It was a sharp, sibilant noise, declining into sadness.

Toby felt squeamish, and trembled. 'How did he get them?' he asked.

'There was still a trade in shrunken heads,' Sophie said. 'It probably still goes on illegally.'

Jorge knelt and pushed away the hair from the faces as one would do with the drowned or murdered. The blinded heads, pitiful and absurd, faced outwards at angles to each other, their features collapsed in on themselves.

'This is it, you see,' Sophie said, a tinge of self-satisfaction in her voice, 'this is what we were up against. These heads were products of a culture. They had their enemies gutted, boiled, shrunk. Dexter had to bring things like this back otherwise he wouldn't be believed. Once you show people what you're fighting against, they will give you the funds you need.'

Toby thought Jorge was going to cradle the heads, lift them up in his hands like injured birds. But Sophie leaned forward and picked one up by its long black hair. Disgust showed on her face. 'This is what people did to each other.'

'And this is what people will buy,' Jorge said suddenly, but without emotion.

The head swung by its roots, seemingly with little weight. It looked artificial, like a bizarre toy.

Later Jorge helped Toby carry the seven volumes of Dexter Parnaby's diary down into the library, where he had cleared the desk in readiness. He arranged the volumes in order and scanned each very quickly, assimilating the dates and geography of Dexter's travels. To assist him he had a large atlas of South America which he had found in the library.

Time passed quickly. He sat on his own, flicking through page after page of notes and observations.

Outside the window the sky had darkened. Toby did not notice the time. He had been straining his eyes for a while before he realized that he had remained much longer than planned and that it was now too dark to work without artificial light. And Lucy would have been waiting for him for a couple of hours.

He rubbed his hands across his face and looked down the library. Gradations of dark and gloom had crept across the shelves of books, but at the far end of the room a flush of rose danced through the rear window and on to the ceiling. Toby closed the journals and walked towards it.

Down in the garden there burned a small but fierce bonfire. Sparks flew from it in tiny showers of intense light and smoke streamed darkly upwards. Jorge stood beside it, a few sparks of wood and a small sack at his feet. Through the window Toby could hear the whirr, crackle, spit of the blaze.

Jorge stood close, the heat on his skin. He tried not to flinch, not to narrow his eyes as he gazed into the fire's heart. Heat fanned outwards, bending light around it, and the shadows of the rose branches shimmered and shifted on the walls.

He felt himself observed. He turned, looked up, saw Toby's image in the window. It was still and pale, the red light touching it only slightly from below. He looked like a ghost gazing into the world of men.

Jorge's expression did not change. He looked back at the fire and added some more wood. Flames licked round the wood, ate it. The breath caught in his throat; he understood that the air he breathed was required to feed the flames.

When the fire was at its fiercest he stood as close as he dared. The heat seared at his face and hands; it made the legs of his trousers so hot that he tried to stand so that his skin did not touch them. The heat roared at him, stinging him. He raised the sack and lowered the heads into the centre of the flames.

The sacking burned and shrivelled and fell away. For an instant he saw the dead faces. They were pathetic and tiny. Their features began to change, as if expressions had suddenly returned for their last moments. It could have been the light, or the heat expanding them from within, but they began to reform themselves. And then the fire swallowed them and they blazed, featureless and unidentifiable.

Jorge waited by the fire until, quite suddenly, it exhausted itself and collapsed into embers and ash. He looked up but Toby had gone and the window was empty.

He walked back into the kitchen smelling his hands. Beneath the smoke and the ash he could detect the odd, musty smell of the heads.

Becky edged away from him. He smiled wolfishly at her. Soot had smudged his face and he could taste it between his teeth.

'They were horrible,' she said.

'Shuar. Books call them Jivaro.'

'What?'

'They used to do that to their victims. The heads were called *tsantsas*. There was a celebration about shrinking them. The Shuar believed that the dead man's spirit lay in the hair.'

She looked at him as if he were mad.

'I learned all this from the library. Where I come from there is no ceremony such as that. And once the Shuar did this, they lost all interest in the heads. They were no longer important. That is why Dexter Parnaby could buy them so cheaply and send them back here to horrify and amuse his friends.'

Jorge had expected some kind of release by his cremation of the heads. Instead he felt angry and bitter.

He strode across the room to Becky and took her by the collar. She gasped and flinched away.

He put one finger up to her face and drew a straight line of soot across her pale skin. He felt her shake as he did this.

'There is a book from the libary I must show you,' he said.

8

When Jorge dreamed he spoke again the languages of his childhood, but when he awoke they had slipped away from him, as insubstantial as the dream had been.

But one night he dreamed of Sophie and Toby. He lay in bed and knew that he dreamed, but the vision was too insistent for him to let it go. He followed it.

They stood among leaves and water. Sophie's face was smudged, bent out of true. As if a holy man had pushed her face awry with the paint on his fingers. And Toby's form was irresolute, perched at the very edge of being. A falling leaf cut through him, came out the other side, and he was unharmed.

When he woke Toby was still there, standing in the corner of the room. Half his body was dead and Jorge could see ribs, eye sockets, the coil of entrails, but the empty spaces of his body had been filled by his ghost, making the half body whole. Jorge wanted to hold the vision, but sleep closed his eyes, maybe only for a second, and in that time Toby had gone.

Jorge brooded all day, like his tribesmen did over their dreams, for ever seeking some coherence in them. That evening while he walked along the Embankment he was still thinking about it.

The river was choppy and grey. Jorge smelled salt, as strong as a handful held to the face. It was overwhelming and scary and it carried the taste of high grey northern seas. The river washed up over cold concrete ramps, rust, burned oil, dead wood. Whatever the time of year, Jorge smelled winter in the sea.

He disliked the winter. Most of all he hated the cold. It was cold that crept down into the lungs, claws as sharp as a parasite's, inhabiting the blood. Cold clung on to houses and gutters in icicle boles. It suffused the air. It rose from the river in a mist that would stop the heart.

Jorge remembered the first time he had seen the sea. He had been crazed by its width. It made his eyes feel as if something were tugging them outwards at the sides. The water broke as if huge invisible river steamers were ploughing constant wakes through it. Birds cried at him and the whole air was salt. He fell on his knees and closed his eyes and put out his tongue. The salt showered it in tiny droplets.

By then he thought he was used to the ways of the world.

At the mission station they had told him of the peculiar wonders it held. They had photographs and paintings of aeroplanes, skyscrapers, hospitals, power stations, banks. He had seen films (and he never forgot the queasy fascinated terror he felt when first he saw pictures on a screen). Even though he thought he knew what to expect, the sea still stunned him. As, later, cities were to stun him with their size and noise and sudden changes. Colours dipped and flashed, the air was full of tastes, temperatures soared and plummeted among the buildings.

He grew used to it, of course.

Not only did he discover finance and health and food, but the church educated him in appreciating them. He felt more and more at home with things that had seemed terrifying, unreal and worthless when first he saw them. If some had expressed surprise at this, Sophie had usually countered with examples from other worlds. Why should such adaptability come as a surprise, she would ask, when everyone knew how people from tribal backgrounds rapidly learned to shoot guns and service cars? Given the chance, surely they would all be eager to learn about city transport, banking, law? As for religious feeling – well, everyone knew that the strongest, purest Christian beliefs were held among simple, hardy people. They were the ones who were closest to God.

In the mission station they had told him all about God.

God was everywhere but somehow more present in certain special places. Holy places. You couldn't see Him and you couldn't feel Him, but some people said they could hear Him talk to them. Jorge had thought that God must be like the butterflies in the forest, spread throughout it but often concentrated on particular plants. No, they said, God was more than that. There could be a tree without butterflies, but there was no place without God.

Although sometimes they weren't sure.

There was a thing called the Devil. He seized those who fell from God, took them away to somewhere where the spirit was always struck by lightning. The spirit split like a tree and burned, for generation after generation. You had to believe in God, or the Devil would come and get you. While you lay in your hammock asleep, the Devil would creep in the door, wrap the hammock about you so you couldn't move, carry you away with your mouth full of stones so you couldn't scream.

Christ came between God and the Devil.

It was Christ who was closest to the priests. Christ had been killed on a wooden cross (a waste of good metal nails, Jorge had thought). Crosses of wood and metal hung on the priests' necks, above doors, in the schoolroom, at the centre of the chapel, in alcoves, at the boundaries of the station. Sometimes Christ hung on them, thorns around His head, His bearded face sunk down upon His chest. His ribs often showed through the taut skin, and sometimes His heart, scarlet and huge like the throat of a courting bird, glowed under the chest wall.

He could never escape from this. Everywhere he went, Christ was nailed and hung up on these fragments of a tree. He was there in the crucifixes, in paintings, in the illustrations in the books they called Bibles. He was crucified in the talks given to them by the priests, in the films they were sometimes allowed to see. And, once a year, they crucified Him themselves.

It was at Easter, although the preparations went on for several weeks beforehand. The station was united in its anticipation of, and excitement for, the re-enactment. There was a sense that the old mysteries were showing themselves in a new guise. Just as a god could change from bird to monkey to fish, so He could change His faces. Just so long as He was with His people.

There was much competition for the parts. Many wanted to be soldiers, or governors, or disciples. The priests handed out scraps of equipment and old theatrical props – wooden swords painted silver, helmets that were the colour of flaky gold but were light enough to blow away in a wind. Only the cross was real.

The priests always made sure that the least likely person was Christ.

In the West he had expected that this figure would always be present. All the statements that He had died and ascended bodily into the skies were outweighed by their assurances that He, too, was everywhere. Not that Jorge was naïve enough to think of Him as a constant physical presence. But he often saw this crucified god as something like the spirits of his childhood, who could be seen in the distance fording rivers, or heard through the forest at night, or who came among them in disguise during the holy dances. So Jorge would have been surprised, but not shocked, to see a Christ in run-down cafés, underground trains, coach stations. Sometimes he thought that if he closed his eyes, narrowed his mind, concentrated enough he could summon this god into existence. There He would be, slightly forlorn, sitting among waste bins and advertising signs, His halo glowing, the crown of thorns about His head.

Sophie had placed a crucifix in his bedroom. On it hung a Christ who was anorexic, His ribs as prominent as those on a stripped carcass. Like all the other carvings, it never gave any sign to Jorge.

There was a full-length mirror in the bedroom as well. It was set in a frame of ornately carved teak. It had been made when Sophie was a child, but she disliked it so Jorge had manhandled it downstairs to set up opposite his bed.

He habitually stripped to study himself in this mirror.

'You're always looking at yourself,' Becky said quietly.

He ignored her.

When he had first come to the West the tastes of refined sugar, candy, chocolate, cream had made him sick with their excess. He quickly became accustomed to them. And then interested, and then obsessed by their richness. He ate hamburgers, hot dogs with relish, fried chicken, pancakes with syrup, ice-cream with chocolate sauce. Sometimes he was sick, but the church was always keen that he should enjoy the benefits of civilized life to the full and its funds were always available. Jorge could always get more.

So he put on weight. He ballooned, he bloated. He was tired, sluggish, lazy, interested only in some new delight for his palate.

Only when he took the trouble to examine himself closely did he realize he was becoming a casualty. Then he began to regain control. Now, although by his earlier standards still overweight, he was almost back to what he had been when he worked for the Spanish family on the South Atlantic coast. And he had begun to regain his senses. Instead of being overloaded they were sharpening, becoming more subtle and flexible and alert.

His back teeth had almost become permanent casualties. At the front they were still strong, but sugar coatings had attacked those at the rear. When he stood at the mirror and tilted his head he could peer inside his gaping mouth to see gold fillings in their centres. The church had paid for those, as well.

'Are you worried about them?'

'One day I'll go back. On that day I want to be as healthy as I was on the day I left.'

He turned to her. Becky looked frail and breakable.

'I hope that day will not be far away,' he said.

'No,' she almost whispered.

He watched her. She was lying in bed, the closed book beside her under the light. There was only the slightest movement in the muscles of her face. A momentary release, and that was all.

Jorge knew she was scared of him. At times he felt guilty about this. He could, he thought, try to be understanding, less domineering. He would cease to be master to Becky's slave. But deeper passions ran within him.

'The book,' he said.

She opened it. He noticed that, in reaching for it, her arm shook.

If Becky feared him it was because she saw him as a wild man. A creature of violence whose only disguise was an imperfect veneer of civilization. Sometimes, he knew, he gave her cause to think this. He had made her his mistress. She had acted as if there had been no choice in the matter; as if she would be beaten or blackmailed if she refused. She had asked him if he would sack her if she did not agree. He'd smiled and lied that of course he would.

Whenever they coupled he knew she thought of it, not as lovemaking, but as mating. Simple and animal-like, a structure of stimulus and response. This delighted him. He wanted no affection to cloud the issue. He merely wanted gratification and, at the same time, exploration.

He turned the pages over.

This was why they followed Artetino's postures. Page by page they exhausted the book. They explored all the accumulation of detail, all the centuries of experience. He would arrange their bodies carefully so they paralleled the couplings in the engravings. Many were variations on the same basic theme – several pages, for instance, were devoted to fellatio. The positions of the bodies changed (the male recumbent, or seated, or standing: the female lying, kneeling, bent double), but the central action remained the same. Nevertheless they followed these, in sequence, without deviation.

He thought of all this as an exercise in objectivity. Of isolating the body from the mind and feeding it stimuli. Of watching its response.

But despite this the mechanisms of the body sometimes would not let him be, and he seized Becky roughly by the throat, the hair, arms, breasts. She tensed with fear. Once he had grabbed her between the thighs, gripped hard as if all that moist warmth could be torn out by the root. She gave a cry of pain but fell back as if accepting her fate. Her head craned backwards and her throat, long and white, lay exposed as if to an executioner's knife.

He reached the page, held it open for her. 'Get up,' he said. She struggled into position.

She had looked forward in the book, trembling at what awaited her. But Jorge would not be thwarted. This was the whole of the Western attitude to sex. He did what the book demanded, knowing he was capable of everything that was in it.

Before him she had experimented, cautiously and provisionally, with one boyfriend. When she had joined the Parnaby household she had been, technically, a virgin. But now the experimentation of centuries would not let her go. She opened her body, held tight her mind; the catalogue went on.

Jorge took her legs and opened her a little more. Beneath his brown fingers her skin looked bloodless.

Towards his climax he felt his lips move back over his teeth, like those of an animal about to kill.

Afterwards they lay together, separate and not touching, recovering from the exertion. Becky quivered several times.

'The book,' she said after a long time, 'is it really valuable?'

Jorge was drifting into sleep. Around him grew the trees and grasses of his childhood. 'Yes,' he mumbled, dozing, 'they say so.' She did not recognize a word he said; it was in a language that sounded like nothing she had ever heard.

A short time after he had fallen asleep he began to dream. Becky lay and watched the eyes tremble beneath the lids and the fingers and toes jerk and twitch.

On the next night he discovered that she had taken the book and, with the exhaustive persistence of a child, had coloured the drawing of the male on the next plate.

Both the partners were anatomically exaggerated. The woman was over-voluptuous, wide-hipped, with long eye-lashes and cupid's-bow lips; the man was athletic, muscled, with a profile too sharp and a chin too strong. Now he was also coloured brown. Not bronze or copper, but an unattractive dirt brown, which had been applied thickly over all the body surface, including the eyes. His outlandish genitals extended in front of him like some hideous brown excrescence.

Jorge flicked over the pages. Only that night's had been defaced.

'You've ruined the book,' he said simply.

She was sullen but unmoving. He detected fear beneath the sudden bravado.

'I do not know enough to say how much you have ruined it. Our cataloguer would tell you that. He is very concerned with such judgements.'

Her jaw moved, quickly and in a reflex, as if she was chewing something. 'He looks ridiculous now,' she said.

Jorge looked at the man. 'True,' he agreed. The man looked like a pasteboard creature slapped into the wrong setting. Now that this had been done to him, he looked unnatural and artificial. 'Maybe you should have coloured the woman brown. And left the man white.'

'But that would have been stupid, wouldn't it?'

'Perhaps it would say more about what has been happening. That is what you wanted to do, isn't it? Say something you could not put into words?'

Becky did not answer. Jorge held up the book and stared at it. 'I thought you might be upset. After I'd done it, I thought you might hit me.

He shook his head.

'I didn't even think about Toby. I wouldn't want to make him angry.'

'Did you decide on this a long time ago?'

'I've told you, I didn't even think.'

'I don't think you need worry about Toby. His interests are taking him elsewhere.'

'You're not answering,' Becky said.

He looked at her, surprised and innocent. 'What do you want me to say?'

'We could go right through this book and in the end it would have got you nowhere.'

He watched her.

'You know I'm right. What purpose does this serve?'

'Pleasure?' he suggested.

She shook her head. 'No.'

'What else then?'

'You're using me, that's all.'

Jorge closed the book and placed it on the table.

'Do you have slaves where you come from?' she asked bitterly. She was breathless and her eyes had dilated.

'But Becky,' he said with an air of reason, 'this is nothing like where I came from.' He smiled at her. 'That's why I do it.'

She raised herself up, and for a moment he thought she would strike him. But he knew she was more frightened than violent. He knew, also, that he had it in himself to terrorize her a little more, and that still she would be too frightened to hit back.

'Things are different from how you think they are,' he said, 'every kind of life is complicated. Even the one I came from.' He stood up and walked to the dressing table. 'Have you looked in here?'

'You warned me not to.'

'And I thought everyone wanted to do things that had been forbidden. No matter how tiny the sin, no matter how small the crime. That is why you have laws and politics, isn't it? And, they have told me, that is why Jesus must come and die again.'

'I don't know what you mean.'

'I can quote you chapter and verse. Would you like that?'

'You're a bit like an animal. You want to play with me. Like a cat. I know you're testing me. I know that.'

He smiled at her. 'Right, Becky. I must exercise myself. I have to keep my mind sharp.'

'You're backward, George,' she said miserably.

'Backward?' He pronounced the word as if he found it amusingly appropriate. 'Ah,' he went on, '*now* I know what you mean.' He tapped the side of his head. 'It's the primitive mind, Becky. Don't worry about it. You are used to technological marvels, abstract concepts, rapid change. I am not. You live with a subtle, complicated God. A perfect God who created an imperfect world then sent His son to take on its sins and die for it. That's what He took on. The sins of the whole world. Enough to break the back of you or me. But only by taking on sin can you be saved. And you think you are superior to me?'

'I never said that. I never even thought it.'

'You must think of me like that. Especially when I force you to do things you hate. It's the easy way.' He slid open the dressing table drawer. 'Do you know what is in here?'

'I've never opened it.'

'We found it among Dexter's things. I find it interesting. Sophie lives for a dream and Toby lives for dead words, but this – '

He unwrapped the revolver. She drew in her breath and shrank back.

'Don't be scared. Do you know anything about guns?'

She shook her head.

'We had to hunt food with guns at the mission station. We used rifles. You can see that this is a revolver. But don't worry. It is not loaded.' He stared hard at her. 'It *is* empty.'

'Didn't you use . . .'

'What?'

'You know, bows and arrows, poisoned darts, things like that . . .'

'Rifles were an advance on traditional methods. The priests made us depend on rifles.' He turned the revolver in his hand, held it as if about to fire, took a sighting at the floor down the barrel. 'If they did not break the tribe then our beliefs would never be true.

They had to make us throw out the old ways of doing things. They gave us new ones. They took certain people and made them more powerful than others.'

He snapped the gun apart.

'You see?' he said. 'Not loaded.'

'Yes.'

'There was one revolver. It belonged to a priest called Peter. An American. If you saw them now you would not think any of them were priests. They wore shirts with open necks, tunics of green and brown, caps with baseball teams on them. We envied the clothes they wore. How bright they were! They were not all like the priests I have seen here.'

'What are those?' she asked, seeing him take something else from the package.

He held a bullet out to her, balancing it between thumb and forefinger.

'It fits into this part here. There is no problem. It just slides in. You follow the principle?'

He saw her lick her lips quickly.

'Peter chose his own name. He said it was the best possible name for founding a church.'

'Is that loaded now?'

'Yes.'

'It's ready to fire?'

'There's nothing to be frightened of. Guns are only frightening to those who do not know how to use them.'

'George – '

'Peter's revolver was like this. Almost the same. The balance is a little different. He said that there was no point in carrying the gospel naked to the unbelievers. God had made sure that His followers had become the lords of the earth. To spread the good word it was necessary to use all the advantages He had given them – machines, radios, books, medicine, tape recorders, guns. To do otherwise would be to delay conversion by years. Generations, perhaps. And the important thing is to get as many as possible baptized as quickly as possible, for only then can their souls be saved. And the more one saves, the more one grows in the sight of

God. There is a phrase for all this. I learned it many years later. The end justifies the means.'

'Look, can you please put the gun away? It's dangerous like that.'

'Peter had been spoken to by God. You needn't look so wild, Becky. I am not taunting you. God had spoken to him. Peter knew that to be the truth.'

She edged towards the door but he waved the gun barrel at her in a leisurely, practised movement. 'Sit down and don't be so silly.'

She obeyed, her eyes fixed on the barrel. Half-amused, he lifted it and watched her head move in response like a puppet's. 'It happened when he was a boy,' he said. 'Just an ordinary child, with a checked shirt and jeans, sitting by a river with his fishing line. Somewhere in the middle of North America. He woke up on the ground, gazing into the sun, and God had spoken to him. At that moment he knew what his future was. He knew it was God's plan to come into the forest. On the way he met Dexter Parnaby, who persuaded him to buy a gun just like this one. Said it was necessary, that this model was best for the climate, that his own had never failed him. You can see – after all these years, it's still as good as new.'

He took the chamber and spun it. It rotated freely, giving a short metallic whirr.

'Do you know where the bullet is?' he asked.

'In there.'

'Ah, but which one? That's the question.'

She shook her head dumbly.

'You don't know?' he asked in mock surprise.

Again, she shook her head.

'My talent is to know that. The bullet is now two firings away. I could pull this trigger twice and the hammer would fall on an empty chamber. Should I do that?'

'For God's sake,' she said, shaking her head rapidly.

'Some would say that it is God who tells me these things.Two falls. But on the third – bang.'

'What are you going to do?'

He drew his lips back across his teeth.

'I'm going,' she said, 'you can't stop me.'

He strode across the room and took her by the hair at the side of the head, just above the ear. He looked fierce and brutal and she was terrified. She wanted to scream but she thought it might make him worse, thought it might make him actually use the gun, so she did not call out but gasped in pain and fear.

'They thought it was a gift from God,' he said, 'but all the time I knew it was my own gods letting me know they still were with me. I put a bullet in the revolver. I spun the chamber. I *knew* where the bullet was. I put the barrel to my head. I pulled the trigger. The forest sang with birds and danced with light. The hammer fell on an empty space.'

He tightened the grip on her hair. He could feel its tension against her scalp. Her mouth was open, saliva ran from the corner of her lips. Her eyes were staring.

He let go of her. She collapsed with her head in her hands and her legs and shoulders shaking violently.

'You ask me nothing, Becky,' he said bitterly, 'we are lovers and you ask me nothing.'

She spoke with a voice that was beginning to break into sobs. 'We're not lovers. I'm just someone you can use to hate. I'm the easiest target. You care for nobody, not even Miss Parnaby, and especially not for me.'

Jorge felt suddenly exhausted and frustrated. His games with Becky were purposeless, he thought. He sat down, broke the gun apart, and slid out the bullet.

'Becky,' he began, but her sobbing increased so he doubted if she could hear him.

He put his hand on her arm to steady her. At first she flinched away but he grasped her lightly, almost tenderly.

'I was a stranger there,' he said. He looked at the bullet, turning it over in his free hand. 'I am a stranger everywhere. At one time I thought that God united, making all men brothers, all women sisters. God divides. He separates.'

He put the bullet back into the wrapping.

'It was a long time ago when Sophie Parnaby rescued me. She sees a divine plan in that. That is why I have been brought away, educated. And why I shall shortly be returned. She sees me going where Dexter could not go. She sees me taking light into darkness.' He put his hand up to his lips and bit the edge of his palm.

'She thinks I can return to my own people,' he continued. 'But she is not even sure who my own people are. The river tribe who captured me have quarrelled with many groups. They call them all the enemy. I cannot remember any of the words I spoke as a young child. And the mission has moved up-river. Now it is among the river people. The people among whom I was raised have had their lives changed by the coming of the whites. Sophie says that their belief in God is being put to the test. Belief in God will carry anyone through.'

'She's right, she's right. If you truly believed you couldn't act as you do.'

'But you don't know anything about it, Becky. Nothing at all.'

She shook her head.

And Jorge thought that he, too, now knew very little. Just dim memories, and things he had been told or had read. Pieces from another world, and a lost childhood.

9

Toby told Lucy he was working on the biography and would be home late. Then he caught a train to the campus.

Rachel picked him up at the station. Toby sat in the passenger seat as she drove to the university. He felt nervous and heady, full of a tension that could only be resolved by action or illness.

Rachel's room had a bed, chairs, a desk with a swivel lamp. A calendar with highly coloured tropical frogs was fixed to the wall. They had waxen skin and peeled-back eyes. On the other wall was a chart like an industrial plant flow-chart, but showing instead the interconnection of mythic structure and culture. It was in French.

'This is it?' she asked as he handed the volume to her.

'Just one part,' he said, 'they're all about the same.'

She sat on the bed, back to the wall and knees drawn up, and began to read the journal. Toby sat beside the desk and watched her. Her eyes moved rapidly over the pages; it was obvious to him that she was not reading it all, but picking out sections that caught her interest and skimming lightly over the rest. After a while he began to study the items on the desk – a zipped-up portable typewriter, a book on Bororo legends, two technical journals, a few folders with sheets of paper in them. One folder was fixed under a ceramic paperweight on which was drawn a stylised insect the colour of ebony.

'What do you think?' he asked after a while, but she made a sound in her throat to indicate that she was too involved to answer him.

Toby looked out of the window at the broad sweep of the university grounds. Thin rain slanted across them. He could see the artificial lake with the line of willows to one side of it.

Eventually she put down the journal and looked at him. Then

she put one hand in her hair. 'Did you expect me to be impressed?' she asked.

'I thought you would be interested. I wouldn't like to say what you would feel beyond that.'

She nodded. 'And you have the book mapped out?'

'I have it divided into sections.'

'But unwritten?'

'The scheme's there. That's all, so far. It's a very simple scheme – youth, army and university, first expedition, that kind of arrangement. I'll group information on each part.'

'As good a procedure as any. You've followed up the references I gave you?'

He nodded.

'But the journals will be at the heart.'

'Tell me what you think.'

She pulled a wry face. 'I was disappointed.'

'Why?'

'Oh, they're essential, that's true. What he did, where he went. Estimations as to his position. How the food supplies were organized. What kind of trees there were. A few insights, not very deep ones, into the nature of the country. Some facile judgements about the Indians. A lot of misquoted favourite poems and sayings, all sentimental or simplistic or both. A lot of speculations on the sources of rivers, on mineral deposits, on mad rumours about golden cities and white tribes and Indians speaking European tongues.'

'And a few hints, hardly developed, about what he was doing there.'

'Go on,' Rachel urged him.

'I mean about the deeper purpose of his travels. I suspect he didn't really know *why* he did what he did. He was always in search of that answer.'

Rachel laughed unbelievingly. 'He knew all right. He just didn't want to put it down.'

'It's not as simple as you said. It can't be.'

'Of *course* it is. They mystify their reasons, that's all. They still do today. Forget about the soft centre, his heart or whatever you want to call it. Dexter is part of a process that is culminating only now. Theft, genocide, destruction, the appropriation of other people's wealth – that's the end that Dexter had in mind. And that's what is happening, now, this very minute as we speak. You must come to terms with that.'

Toby shook his head. 'I don't know,' he said. 'Don't you get the impression that he circles round things, observes them, yet doesn't know exactly what they mean? Isn't that one of the reasons why the journals are so unsatisfactory? I've read them all. And you get the sense that there's something building, almost as if it was unknown to Dexter himself. That, somewhere, there should be a culmination.'

'When were you told about the missing one? Before you read them?'

'Yes.'

'Then it's a quality you have impressed on your own reading, Toby. There is no build-up and no culmination. Just a lost final volume that would have been the same as all the others.'

'I keep thinking it will turn up.'

'It was with him in the plane?'

'That's right.'

'Then it can't. It will have been burned to ash, or it will have rotted, or been shredded in some river.'

'I know you're right. But I still have a fear that it will turn up, and prove me wrong. That one day someone will be browsing in Lima or La Paz, on a bookstall or in a library, and there will be Dexter Parnaby's last journal. Just sitting there waiting to be found.'

'It's not possible. You know why you think this? It's a feeling of insecurity, that's all. All biographers must be terrified that they might miss the main primary source. It's a common enough nightmare.'

He spread his hands. 'I just wonder if it really was a synthesis. A culmination.'

She sat forward. Her face was only a few inches away from his. 'Things don't work like that. Lives drift to an end, or get chopped off, or fall into silence. You've spent too much time among books. The notion of a culmination, of a meaningful end, is just a literary conceit. Dexter's last diary would be the same as all the others.'

'Yes,' he admitted, 'but I've been thinking something else.'

She said nothing. Her eyes were determined.

'What if it was deliberate?' he asked.

'Suicide?'

'He would have written something then. And we'll never know what it was.'

'You can't believe that. He wasn't the type. Dexter Parnabys never kill themselves. You're just seeking ways to romanticize him, when there was nothing romantic about him.'

Toby had been thinking of a handsome, determined pilot heading his plane full throttle towards a canopy of leaves. But even he had to admit that this was unlikely.

'Yes,' he said, acknowledging defeat.

'Face up to it, Toby; the man was a bastard. That doesn't mean you shouldn't write about his life. Exactly the reverse. But it does mean you must bite the hand that feeds you.'

'Sophie?'

'It's essential. You must prevent her from seeing what you're doing. Write a few hagiographic pages just to throw her off the scent. She mustn't know what you're doing until it's too late for her to stop it.'

'She tells me I'm a free agent. That I must write it as I think fit.'

'And you believe her?'

'I thought she had an interest in the truth.'

'She has an interest in her own fantasies, believing them to be the truth.'

'You've never even met her.'

'I don't have to meet her to know what she's like. Just as you don't have to have met her brother.'

'She had kept all his things in the attic. As if she had waited for years for someone like me to come along. I think she expected me to ask about Dexter's biography. And there all his stuff was, locked away. Just waiting for the right person.'

'You're daydreaming. These things are accidents, that's all. Coincidence.'

'There was a collection of erotica in the attic, as well. The kind of thing she would have had burned if she had only been interested in one view of Dexter.'

'Packed away. Things he had put behind him. Like all converts.'

Toby stood up and went over to the flow-chart on the wall. He couldn't understand any of it. 'You're too dismissive,' he said.

'I'm a realist.'

'He can't have been as black as you paint him.'

She shrugged. 'Hitler loved children.'

'Why haven't *you* done something like it?' He turned and looked at her. 'You have the contacts, you have access.'

'And you have the Parnaby journals.'

'I didn't mean merely on him. I meant about the whole thing. The movement you see him as a part of.'

She stood up and looked out of the window. 'I have my fair share of vanity, that's true. I would like my name to be on a shelf, just like you. But I keep finding excuses not to. Lucy once said that you were like me.'

Toby was stung by this. He hated comparisons that were unfavourable, and reacted swiftly to them without ever considering if they were true. 'That's stupid,' he said, and, after a pause, 'you talked about me?'

'A few times.'

'When?'

'Over the years. Ironic, don't you think? Lucy and I are further apart than we ever were. That doesn't stop people confiding in each other.'

He took her by the elbow. She looked at him as if he had done something daring. He relaxed his fingers, about to let go, but then tightened them again.

'What did she say about me?'

She put her hand under his, lifted it from her elbow and put it on her shoulder. He did not know whether or not to draw it away. She moved her head in an exercise to loose the neck muscles. Her hair brushed his knuckles.

'Well?'

She looked into him. 'She said you were like me. That you drift from one enthusiasm to another, and justify yourself as you go.'

'We're nothing like each other,' he said, but he wished he had Rachel's poise and confidence.

He began to lift his hand but she caught it by the wrist. He was surprised at the strength of her grip.

'I can tell you all about the Tupi-Guarani, the New Guinea millennialists, anything you say. Just as you could tell me all about things that are important to you. I wish I could do nothing else but record whatever's left of native cultures. Your Parnaby book will be available forever, but their lives are slipping away, their myths are dying. There's not long left.'

'You couldn't do it?'

'All the great works of synthesis have been done. There can't be any more James Frazers, sitting in their libraries and making links. The days of Malinowski and Lévi-Strauss are over. Perhaps there's only fiction left.'

'Then maybe that's what you should do.'

'A poor substitute. Truth is stranger.'

'The truth about Dexter Parnaby? A good title?'

She moved her hand fractionally down his arm. 'You do it. Remember all that I've said.'

'I'll do that.'

She leaned a little closer. 'And you know, of course, that close to you there's a much more interesting story.'

For a wild second he thought she was talking about herself, but then he realized. 'Jorge.'

She let go of him and sat back down on the bed, looking thoughtful. 'Dexter is interesting because he is the representative of a particular type – the public school masochist, the Sandhurst graduate who loses himself in the wilderness, the hardened traveller with mystical trimmings. Like Burton, Speke, Lawrence, Wingate. But Jorge, on the other hand, is an individual.'

'I know.'

'You know how he got here?'

'He was rescued by Sophie Parnaby.'

'*Rescued*. That's a strange word.'

'But the right one.'

'I always doubt everything like that. He was taken from his own people and brought up on a Christian mission. As if Christ belonged in a rain forest! Later, he moved to the city as a houseboy. His powers of adaptation must be very strong; he survived and prospered. And then the church took him to New York. The church that Sophie helps fund. He was proof of their good work.

Proof that if your mission is to convert the heathen then God will smile on you. That if you're a hard-line, unthinking fundamentalist then you're following God's path. And, after that, he came here,'

'To Sophie.'

'To the Great White Mother.'

'You've researched him, as well.'

'I can give you two more references before you go. It's all in there. Even a photograph of him in his lounge suit, with a broad grin for the flashbulbs. He's a prize, a prophecy, a symbol. The church loves him. Dig deep in your pockets, brothers and sisters, and let us have more successes like Jorge.'

'And are there more?'

'There will be. And for every Jorge there will be a thousand left in squalor and without a culture. He was obviously the most adaptable of them all. That's why he would be selected. He's taken on the colour of whatever has surrounded him.'

'And all the time he's been a kind of servant?'

She nodded. 'Exactly.'

They fell silent. Rain could be heard striking sharply on the window.

'He's your kind of subject,' he said, 'Dexter's mine.'

'Perhaps.'

They sat there and said nothing. Toby felt that the light coming into the room had dimmed. He could hear her breathing, regular but quick.

When they made love it was hurried but efficient. Toby, distanced from the energy and intimacy of the act, had the curious sensation that all this was happening to someone else. The narcosis was so strong that he was even vaguely surprised when he ejaculated; he noted that his breathing had become shallow, that his legs gave slight tremors, but he had a detached, impartial view of himself.

Afterwards he thought that he could have re-created the act in all its precise detail. But he felt no guilt over it. And, even more surprisingly, no sense of triumph. He had fulfilled a biological need, that was all. He had acted as a creature of reflex and response.

He wondered if, at some time in his life, he would suffer a wild, blinding passion that would make everything change.

Rachel lay and stared at the ceiling. She seemed content. Toby was struck by the fact that she had very pale skin, despite the blackness of her hair. He supposed that she, too, spent a lot of time (too much, Lucy would say) away from the sun.

A few minutes later she stood up beside the bed and began to dress. In a reversal of what he felt things should be like, Toby grew erotically more interested in her the more she put on. When she was almost fully dressed he found the imagined nakedness of her body sharper and more affecting that its reality had been.

'I need a shower,' she said, preoccupied. It was as if she needed to wash his smell away. He put his feet down on one side of the bed and began to dress quickly. Too quickly; his movements were awkward and he almost stumbled and fell headlong across the carpet.

'I should tell you', she said, 'that I spoke to Lucy the other day.' She spoke with such an air of concentration that it sounded oddly defensive.

'You what?'

She walked to the mirror and studied her hair.

'When?'

'You weren't in. I left a message for you to bring a book for me. Dillons have it in stock. But you don't seem to have brought it.'

Toby felt sick. It was the nausea of someone frightened by something expected, like a fairground ride finally taken. 'I didn't get the message,' he said.

'She would wait to see if you were going to tell her about coming to see me. She was testing you.'

'*Christ.*'

Rachel shrugged. 'You should have told her, then nothing would have happened.'

He walked back and forth across the room. 'What do you mean?'

'You didn't bring it. You never mentioned it. That means you never said you were coming here. That's how I knew that you were interested in me. Sexually. That was the confirmation.'

'You mean that you were organizing a test, too?'

'Not consciously. But that was how it turned out.'

Toby shook his head. 'I can't believe it,' he said.

She smirked. 'Come off it, Toby; you enjoyed it. We both did. There was no reason why we shouldn't have. No one has been harmed. And it will have done you good. Your relationship with Lucy was drifting, mine has gone. You need to be freed a little.'

'There are rules to these things. You don't play by them.'

She gave a derisive snort. 'Don't sound so bourgeois.'

He picked up the Parnaby joural. 'This is what I came for,' he said, 'nothing more. I wanted your opinion on it. Your professional advice. Everything else that happened was just an accident, or so I thought.'

Her silence was challenging. He felt that his own objections were beginning to sound like bluster.

'It's as if you arranged it all,' he went on bitterly. 'I feel that I've been taken in.'

She shook her head at him. 'Poor Toby,' she said, 'forever searching for the wrong patterns.'

After he left her he walked by the lake. The path was muddy and wet but the rain had eased, although he could still feel it in the wind. The water was choppy. Two moorhens, their beaks bright and their plumage black, bobbed on the waves. Most of the rushes had died and lay at the edge of the water in sodden heaps.

He walked around to the humpbacked wooden bridge that spanned the exit stream. To one side of it, where everyone always stepped, there was a wide depression in the mud that was full of water. He stepped carefully around it and walked up on to the wet planking. At the apex of the bridge he stopped and leaned on the handrail; it was made of branches sheathed in rough bark. A tiny section of the dead bark flaked away and fell into the stream. The water, rushing headlong, sucked it away.

For some time he looked into the stream. He tried to concentrate on what he should do now, but he kept thinking about Dexter Parnaby. About the fact of his death. About how he had fostered destruction until he himself had been consumed by it. As he did this he also wondered, vaguely and without strength, if he was merely delaying his own return.

He felt the faintest sense of motion on his hand – a breath of wind, a tickle, a misfired nerve. But when he looked down he saw it was an ant which had crawled on to him from the wood.

Exploratory, hesitant, it crouched on the skin between thumb and finger. He dashed it from him and it tumbled into the stream. He lost sight of it before it reached the water.

He walked away from the lake and began his journey home.

When he returned to the flat there was a note stuck up on the mirror. Lucy had taken a couple of days holiday and gone to join her parents. She apologized for the suddenness of her departure, but thought that she should get away for a couple of days. She hoped Toby wasn't inconvenienced too much. And she had told the school that she would be away ill for a short while. In a postscript she said that she hoped Toby had enjoyed his day with Rachel.

Toby walked around the flat cursing her in a self-conscious, actorly manner. He dredged swear words and derisory names from his memory and applied them all to her, but none of them seemed to fit.

She rang the next day. It was a stilted conversation. He knew her parents would be within earshot. He wanted to appear indifferent, but did not know if this was because he wanted to portray himself as disinterested or as innocent. Afterwards he felt like phoning Rachel and telling her some story about how he had played it really well; he dialled but hung up the phone before she could answer.

He played outrageously on Becky's sympathy, told her white lies about Lucy's departure, made himself appear wronged. Jorge watched all this with an unchanging expression, but did not object when Becky made him a larger than usual meal, nor when she slipped some food into containers and gave it to him to take home. Toby was gracious with his thanks.

Walking through the streets, plastic bag of food in his hand, he decided to visit a prostitute. He had not done this before and his nerve almost failed him this time. Finally, after much hesitation, he picked a girl with her name on a card tacked up under the doorbell of a house down a side street. As with Rachel, only more so, what he felt was more narcosis than pleasure. She had made him wear a sheath, and afterwards, as she dropped it into a flip-top bin, he noticed that there were several others in there, like sloughed skins.

But when he got back out on to the street he felt freed of his responsibilities to both Lucy and Rachel. And by the time he reached the flat he was light-hearted again, and optimistic. No matter what happened to the other people in his life, he was on his way.

10

Toby had been living in the Parnaby house for several weeks by the time Sophie's church met.

Lucy had finally left him. She said she had given him lots of chances but he'd refused to take them. He would neither confirm nor deny his affair with Rachel; he sat there, hardly speaking, sending her further and further into frustration and anger. He'd trained himself well. Although she shook with the rage which transfused her, he remained silent and infuriatingly calm. By the end he could tell that, although she would not express it in words, she was begging him to ask her to stay. He knew she did not want to go. She wanted reconciliation, peace and love. But he wouldn't give it to her. He was too detached. His nerve ends felt cauterized, numb. He did nothing.

She took a long time to go out of the door.

After a while Sophie had taken him in and given him the spare room next to Becky's in the downstairs quarters.

He was quite happy. He spent almost all his time either there or in the library, working away on all his sources for his Dexter Parnaby biography. He had books, photocopies, charts spread out in the libary and his room. Sometimes he would meet Sophie and she would ask how he was progressing. He would reassure her that progress was good, that her brother was a *fascinating* character, that this was a major biography in the making. It would sell all over the world.

'But I need more than this,' he said.

She pressed a hand to her temple. 'I know. You must meet and talk to the people who knew him.'

'Are you all right?'

'A feeling of unreality, that's all. A sense that everything is without substance.' She smiled at him. 'It's the soul. I know it. But soon I'll be back in the world.'

Toby shifted his weight, feeling rather uncomfortable. 'You realize that some people are critical of him? I would have to listen to their views, as well.'

'If you do God's work you cannot expect the Devil to be silent. That's why Dexter has his enemies.'

'Yes. I see. So . . . Interviews.'

'You want to talk to me about him? His childhood. What he was like. How we searched for him.'

'Yes. I'll have to devote a lot of time to that. And there are others. But they're difficult to get to. I'll have to do a lot of correspondence work, I suppose. It's not a very satisfactory method, but there is a value in having a written text to which you can refer.'

'You mean people like Peter. From the mission.'

'He's still alive?'

'He came down-river some time ago just to see me. It's a long journey and a tiring one. He asked me to come up to the mission to see how things had improved. I said perhaps next year. But I, too, am growing old. I do not know if we will meet again.'

'But you want to go back?'

She smiled. He wondered if she had read the flicker in his eyes.

'We are not placed on earth just to squander our lives, Toby. You will gradually come to see that. You need to do what you know is important and so do I. Jorge is ready to go back. We all have tiny parts in a scheme so large we cannot comprehend it.'

Over the next few days she quizzed him about people who had known Dexter. He cited at least a dozen, all (as far as he knew) still at work in South America. She got him to repeat the names. Three of them she knew personally. Each was resident in different parts of the continent. Of the others, one had died in an accident, another had died before his time because of one too many fevers.

'He left a scattered trail,' he said.

'I know what a problem it must be. He can't be an easy subject.'

Three members of the church council arrived during a period of prolonged frost. Ice lay across the windows in long graceful fingers; the taxi that brought them from the airport had skidded on a corner. Toby looked down on them from the library's front window.

They got out of the taxi with the collars turned up on their dark coats. They carried briefcases and overnight bags. They were models of unobtrusiveness and sobriety.

Toby returned to his task. He leaned against the radiator under the window. Inside the house the central heating was turned up full. The pipes murmured. He could feel the vibration in the radiator of the pump that drove the hot water round the system. The whole house was filled with a low hum that was just within the threshold of hearing.

He had been told to keep away from Sophie and the visitors. He tiptoed downstairs like a child forbidden to join adults. On the ground floor he halted, standing motionless in the gloom, breathing shallowly. He could hear the measured, grave, American voices of the visitors. They spoke carefully and with poise, but without humour.

Inside the kitchen Jorge and Becky mastered their roles in relation to a chef and one assistant brought in specially for the meetings. Steam rose from pans, noises of sizzling and slow bubbling filled the air, the chef talked quickly in a laboured French accent, there were clatters and scrapes and thumps. A mixture of smells, heady, sharp, spicy, filled Toby's nostrils.

'Please, Toby,' Jorge said to him with unaccustomed emotion, 'leave us be.'

Toby stood there for a moment. 'Any food for me?' he asked.

'It'll have to be later, Mr Toby,' Becky called, 'is that all right?'

'Don't bother about me,' Toby said, as if he had been hurt.

He sat in his room and doodled on a sketch pad for some time. He had worked for long enough on Dexter Parnaby's biography; he needed recuperation.

After about an hour Becky knocked on the door and brought in some food for him. She was flushed and nervous.

'What about you?' he asked.

'We haven't time,' she said, 'Miss Parnaby stressed these visitors were *very* important.'

He wondered what they would talk about. Crucifixes erected in the jungle? Bibles smuggled to the communists in the false bottoms of suitcases? Missionaries axed down by tribesmen?

More of them arrived the next day. Three cars full of them.

Their breath turned into plumes in the icy air. They rubbed their hands and stamped their feet as they crossed the square.

Toby turned back from the window and sat at his seat in the library. Then he put his feet up on the table and studied them gloomily. He wondered what they were saying about him downstairs. He daydreamed testaments of praise from Sophie, just as he sometimes daydreamed adulation from gossip columinists, university lecturers, publishers.

'Mr Savage the biographer.'

He looked up. Jorge stood at the door. He had not heard him come in.

'What do you want, Jorge?'

'It is what the church wants, Toby. Mr Savage the biographer.'

His heart lurched. 'Now?'

Jorge nodded.

Toby took his feet off the table, stood up, darted to his time chart of Dexter's life, stood away from it, looked at Jorge.

'Quickly.'

'What should I take?'

'I do not know. They only wanted to see me. They did not wish to see any documentation about me.'

'*You've* been?'

'Yes.'

'What did they want? Is it an interview, or something? Does Sophie need their approval to employ us? Is she showing us off?'

'All this was expected of me. I have been waiting for it.'

They descended the stairs together. 'What do they want with me, Jorge? Should I have brought my work?'

Jorge sighed gently. 'I do not *know*, Toby. If they wanted to see your work they would have asked for it. They only asked me to bring you.'

The church council was ranged around the long table. They were a strange mixture of people. All wore dark clothes, but only a few had crucifixes round their necks and only one had a reversed collar. They looked more like magistrates than churchmen. Two or three had drawn, unhealthy looks, as if they had been in great pain, but others had wide, cheerful, open faces, the faces of midwestern evangelists. Sophie sat at their head.

Briefly, she told them how Toby had begun as a temporary employee whose duties were to catalogue the library. Now, however, he had begun to work on something much more important.

'You speak as if Mr Savage were some kind of butterfly newly burst from a chrysalis,' someone said. Toby looked sharply at them, but there was no hint of irony and no one laughed.

'Yes,' she agreed, 'perhaps that *is* a good image. A moot point for our theologians – does the chrysalis know it is to become a butterfly?'

'God can illuminate even the simplest of creatures,' another said. 'The butterfly is an unknowing testament to God's glory. But even the chrysalis, dumb and senseless, can feel divine power. Even something as lowly as this can be illuminated, and know how it exists, and why.'

There were several murmurs of assent.

'Toby,' Sophie continued, 'let us hear about your – project.'

He told them all about Dexter Parnaby, about his meeting with Peter; no one interrupted him but he suddenly realized they must already know it all. He told them about how there was such a rich diversity of material that Dexter's life cried out to be written down. He told them his plans and sketched out how far he had progressed.

He exaggerated all this.

'And now', she said, 'the difficulties.'

He told them about the scattered sources but did not mention the missing diary.

'Tell me, Mr Savage,' one of them asked, 'are you a free man?'

He wondered if this, too, was a theological question. He hedged. 'That depends very much on what you mean by the term.'

'I mean in the material, wordly sense, At the moment you are working within limitations. Not only with regard to source material, but as regards finance, place, environment. Would you have a problem of reconciliation if those limitations were removed?'

'I like to think of myself as adaptable.'

'So do we all. Let me put a hypothetical question to you. Suppose you were researching life among, say, New Guinea tribesmen, or Nepalese Sherpas. Would you hesitate about going to live with them for two or three years?'

'Of course I wouldn't. That would be my job – wouldn't it?'

Another member of the council took up the question.

'But if it were not strictly your job, Mr Savage?'

'Are you offering to send me out there? To South America?'

'We have made no offer. None. We are merely seeking your response to some hypothetical questions. You are, after all, a literary man. You need literature. Is that not so?'

'I'm used to working with books. Maybe there's a distinction.'

'And a world without books? Could you survive in it, do you think?'

'There is an argument that one should concentrate on only one or two books, that variety stunts the appreciation. Dexter Parnaby always took only a couple of books with him.'

'I don't see you in anything like the extremities of danger that Mr Parnaby faced.'

'No,' Toby said, a little abashed, 'of course not.'

Later he walked through the kitchen; the new chef and his assistant were still masterminding everything, although their efforts were now directed towards producing a less rich meal in greater volume. 'Jorge,' Toby said, and Jorge glanced sideways at him. 'Jorge, what's going on?'

'*Later,* Toby.'

It was a couple of hours later that he managed to catch Jorge when he was relaxing. Jorge was standing out in the garden. The air was already darkening and frost, still present throughout the short, pale day, had begun to settle in an extra icy layer across the roofs and walls and grass.

Jorge wore a thick coat and yet still hugged his arms around his own body. He nodded to the sky. A bright star had begun to shine. It was just visible over the top of the high wall at the back of the house. 'I grew up with trees shielding the stars from us,' he said, 'although we sometimes drifted out to the middle of rivers to see how wide the sky was.'

'You don't see much of stars in cities. I once went to a farm in Yorkshire. It was in the middle of nowhere. The stars there were fantastic.'

Jorge said nothing.

'Actually, I think that's a planet.'

Again, nothing.

‘Are they sending you back, Jorge?’

Jorge looked directly at him. ‘It is time, Toby. I have lived long enough in the West.’

Toby cleared his throat. ‘I think they may ask me if I want to go with you, I don’t know why. I just get the feeling that they will.’

‘For Dexter’s book?’

‘For the book *on* Dexter. Yes, I think that’s the reason.’

‘Sophie will take me back. I do not know how far she will come with me. The mission station where I was brought up was changing fast when I left. The priests had lost their rights over the land and others were moving in. Now the mission has moved up-river. Peter will be with them. They are among the people who kidnapped me as a child. I think Sophie wants to see him before it is too late.’

‘And you – what will happen to you?’

He smiled. ‘I am to spread the word of God. I am to take it further into the unknown. I am, they think, one of the natives. One who has seen the future, has lived in it. *Native*.’ He pronounced the word as if it were distasteful. ‘I am my own man,’ he said quietly, ‘no one else’s.’

‘You, too, will be a missionary?’

‘That is the plan.’

‘I don’t believe it.’

‘Believe what you wish, Toby.’

‘I don’t believe that you’re that committed. Is that right?’

‘It’s time for me to go back in. Be careful you do not stay out here too long. It is far too cold, even for an Englishman.’

Toby caught hold of Jorge’s arm. He felt bold and confident. ‘You’ve been stringing her along all these years, haven’t you?’

‘I do not know what the word means. Let go of me, Toby.’

‘You’ve made everyone think that you’re part of the same game. That you share the same belief. Whatever belief you had you lost long ago. You don’t believe in anything very much, do you?’

‘Let go of me. Please.’

Toby dug his hands into the cloth of the coat. He felt he could draw Jorge to him, a gangster threatening a victim.‘You can confess it to me, Jorge. Go on. I won’t tell anyone. And I really would like to know.’

Jorge raised his arms and broke Toby’s grip as easily as snapping a twig. Toby felt his arm jar with the shock. He stepped back. The bone tingled and began to go numb. 'Jesus,' he said.

'Do not come with us, Toby,' Jorge said, 'you have no business out there. It is not your country. Stay here with your books.'

'But what will you do?'

'That is something that is no concern of yours.'

'It just strikes me that you're in a unique position. And I find that very interesting.'

'Do you see me as a subject, Toby? Is that why I have suddenly become interesting to you? Is there possibly a book in me?'

Toby took a deep breath. 'That could be the case,' he admitted.

Jorge turned away. Toby reached out and touched his sleeve. Gently.

'A friend of mine said to me that you would be much more interesting than Dexter Parnaby was.' He spoke in a rush, words falling over each other.

'Leave me alone.'

'What happened to you there? Why was it you who was kidnapped?'

'Chance. Just chance.'

'And the marks? The marks on your arms?'

'Has Sophie not told you?'

'Tribal markings? Like raised weals? Tattoos?'

'I am of no interest to you. You cannot catalogue me as you will catalogue Dexter Parnaby.'

And suddenly the solution hit Toby. It was so obvious that he wondered why he hadn't realized it before. He was trained to tease the important fact from the surrounding detail, to appreciate the importance of evidence, and yet he'd missed it. He was momentarily shaken by his own lack of insight, then triumphant at his breakthrough.

'I *know*,' he said.

'You have been told.'

'They're ropeburns, aren't they?'

'Toby – '

Toby grinned widely. Jorge's eyes glittered in the dusk. Behind him the star shone as bright as a landing light. It seemed brilliant and close, as if it was just over the wall.

'The marks are scars left behind when thick ropes were wrapped round your arms and wrists and a lot of pressure was put on them. Pressure that was so hard that they burned into your skin and marked you permanently.'

He could hear Jorge breathing, sense the tension in his frame.

'What happened?'

Jorge shook his head. 'Sophie knows all this. She thinks it is what helped her draw even closer to me.'

'It must have been torture,' Toby murmured. 'How long did it go on?'

'I wonder if it was deliberate or accidental. They did not know what to think of me. I was a stranger. I had a strange tongue, strange powers.'

'And?'

'The celebration takes place every year. Perhaps in Europe they pick the popular man or the one with the most standing in the community. In the mission the priests make them pick the misfits. The ones who were less intelligent. Those who were somehow different from the others. The stranger. Me.'

'It happened to others?'

'No one was scarred as deeply as me. The others suffered pain, yes. But not agony. They were bruised. Afterwards their bodies changed colour with the bruising. But the torn skin healed.'

'Why you?'

'Some said it was a special sign. From God.' He smiled and put his fingers to the corners of his mouth as if it had not done what he wanted it to do.

'It was accident or design, though?'

'I helped cut down the tree myself. We lopped off all the branches and then cut it to the right size with two-handed saws that the priests lent us. The wood was still heavy. I had to drag the crosspiece around the perimeter of the mission. They whipped me with fake whips. It was like being struck with grass. I had a band of thorn fastened round my head and one of the priests put trails of false blood down the sides of my face. They made the blood out of *urucu*. I was exhausted by the time we got to the execution site. They put ropes round my arms to fasten me to the crosspiece, and hauled the crosspiece on to the upright. I screamed with the pain.

I could not help it. They thought it unmanly, but the pain was so severe I blacked out several times for a few seconds each. I thought my arms were being cut apart at the wrists and elbows. All my weight was on them.'

'My God! How long did you hang there?'

'Not very long. An hour or so. I remember losing all feeling in my arms and looking across to see that blood was running from them where the ropes cut into them. My chest felt as if it were trapped under a fallen tree and I could hardly breathe. I took as much of my weight as I could on my feet but there was no support where there should have been one, and my feet kept slipping on the wood. I just hung there. My bowels were loose and my head felt as if it would split apart.'

He paused for a few seconds. Toby felt himself tremble.

'I was not very far from the ground. I prayed that I should be let down on to it. But nothing happened and I stayed there.'

'Couldn't the priests stop this? They must have seen what was going on.'

'This did not belong to the priests. It belonged to the people. I could see them gathered round me. It was as if I should have been able to bend over, reach out and touch them. They were wearing bits and pieces that the priests had lent them. One had a wide belt buckled at his side. Some wore scraps of cloth knotted round their loins or necks or heads. Two or three wore fake helmets. Some carried wooden swords that had been painted silver. They were all out of reach. They stood there with their faces turned up to me. I couldn't curse them. I had so little breath in my body. I just felt despair. I did not think I was going to get off the cross alive.'

He stopped talking for a while. He was staring up at the stars now. His face looked cold and ghostly.

'After a time they raised a drink up to me. It was the kind of drink that they had used in celebrations and dances before the whites came. The priests got them to stop making it; they said it made men forget and women mate. But they let them use it for the drink on the cross. They poured it down my throat and I was terrified that with all the weight on my chest I would not be able to swallow. I thought I would drown. When it was taken away I began to cry. Tears ran from my eyes. My nose ran. Fluid ran from my mouth. By the time they pretended to put a spear in my side I was almost unconscious. When they took me down I did not know where I was. I did not know if I was alive or dead.'

Toby shuffled his feet. He felt unsure of his own reactions. Jorge looked at him and he glanced down.

'They stood me up for the end of the ceremony. I was weakened, in pain, drugged. It is difficult to know how I felt. I remember falling on all fours and being sick. And afterwards the priests took me and did their best for me. They had a tent they used as a kind of hospital. They kept me there for days. I dreamed, I lived it all again, I woke up in terror.'

'And the next year?'

'The next year they checked the cross very thoroughly. They made sure the ropes would not burn. They cut the cross exactly. The man who hung on it was a man with the brain of a child. I stood and watched. I wore a bright red tunic that the priests let me have because of how I had suffered the year before.'

'It was an accident. Nothing more. And there are other people that it's happened to. All over Europe, all over the Christian world. You were just unfortunate, Jorge.'

'The man with the brain of a child was a good Christ. They all said that. He did not scream or faint or vomit. He did what he was supposed to do. He would be a good Christ for the rest of his life.'

The sky had deepened and more stars began to shine. Above their heads, silent and with distant stateliness, aircraft lights tracked across the dark.

The two men fell silent.

Toby shivered and turned back to the house. The night had made its geometries strange, reducing them to vertical perspectives without depth. Frost transformed the windows into dead eyes and, beneath the guttering of the roof, just outside the attic, there was a bole of ice. It had grown over the past week. Its chilly, jellyfish colour was oddly disturbing.

He turned back to Jorge. Their eyes met.

The kitchen door opened. Becky stood in the light.'Toby?' she called.

Toby realized she could not pick them out in the dark. The two of them were indistinguishable. 'Yes,' he said.

'Miss Parnaby wants you back at the meeting, Toby.'

'Yes, of course.'

11

The fog slowed everything down; it scooped out the pith of every noise, leaving a hollowness. It surrounded all the lights, making them diffuse and thin. Lucy was ten minutes late when she walked up the steps. Her collar was turned up and her hair was protected by a scarf.

'I'm sorry if I kept you waiting,' she said.

Toby stood in the hallway with his hands in his pockets. He looked pale. 'The phone rang up the stairs,' he said, 'I wondered if it was you saying you couldn't make it.'

'It wasn't for me?'

'Someone came out on the landing and answered it. I think it must have been for him.'

She let him into the flat. While she was taking off her coat she saw him glance round it. It was comfortable, even cosy, with a gas fire and a window that looked straight out on to the road. There were four shelves stocked with books in an alcove.

'Some of those are mine,' Toby pointed out.

'They were *ours*. Should we divide them or haggle over them?'

He waved a hand magnanimously. 'Keep them,' he said, 'I can't take them where I'm going.'

'All right.'

Toby smiled his best smile. 'May I sit down?'

She indicated a chair. He sat and locked his fingers together. 'You're quite comfortable here,' he said.

'It has its advantages.'

'You've done well. I mean, as regards how you live.'

'You must be thinking about such things quite a lot,' Lucy replied, and saw him considering his response. 'Because of where you'll be living in a few months' time,' she went on quickly.

'Yes.'

'You're doing the right thing?'

He nodded. 'It won't be as tough as it was in the old days. It's probably all very civilized by now. There's a boat up to the mission, for instance. I won't have to go trekking through the jungle.'

'But you'll be away for a long time. Years, maybe.'

'I don't know how long it'll take me.'

'When you come back everything may have changed.'

'I'm not much good at friendships. You know that. No one will miss me much.'

She could tell he wanted her to deny this. He would have been happy if she said that lots of people would undoubtedly miss him. 'No,' she answered, 'some people have short memories.'

She watched his eyes continue to dart round the room. Now they rested on a large portfolio that stood under the bookshelves. 'You still have your pursuits,' he said.

'If that's what you would call them.'

'Hobby, then. Talent. Whatever you want to call it. Have you been working a lot?'

'I've had time on my hands.'

'What are you doing – portraits? Studies?'

'If you mean am I drawing a vase of flowers and an apple, then the answer's no. I can work from memory. You know that.'

'May I see them?'

She sighed. 'Toby, you were never that interested. You needn't try to be nice to me.'

They were sitting opposite each other, a good distance apart. Lucy had wanted to see Toby before he left but suddenly she wished that the meeting was over. She would feel easier if he stood up, said goodbye, and closed the door behind him.

'What you say now will make no difference,' she said quietly. 'This is more like an official farewell than anything else.'

'I thought you might have some drawings of me.'

She held his gaze for a moment, and said, 'No. They're of the farm.'

'Ah.'

'They're competent enough, I suppose.'

'But not good?'

'Not brilliant. I could never make it as an artist.'

'But people never know how their lives are going to change. You shouldn't lose confidence in yourself. Look at what happened to me. I could never have foreseen this. It's the same for everyone – you never know what's going to happen.'

'But I do,' Lucy insisted. 'I know exactly how I'm going to live my life from now on.'

'I don't think so.'

'I don't have outside influences, Toby. I won't be diverted and guided like you. There are no Sophies in my life. No Jorges.'

He shook his head. 'You never met them. You don't know what it's all about.'

'You never gave me an opportunity to meet them.'

'This is my big chance, Lucy. I've not had one before and I probably won't have one again. Everything has started to come together for me.'

'I'm pleased for you,' she said without emotion.

'He was a fascinating man. He must have been. And yet nothing substantial has been written about him. Now I have the opportunity to read his journals, follow his trail, meet his friends. It'll make my name. Surely you must see that.'

'Of course.'

'There's a priest called Peter. He lives among the tribe who captured Jorge. He's the same man who met Dexter years ago. Sophie's right. Everything connects with something else. It'll be my job to find those connections, put them down, evaluate them.'

'You could get out there and find it all very different. It could be the biggest mistake you'll ever make.'

'I don't think so.'

When he smiled like that Lucy thought he looked as smug as she had ever seen him. 'You would still have gone if things had been different, wouldn't you? Even if we'd been married and had children. You would have pursued something that isn't very important and forgotten about something that is.'

'But I never wanted to be married.'

'You wanted its comforts, though.'

He shrugged as if he could not be bothered to answer her.

Lucy leaned forward. 'Toby, don't you think that we're coming into our prime?'

'Who's *we*?'

'You, me, Rachel even.'

Lucy watched his face as she mentioned the name but he did not react.

'Dexter Parnaby's days are over. So are his sister's. They're people who are finished. Of all that household, you should be writing about Jorge. He belongs to the present.'

'Maybe.'

She thought for a moment, and said, 'But you wouldn't do that.'

'Why not?'

'It's not your type of material.'

He laughed as if to ridicule her. 'Of course it is. Everything could be.'

'But you need to have something written down. A source. A diary, a journal, someone else's book.'

Toby looked at her but said nothing.

She felt herself flush; a necessity to speak the truth had brought blood to her cheeks. 'You're helpless without a text, Toby. You used to say it yourself. You catalogue things, compare them. You don't create.'

'That's how I started out,' he said evenly.

She paused. 'I shouldn't complain.'

'No,' he replied coolly.

'You are what you are.'

'That can't be denied.'

'Stop playing with me!'

She had surprised herself with her own anger, but she held his gaze until he looked down and pretended to pick a loose thread from his shirt cuff.

'I thought you were more than you are, that's all,' she said. 'But you're just like a sponge.'

'Spineless, you mean?' he asked cuttingly.

'No. Not that. Just that you take up all kinds of interests and fads. They satisfy you for a while, then something else takes their place.'

'And the cell walls are made of text? You've been spending a lot of your time dreaming up ridiculous similes, Lucy.'

'Not all all. I've been working hard. It's just that I can't stop thinking about you. I try to, but I can't. Oh, don't think I'm still the same; I'm not. What's past is past. But you were part of my life for such a long time that I need a while to adjust.'

'Of course.'

Again, she felt angry at him. 'No doubt you've had no trouble adjusting.'

'I've coped.'

'Because you were bored with me. And for you that's enough justification. But how long will it be before you're bored with the Parnabys? How many days will you be out there before you're bored with that?'

Quite suddenly he stood up and began to walk around the room. 'You make me sound empty,' he said.

She watched him walk.

'I didn't want an argument,' he went on.

'Am I supposed to be grateful for that?'

He shook his head.

And, without warning, she felt sorry for him. He seemed so helpless. It seemed he could never settle. If he ever found someone or something to give him the stability he so badly needed, then he would still refuse help.

'You must know it,' she said quietly, 'in your heart of hearts, you do. You take on the colour of your surroundings. That's what you live for.'

'I thought I was special to you.'

'You were.'

'You're just saying that because you want to sound sentimental.'

'No, it's true.'

'Look, I came to say goodbye. Nothing else. I certainly didn't want all this. It's too personal.'

'How else could we talk if we didn't talk personally?'

'Just look at it in an impersonal way. As a pattern.'

She stood up and faced him. 'But I'm not part of a pattern. That's an avoidance of responsibility.'

He made a tiny noise of exasperation, his tongue between his teeth.

'I can't be abstract about myself,' she said, 'and I don't want to be.'

She reached out and caught his hands. Toby looked down and then away, as if he had been trapped in an embarrassing stance.

'I was late because I was praying for you,' Lucy said.

'Thanks. But I don't need it.'

'Whenever I take communion it makes me feel peaceful. I don't know if I believe or not, but the feeling is important. So I prayed for you. And for me. And for your safe return.'

She tightened her fingers on his. At that moment she thought that if he broke, if he repented, she would take him back. But then she felt his fingers tug away in an effort to break free, and she let him go.

'I'll write to you,' he said.

'I don't think you will.'

'Hang on to whatever I write,' he said, and smiled. 'It may be valuable some day.'

She nodded, but did not believe him.

He left a short time later. They shook hands in a formal manner, and then Lucy kissed him on the cheek and wished him luck.

Afterwards, when she had thought about him for several minutes, Lucy put him to the back of her mind. When she went to draw the curtains, however, she thought that she could see him standing outside. A pale, almost featureless face was peering from behind the fog-blackened trunk of a tree that stood on the pavement.

Lucy watched it for a few seconds, doubted if it was him, and then, deciding that it was, became exasperated by such a trick.

She closed the curtains on him.

Part Two

12

Sophie was ill before they set off. She sat with her head pressed between her hands, looking tired and pale. Becky tried to help her but was unable to. Eventually it was Jorge who carried her to the bathroom and helped her vomit until she could vomit no more. Afterwards he carried her out. She looked frail, not the kind of person to go on such a journey. It was as if all her strength had gone. 'Clean her up, Becky,' Jorge said. Toby could not decide if his brusque manner disguised a tenderness. Becky, hesitant at first, but with increasing confidence, cleaned Sophie. After a few minutes she was talking to her like a practised nurse. Sophie lay quiet, breathing steadily, her eyes flicking round the room. Her hands trembled a little.

'Nerves,' Jorge explained to Toby as he ran the taps in the bathroom. 'I have seen her like this before, but never so bad. She is getting old.'

The last days were spent arranging to leave the house empty for three months. Becky was to be paid a retainer to maintain it; accountants, solicitors, the police had all been instructed.

Toby begun to wonder if he was being foolish. He looked up books on guerrilla movements, Indian resistance groups, and tropical diseases. He feared that if these didn't get him then an accident might. He read accounts of adventures where it was necessary to take water purification tablets, compasses, machetes, insect repellent, hammocks, zinc talc, jungle boots, trade for the natives. He even located, unintentionally, one of the childhood books read by Dexter. In it the heroes faced perils he thought might finish him. He recognized that this was idealized, romanticized, exaggerated, but felt that reality would be even more fearsome and perilous. In the book's simple but accomplished illustrations, heroes with stylized, handsome faces leapt free of alligators, piranhas, lost tribesmen, evil prospectors, giant snakes.

And if they didn't get him there were other, more insidious dangers that could. Beetles. Parasites. Vampire bats. Anything.

On the day of their departure Sophie had recovered, but she still had an oddly nervous look. Toby wondered if she thought her life was ending just as his, and Jorge's were restarting.

When Becky waved them off she looked impossibly young to leave in charge of such a large property.

Toby had flown only once before, on a charter flight to France that Lucy had paid for. He was unused to the ritual, to the lift in his guts at take-off, to the long, long hours with nothing visible out of the window. And, although he half-expected it, the texture of a tropical day was still a surprise to him as he stepped out of the aircraft.

The departure lounge was the same as the one they had left, except that here the racial blend seemed a little different, more tilted towards dark hair, brown skin. And there were objects in the little shops that he did not recognize.

They took a connecting flight on a small aeroplane that had been in service a long time. An Indian woman in a wide-brimmed straw hat and striped cloak sat motionlessly on the seat in front of them.

The city had roadsides lined with palms, and buildings that were old, the colour of ochre or sand. One or two new buildings, as white as quartz, stood on the access road to the airport. In the city centre a futuristic tower block that was brutal and blank on three sides had a fourth side that was tiled with glinting colours. During the few days they were there Toby grew used to the blaring traffic, the old lorries belching oil fumes, the soldiers who marched with guns slung over their shoulders and their heads encased in olive-green helmets. He grew used to the local and the international jammed together in shop windows, advertising signs, clothes.

On a small hill in the centre of the city there was a cathedral the colour of dirty chalk. A long stair of broad shallow steps swept up to it. People walked up and down while penitents crawled painfully up on their knees. In a few weeks' time, Jorge said, at Easter, the steps would be a carnival of worshippers, of masks and singing and coloured smoke and musical instruments. Christ would hang before the cathedral doors among incense and sugar sweets and fireworks.

They stayed with the family Jorge had served in his apprenticeship for the civilized world. They were stately and courteous. The man wore embroidered jackets and looked like a liberal grandee. He spoke with dignified passion about national self-realization, the need to modernize, the strength of old moral values. His wife was small-boned but strong and almost haughty. She affected a paleness of the skin. Both children were away in the USA and raising families there. They went to see them whenever possible.

Jorge was uneasy as a guest. The ornamental shrubs in the inner garden he had kept watered when they were small. The silver he had polished when there was little else he could do. He was embarrassed, even guilty, that another two Indian faces were now at work in the kitchens of the house. He found that they were from the mission station. He remembered them as infants.

They did not know him, but had heard about him, and were in awe. Perhaps they, too could follow where he had led – out into the world of banks, cars, available white girls, food they had never eaten, drinks they had never tasted. They asked him about New York, which to them was a heady myth of violence and opportunity and wealth.

He tried to tell them the truth.

For the first day he had difficulty remembering their language. His brain seemed immobilized, as locked as frozen water, but slowly he began to remember. Haltingly at first, and with long pauses, he began to use words he had last used as a young man.

He asked them about the mission station and they shook their heads as they had seen civilized people do. 'The priests tried to keep us away from all the good things,' one said. 'We did not know how rich the world was. We had only been given parts of it – clothes, guns, axes, mirrors. We did not know about radios, drinks, television, cars, bulldozers, supermarkets, hamburgers, Coca-Cola, holidays, the sea. They kept all these things hidden from us. As if we were children.'

The Indians worked for a chief steward who was part Spanish. He took them to a brothel. 'Come,' he said to Jorge, 'the girl is on me.'

The city football team had won an important match that night, and the streets were jammed with hooting cars. Young people danced in their headlights and waved the team colours and raised their arms in victory. Inside the brothel the girls were naked but for the team shirts and high-heeled shoes. They moved between the gamblers and drinkers with feline grace. Sometimes they pulled down the collars to expose one breast, or hitched the shirt up at the back to show naked buttocks.

Jorge drank so that his blood was warm and his face felt like a mask. The girl he chose had hair that was as black as a cat's and shone. She took him upstairs to a room that was quiet and cool and smelt of perfume. She told him that the man who had scored the winning goal was three-quarters Indian, that tonight was an Indian's night. They copulated in front of a huge mirror in a heavy gilt frame, watching themselves. They laughed and were easy with each other. When she straddled him he felt comfortable and happy, knowing that he was bidding a farewell.

At the house, in the cool, civilized calm of the wide rooms, Toby and Sophie talked with their hosts about Dexter Parnaby.

'He was always welcome here,' the man said, 'he used this house as a base. As you yourself did, Sophie.'

'And still do.'

The man spread his hands to indicate that this was natural and welcome.

'He was here before his last journey?' Toby asked.

'He arranged it from here.'

'Was he any different? Was it just another expedition, or did he feel that there was something – special about it?'

'All expeditions were special,' the man murmured.

'Yes,' the woman said, 'I noticed a difference in him. He always had a sense of purpose, but this time he knew he was doing something right. He had direction. Confidence. There was a kind of destiny about him.'

Sophie shook her head. 'I wish I'd been with him on those last days. Perhaps he became happy at last.'

The man sighed. 'I have my own theory about this,' he said. And waited to be asked.

'You have told me this,' Sophie said. She turned to Toby. 'Ask if you wish.'

'Go ahead,' Toby urged.

'Do you believe in God?' the man asked.

Toby was on his guard. 'Possibly not in the same way as you,' he said.

'Then you will know how God can illuminate one's life. Quite unexpectedly and suddenly. Without warning. Dexter had distant flashes of God's purpose. When he met Peter it was only years later that he realized that this was no accident, but part of a grand design. And he would lose that insight, it would fade from him and he would spend years hacking through jungles, crossing dangerous rivers, going among primitive tribes just to catch a glimpse of it again. You have read his journals. You will know that what I say is true. There will be a thread running through them, sometimes difficult to discern, sometimes obvious. Before his final flight I would see him writing in his last journal. He wrote quickly and with confidence. But I never saw what he was writing. He took it with him in the aircraft.'

'You think he saw something? What?'

The man studied his hands. 'I think he saw that he was going to die and was happy with that. I think that God made him see that there was a working out of a divine plan. That it was his place to die so that Jorge could be saved, so that we, the mission, would move further into the rain forest, so that Sophie and Jorge would return here. And that Jorge would move into the jungle among his own people carrying the torch of Christ to illuminate their darkness. And that you would be here to document it.'

'I'm here to document Dexter Parnaby's life.'

'Ah. But only God knows why you're *really* here.'

Later, when they stood behind wrought ironwork looking out at the lights of the city, Toby said to Sophie that he found such certainty rather disquieting.

'He has a conviction that I often feel,' Sophie said.

'Not about Jorge.'

Sophie turned to him. Her face looked cool and faintly blue.

'I don't know what to think about Jorge,' Toby confessed,'I don't know what he believes in.'

'Nor do I. Not any more. But perhaps the purpose is working itself out in ways that are still unclear to us.'

'Yes,' he said, 'all right.'

Two days later they set off for the interior.

Inside the small aircraft the air was cool and thin and laced with the smell of grease and burned oil and journey after journey. They bounced and shaved the air currents. The body of the plane felt sickeningly thin, and it was impossible not to feel one's life depended on the angle of its wing, the beat of its ancient engine. They sat silent, crammed together in the space behind the pilot. The pilot chewed something all the time, although many of his teeth were missing. He sometimes wiped his hands on a rag. Underneath them a vast savannah slowly unfurled, mile after mile of scrub and, along the courses of rivers that only ran in the rainy season, palm trees.

They hardly spoke during the flight.

Some hours later they landed on a runway of baked earth that threw them about and made them all queasy. There was a collection of wooden shacks, a store with crates full of fizzy drinks, a sullen Indian girl who wore a red shirt and stared broodingly at them. A man in jeans and a filthy teeshirt prodded a stick at a pig that snuffled round the shacks. Chickens scattered out of the way and returned, pecking for grain round their feet.

The boat was waiting for them. They sailed within the hour.

Standing at the rail, Jorge saw a bleak, muddy hillside of felled trees. Smoke rolled from behind it in a wide arc.

He looked at Sophie. 'The mission station?' he asked, incredulous.

'Where you grew up,' she said.

He raised his hands and put them back down on the rail. She touched his arm consolingly. 'Our failure,' she said. 'We won't let them do that to us again. Up-river will be safe forever. We have the finance and the legal backing now. At least we'll be able to save something.'

The boat pushed up-river, the water splitting before it and coursing down its sides.

It was older than its years. Rust streaked the metal and damp scabs of fungus lay in the wood like sores. Tiny unrecognizable insects appeared from nowhere and settled on all its surfaces.

They pushed on laboriously, hour after hour, engines beating against the current. The water was weighty and endless.

At night they could not sleep, but lay in the small cabin looking at each other, their clothes wet with sweat and their eyes wide open but heavy. They were like sufferers in a fever dream.

Toby slipped into a kind of delirium, not knowing, not caring if the images in his mind were real or dreamed. A persistent sense of discomfort began to drag him slowly back from these mysteries. He was seeking a particular word. The word was *invasion*. He surfaced to find himself covered by the small black insects. They were feeding off him. They had invaded him.

Revolted, almost sick, he dashed them from his face and arms but still felt them under his shirt and on the lower parts of his legs.

Toby went up on deck. Mist as thick as a cloud had covered the river during the night. He could not see the water at all. With a sense of eerie dislocation, he realized he could not even see the front of the boat. They floated and were suspended in a strange, blank nothingness. Even the engine had stopped.

The boat was drenched by droplets from the mist. Toby stood on the wet deck, rolled up his trousers and picked the insects from his legs. Their fragile tiny bodies had an odd kind of strength; he could feel their chitinous shells beneath his fingers.

Then he took off his shirt, hung it over the rail, and dashed the other insects from his body. All across the deck the insects lay in the collections of water. It was as if someone had scattered thousands of small grains or iron filings across the boat. Toby wished he could have a shower. Stand naked in hot, clean soapy water that drained away, went down a plughole, vanished. At this moment he did not know if he felt hot or cold.

In the several minutes that it had taken for Toby to clean himself the sun had risen. As it shone more strongly the colour of the mist changed to pearl, then to milk.

Someone was standing in the bows.

Toby felt his heart quicken. He had no idea who the figure was; his rationalism told him it must be the pilot or one of the other passengers, but imagination jostled his calm.

The sun rose and stripped the mist from the boat. It fell away in thick swathes, dissolving as it streamed behind them.

Jorge stood at the bows of the boat, leaning forward into the slight wind. In front of him the banks of mist came away in shreds. He saw his shadow fall on them and then it broke apart. The gaps in the mist became deeper until he could see the side of the river.

There, crowding the banks, was the forest, tree upon tree, green upon green, reaching up for the air, as far as the eye could see.

They waited for the engines to restart.

13

The village waited for them to moor the boat. From down-river they could see Peter standing among the Indians at the very edge of the water. He waved at them as soon as he was able to make them out. The captain of the boat punched the horn and its harsh, penetrating klaxon made birds rise from the tree canopy.

It was Peter who led the Indians in singing a hymn of welcome. The words were slurred but recognizably English, the tune partly buried but unquestionably Victorian. Sophie's eyes filled with tears of pride. She wiped them on the back of her hand and turned to Toby. She looked healthier now, but still strained, and her eyes were sparkling. 'I'm so happy,' she said, 'this is the most important thing that I have ever done in my life.'

She took hold of his arm, and Jorge's, and squeezed them. 'You're both witness to this,' she continued, and her voice was heavy with emotion. 'And Jorge, you're coming home. Back to where you belong.'

He smiled and said something under his breath. Toby thought it was 'Not quite.'

'When you have travelled a long way,' she said, 'and come back to where you began, you can recognize it for the first time.'

Peter had the look of a man who is happy in his age. He stood among the bare-chested Indians in a faded blue work tunic with his head bare. He had lost most of his hair, and what was left had turned white, and his face was tanned and lined, but he had a vitality that made it seem that he had never been in ill health. Confidence shone out of him. One day he would die, suddenly and with no fuss, but until then he would neither fail nor slacken.

They stepped ashore. Sophie and Peter hugged in an embrace that was only broken when he reached out to pull Jorge into it.

Peter even, after pumping Toby's hand, hugged *him* somewhat to Toby's consternation.

Peter was obviously proud of the village. He indicated the communal round house, the new roofs of thatch, the church they had built from wood cut from the forest. The other priests, men younger than he, came to greet them. They wore sweatshirts with the names of Bible-belt colleges on them, forage caps, black and white sneakers. They were serious but pleasant men, with well-fed faces and polite, measured ways of speaking. From one of their huts drifted the plump, satisfied voice of a radio sermon.

Sophie and Toby sat facing Peter under a thatch parasol. Toby found this rather bizarre. It was almost as if the village was about to be marketed as some kind of holiday adventure resort for Westerners. He glanced up dubiously into the latticework, expecting to see insects or rodents as long as your arm, but nothing moved.

Some Indian women dressed in thin print dresses with zips up the back came to serve them hot mango juice. It was sharp and aromatic and made the roof of the mouth feel as if it had been scraped by something not unpleasant. The children, only one of them naked, gathered round the strangers, silent and mystified, until their parents chased them away.

Jorge, too was given a drink. He stood a few feet away from the others looking around at the buildings. At about this very spot, he thought, he had been hoisted into the air by the young brave. He took a sip from the pot of juice and the taste rushed through him, sweeping him back into the past.

He breathed deeply and lifted his head.

He could smell the fence before he could see it. The strong, tarry odour of creosote. At first he was perplexed by the smell, and then, realizing what it was, he walked up the incline away from the river and stood on the top of the earth ramp.

The fence stretched all round the camp, enclosing it and protecting it. It was of barbed wire. There were posts about every eight feet. Inside the wire no trees remained, and outside it they had been cleared in a band about fifty yards wide. The clearance must have been done in a previous year, for the ground was now a no-man's-land of grass and low scrub. Some stumps that had been dragged out of the shallow soil more recently had been piled up in a bonfire. It smoked languidly, slow tongues of flame appearing in the thick pile.

In the fence there were several gaps that served as gates. Sections stood beside them. These sections could be lifted on to simple brackets so that the fence could form an unbroken barrier. Sometimes guards, Indians who the priests felt needed such a job, could be found at the gates. The guards sat beside the openings and often carved at wood with the good steel knives the priests gave them. They had learned that crosses, no matter how plain, pleased these whites. There was no shortage of wood or time. Now a heap of small crucifixes was piled up high as a man beside one of the huts of the compound. None of the priests seemed quite sure what to do about this. It continued to grow.

The Indian guard sat on a sawn-off tree stump just inside the fence. The stump had been coated with tar to prevent further growth, and left there as a kind of sentry post. The Indian wore a forage cap and red shorts with wide legs which when he sat with his knees up, did not hide his genitals. He chewed something methodically and pretended not to notice Jorge, but Jorge knew he was being watched all the time. The Indian was cleaning a rifle. He had already cleaned it several times and was happy to clean it again. He had no ammunition. A sharp metallic smell came from his hands.

Jorge walked back down the hill and sat beside the others. Sophie had been talking about London.

Peter, who had been smiling and nodding, looked up at Jorge as if he expected him to say something.

'Peter,' Jorge said, 'the fence is like a prison fence.'

Peter beamed understandingly.

'Why have you done this?'

'Jorge,' Peter replied with a soothing calm, 'do not be so dramatic.' He turned to the others, as if they were all part of an agreeable conspiracy, and said, 'Jorge always did have a taste for drama. Or possibly we would call it melodrama, I don't know, I'm a bit out of touch with theatrical fashion now. All my adult life has been spent here. Jorge's sense of drama was so acute we used to worry about it, the other brothers and myself. We were often perplexed by some of the things he did. We didn't know if he was acting, shamming, or if it was all real. You've led us some merry dances in your time, haven't you, Jorge?'

'The fence.'

'When you and I were a lot younger, Jorge – well, you were little more than a child and I was about the age you are now; all that long time ago we used to talk about you a lot. Did you suspect that? We used to have little conferences about you. I suppose the people in other walks of life – doctors, say, or social workers – would call them case studies. You were a case and a half. But Sophie here tells me you've made out. You've turned into a God-fearing, healthy, admirable, sensible man. I've followed your progress, you know. Followed it for years. There's scarce been a step you have taken without me knowing about it. Sometimes I even got asked for my opinion and approval. Didn't I, Sophie?

Sophie nodded.

Jorge tried to speak again but Peter held up a hand to silence him. 'A moment, Jorge, a moment. That's all.' He leaned across to Toby. 'Jorge is our standard bearer. You know that?'

'I guessed it.'

'Our flag couldn't be in better hands. I'm sure you'll agree.'

'That's right.'

'You see, Jorge proved something that we all believe in very much. It's at the heart of our teaching, at the very core of our beliefs. That's why we are here. That's why we are prepared to defend this place. That is why the fence has been put around the village.'

He waited expectantly for Toby to urge him on. 'Tell me,' Toby said after a suitable pause.

'The Indian is adaptable.'

'That's it?'

'A simple insight, you think? Perhaps so. But try telling that to the forces which oppress him. Try countering superstition, and ignorance, and violence with that simple insight. Jorge here has been given the chance to adapt. He has seized it with both hands. One of us, Brother Paul – you remember Brother Paul, Jorge?'

'I remember.'

'He was posted to New Guinea after you left. I had a letter from him last year. He is continuing with his good work among other peoples. Brother Paul believed Jorge to be a chameleon. He said he had never met someone so adaptable.' Peter chuckled as if they had all had a good time together.

'Perhaps he was right,' Toby said, glancing sideways at Jorge. The mango juice had made him feel suprisingly refreshed yet nevertheless a little tipsy. He wondered exactly how they made it.

'Maybe so. Certainly I can see that he has become European.'

'I have not felt European,' Jorge said.

'But I can *see* that you are,' Peter replied. 'Sophie – what was he like as a worker for you?'

'Excellent.'

'Reliable? Trustworthy?'

'Completely.'

'And he did all the things you expected him to do – dealt with visitors, bought things, answered telephones?'

'Everything.'

Peter looked back at Jorge and spread his hands. The case was proven.

Jorge put down his empty juice container. Little fish had been painted round its rim.

'Europeans have a horror of barbed wire,' Peter continued. 'They associate it with captivity. With war. In America, of course, it is seen for what is is. A convenience. A boon. These people think it is marvellous. They had never seen it before. We brought it up-river in huge rolls. They were enthralled by it, touching the barbs with their fingers, comparing them to their arrowheads. They were enchanted. It is a great big gift from us to them.'

'They are in debt to you,' Jorge said.

'You know how these primitive gift systems operate, Jorge.'

'They will always be in debt to you.'

'Quite so.'

'You've cleared a lot of trees. Are you building an airstrip?'

'It's the obvious thing to do. We need better access.'

'And these people?'

'They are under our protection. Completely.'

Jorge stared moodily at the lines of fish which completely encircled the drinking bowl.

Peter addressed himself to Toby. Toby, feeling he was being talked to like a member of Peter's congregation, became ill at ease.

'Indians have been murdered in their thousands. Even now, as we speak, they are being killed. By mercenaries, illegal settlers, hired gunmen. They have been shot at from aeroplanes, their food has been poisoned, their clothing impregnated with disease. Their lands have been stolen. It is the same old pattern. We have seen it before, in North America, in Australia. Everywhere we have moved we have been barbarous. Wouldn't you agree, Toby?'

'I suppose so.'

'But it *is* so. And God has entrusted us with protecting these poor souls. Because we know their capacity for goodness. We do not turn our eyes away from their weaknesses – from their darknesses, even – because we know that they can respond to God's message. We know they are crying out for salvation. They can adapt to the good that comes out of civilization. They can become as good as any of us. Jorge here will prove that.'

'That's the reason for the fence?' Toby asked.

'Did you pass the site of our earlier mission station? Yes, of course you must have. A great failure. Not because of what we did, but because of what happened. It was stolen from us. That will not happen again. Now we have lawyers working for us in the cities and contacts in the government. Our values are known. And respected.'

'The government?' Toby asked. 'I wouldn't have thought that they would be sympathetic. They seem much too keen on leasing parts of the forest for development. Or so I'd heard.'

'At the end of the day there will have to be some Indians left. With God's will they will not all be exterminated completely, like the pure-blood Tasmanians. If you were in government, would you rather have a force of feudal dispossessed peasants, or a group of right-thinking, peaceful Christians?'

'This is good, Toby,' Sophie reassured him, 'it's *good*. Can't you feel it in your bones? Can't you see? Look what the Indians have on their arms. Haven't you noticed?'

'What?'

'Take a look at their upper left arms, Toby,' Peter said.

'He means vaccination scars,' Jorge explained, 'they all carry them now.'

'Another gift,' Sophie said.

'Or a prevention of white man's disease,' Jorge said.

'Our friend Jorge would like to act as devil's advocate,' Peter said. 'Do you know what that means, Jorge? I'll explain it to you sometime. The devil's advocate would not, of course, mention the native diseases that *we* fall prey to. And that we have been unable to control. We have a man here called Miguel. When he was a young man he was handsome and brave. He was a peacock.'

'I know Miguel,' Sophie murmured. Jorge looked sharply at her and she nodded. It was the man who had abducted him as a child.

'Now he sits in a room on his own. This, mark you, among a people who find a joy in communal living. He has a disease that the indians call *eschutse.* A literal translation of that, Toby, is 'face-biter'. We know it as leishmaniasis.'

'I have never known Indians suffer from this,' Jorge said.

'Be that as it may, Jorge, when you see Miguel you will be in no doubt.'

'What happens?' Toby asked.

'The progress of the disease is very complicated. It starts from the bite of a fly which is to be found in the forest at night. At first the lesion looks minor. Unimportant, even. No more than a spot. But the lesion grows. It enlarges and it ulcerates at the site of infection – arm, say, or leg. But, and this can be many years later, the parasite can produce secondary lesions, usually sited at the top of the mouth. The disease gnaws away at lip, nose, palate. It destroys flesh and cartilage. The face becomes completely disfigured.'

'Like leprosy,' Jorge said.

'Miguel's face has almost gone now. The eyes are still there, of course, and the lower lip – but the centre – '

'Can't you cure it?' Toby asked, terrified that he, too, might be bitten by a fly.

'If we catch it soon enough, yes. We can give antimonials. There is no problem. With some, of course, the disease is too far advanced. It originates in rodents, you know. The flies merely pass it on to man. It is a disease of beasts.'

'And Miguel?' asked Jorge. 'Is he really a leper?'

'We have a very enlightened view of such things. We know the value of suffering. Miguel himself wishes to keep away from us. We feed him. He emerges at night when no man can see him. We all pretend that this is normal, acceptable behaviour.'

'Is he converted?'

Peter shook his head. 'We continue to hope. Perhaps he, of all people, will become a firm believer in the Lord Jesus Christ. God will give him insight that, at the moment, he cannot achieve.'

Suddenly, blasting out across the village, came the sounds of a gospel choir, full-throated, high and resonant. The volume was high enough for their notes to be distorted at the extremes of their range.

Peter beamed. 'We have an extensive library of tapes. These people appreciate this kind of music now. Don't you think that is *inspired* music? It really is wonderful. It is to the glory of God and in praise of His Son.'

'And their old songs?' Jorge asked. 'Do they still sing them?'

'Indeed no.'

'Why is that?' Toby asked.

'Their songs were barbarous,' Sophie said.

Peter nodded sagely.

'They were as unchristian as it is possible to be,' she continued. 'They sang and chanted and danced about murder, sex, their own gods, death, magic.'

'When we first arrived,' Peter said, 'we recorded some of these songs. We needed them as a kind of bench-mark. An indication as to how we and they have progressed. Some months ago I gathered all the tribe together and played them a recording. They fled from it in pandemonium. They covered their ears and scurried away crying and would not come back until I had switched it off and promised not to turn it on again. I asked them why they were scared. They said that they now realized that what they were listening to was the voice of the Devil speaking through their mouths. That, they said, was when they had lived in darkness and ignorance. Now they lived with Christ the Lord standing next to them all the time. I taught them a new hymn that very afternoon. 'Weary of the earth, burdened with my sin'.'

He sat and looked happily round the three new arrivals, his face bright with achievement. Sophie squeezed his hand.

The choir boomed and clashed around the houses, the huts, the church, the pile of crosses, the wire fence.

However Peter was also at pains to point out that many of the traditional practices remained. 'This', he said to Toby, indicating some large leaves in a patch of cultivated ground, 'is manioc.'

'I see.'

'It appears to be indigenous. Other crops – peach palms, plantains – are possibly not. Maize, for instance, does not grow in the wild. Some hybridization must have taken place many hundreds of years ago, perhaps when the Spanish and Portuguese came to the continent. You see, the invasion had its beneficial effects.'

'I'm sure.'

'Should I show you what they do with it?' Like a teacher with a young pupil he led the way to a shelter under which two women were sitting. The women looked up, smiled, and continued their work. They wore teeshirts and had flowers wound round their upper arms like bracelets. Beside them were two woven baskets half-full of tubers, and in front of them were two funnels made from the bark of trees. Each funnel held a pile of yellowish-white material that reminded Toby of diced cheesecurd, although he was sure the consistency would be very different.

Peter explained how the tubers were dug, peeled and washed, then grated. 'We have provided graters,' he said, and talked to the women in their own tongue. They proudly held up two graters of stainless steel. 'We'll provide other things later. There is, of course, no reason for them to use all these primitive methods. But we find it advantageous to maintain some continuity.'

He went on to explain how the juice was squeezed from the manioc, and that this was the dough which must be dried out. 'We'll come back here tomorrow,' he said, 'I'll show you how they make flour from this, and then bake a kind of unleavened bread. Simple but effective.'

'They eat it on its own?'

'They can do. It's very filling. Usually it is eaten with meat or with nuts. At times, of course, it has been used in ceremonies which we have frowned on.'

'Such as?'

'My dear Toby, I'm afraid I talk too much about these people. You are interested in something more specific. Sophie's brother.'

'I think he visited them. Did he?'

'Sophie believes so. It was she who came up-river all those years ago thinking they might have heard from him again. Poor girl. It took her many years to accept that he was dead.'

'You believe he died in that plane crash?'

'I believe the plane crashed, yes. And I think that he would have been killed straight away. I hope that he was. It is not pleasant to think of another creature's suffering. But when a light aircraft hits a tree canopy such as that, there is really no chance.' He sighed. 'Poor Dexter. He is out there somewhere in the forest. But he is beyond recall. Nothing will ever be found of him now.'

'Everyone thinks of him like that. That he vanished without trace. Permanently.'

'You think that is a fitting end, Toby?'

'It is what happened.'

'You are writing his life. How will you have it end?'

'I'll take his life from start to finish. From his early years, and his fascination with adventure books – Captain Marryat, Anthony Hope, P. C. Wren – to his disappearance. A mysterious ending, possibly.'

'An unsatisfactory one. There can be no fitting end to Dexter Parnaby's life, just as there can be no end to Colonel Fawcett's. Or Ambrose Bierce's. People who disappear elude the essential element of any book. Its completeness. The reader wants an ending. I'm afraid that is true, Toby. It is a problem you cannot solve.'

'You knew him from years before.'

'It was I who began to turn him back towards God. I pride myself on that.'

'You're in his book.'

'I know. He was very complimentary. It was a little fictionalized. Not too much.'

'And his diaries.'

'Really? Interest in the self cannot be called a virtue. I will not ask what you what he says.'

'But you would not stop me telling you.'

Peter looked down. The soil at his feet was sandy. He drew a crescent with the toe of his sneaker. 'We have problems with soil fertility,' he said, 'there must be an efficient way to stabilize the structure, to extend its life.'

'He said you were a certainty in an uncertain world. I believe you astonished him with the fervour of your beliefs.'

'Dust,' Peter continued. 'We would not like the same thing to happen here as happened in the Midwest in the thirties, would we, Toby? My parents knew about that. To them, the dust-bowls were a terrible retribution on mankind.'

'And yet everyone seems to think that Dexter was on to something. That there was some kind of vision, some kind of understanding, that had begun to illuminate his later days.'

'I saw him shortly before he vanished.'

'I thought so.'

'I must be honest. He was the same as he always was. He vacillated between commitment and doubt, between passion and despair. I had no sense of finality when he vanished. It did not strike me as a culmination, as an apotheosis.'

'You surprise me.'

'Would you want me to lie?'

'Of course not.'

'Dexter could not achieve what he wanted in his life. He set his sights too high. He was unrealistic. He did not know what he wanted. He did not know who he was.'

Toby brushed a fly from his ear. It was what the priests called a *pium*. They held the camp in a state of constant siege. The pium, he learned, bred in the waters of rivers. They rose in their millions from them, infesting open sites and clearings. The only way to escape them was to retreat into the forest or into a hut, as they thrived only in sunlight. Already Toby had suffered several bites which had turned into large hard spots on his hands and neck. One of the priests, Brother Anthony, had carefully swabbed the bites for him.

'I thought you would think of Dexter as a hero,' he said, trying to swipe away the pium. Instead, many more began to swarm around them. Peter led the way to one of the mission tents so that they could escape.

Inside were a number of wooden boxes with identification codes stencilled on their sides. Toby sat down on one.

'This is no country for heroism,' Peter said.

'What was he, then?'

Peter smiled. 'It's quite simple. Dexter was doomed to make a fool of himself again and again. He never realized that there could be no end to his wild pursuits. No sense of culmination. All he could do was stop, and he could never bear to do that. In the end, he made one journey too many. That was all.'

'You're suggesting that his life was meaningless? That I'm wasting my time?'

'I'm telling you what you already know.'

'That any work on Dexter Parnaby's life must be limited? Incomplete?'

Peter smiled again. Toby had the sensation of being used, of having a range of facial expressions, pauses, phrases carefully marshalled against him.

'That's *it*,' Peter said. He spread his hands. 'It really is simple, isn't it? There's no need of explication, obfuscation, categorization. You have said it, Toby. *Completeness*. Lives are meaningless unless they are complete. And I mean complete in a moral sense. Where would I be if I did not have a root, an understanding, a belief, a knowledge? My life would be like Dexter Parnaby's. For ever heading somewhere, but proceeding nowhere. Toby, you are not dealing with a life, but with a metaphor. The way Dexter lived his life on earth is a way of showing how man can search fruitlessly, can miss the evidence right under his nose, can go on until a kind of entropy destroys him. *That* is what you must write about.'

Toby shook his head wearily. 'I've had so much of Dexter Parnaby, I don't know what to believe any more.'

'But the metaphor lacks sense unless people know what it means. That is why you must write about us.'

'I don't even know any more if I want to write about *him*. Why should I write about you?'

'Because you are gathering material for a story without an end.

You know how the only really satisfying narratives have a shape and culmination, a rounding-off, a sense of everything coming together in an understandable climax. Look outside. Look at the camp, at what we are doing. That is your climax. That is the only way in which sense can be made of that man's life. He is interesting yes, but what is important is what he points towards. Even his death is an unimportant event. Yes, unimportant. An everyday occurrence. Nothing that would alter the world. What matters is what came after him. The steady, glorious, God-given salvation of the Indian. The rescue of blind, ignorant savages by men of God. I say again – look outside. Look at the protection we give these people. Look at the vaccination marks on their arms. See how we teach them to come to terms with the modern world which awaits them. Look at Jorge, at what a triumph he has become. At the airstrip. They need us to protect them, Toby. Otherwise what is there? Their own beliefs, which are brutal and terrifying? The prospectors and road builders, who are mankind at its lowest, drunken and whoring and killing Indians as they go, or forcing them into prostitution and slavery? If you held the future of the Indians in your hand, which would you choose?'

'I'm not a Christian. How do you expect me to approve of this?'

'That is your strength. You can see how it functions. And, given time, you will see how it can alter a man's mind. Do you think Sophie does not know your doubts, and Jorge's? Surely you don't think her merely an obtuse, unseeing woman? Sophie knows exactly what you feel and why. But, like me, she puts her trust completely in God. She knows that He will do what has to be done.'

Peter leaned back. Again, he looked like a satisfied and happy man, confident that his vision was correct.

Toby sighed. 'If only I could have had that last diary,' he said again.

'One of the preconditions of joining a Christian brotherhood', Peter continued gently, 'is to put aside, forget, renounce the thing you want most dearly in all the world. And the more intangible the thing, the more difficult it is to renounce. I renounced my family ties. I do not know what happened to my parents, to my brother and my sister. I had to cut them from me completely. It was necessary in order to do God's work. You? All you dream of is a thing that can no longer exist. And if it did it would be of comparatively small value. Renounce the idea of the last diary, Toby. You know that it is a false god, a creation of the Devil. Learn from what is around you now. Go outside and *see* things.'

'I suppose it is all rather . . . historic,' Toby said.

Peter gave an expansive, happy sigh. 'When you are ready we will talk again.'

'Yes,' Toby said, 'all right.'

That night Toby and Jorge slept in one of the tents. A large moth with wings as big as a hand burned its wing on the paraffin lamp and then careered and flapped about the tent until Toby killed it. He felt its body squash queasily beneath his heel.

During the night some *maruim* flies bit him several times. Their bites were not felt by him, but within a few hours they had formed themselves into bright red spots which began to itch intensely. Jorge was bitten by them once, and his body showed no signs of the unpleasant effects that made Toby's life so difficult.

'You don't know how lucky you are,' Toby muttered ruefully at him. Jorge smiled and went out of the tent. Some time later Toby saw him, a solitary figure way beyond the perimeter fence, standing motionless and gazing into the green wall of jungle.

But Toby did not wake from his fitful sleep when Jorge slipped outside just before the dawn and walked down to the river.

The river was phosphorescent grey. He was reminded of the dead screens of televisions back in America and England. But the river murmured and swished to itself, its huge weighty bulk bearing down past the camp.

Jorge sat on its bank in the eye-wearying dark. At the very edge of the river, along a sandbank that was grey and undefined, he thought he saw movements, but his eyelids were flickering with the strain of peering into the dark and he did not know if he was right or not.

He had been there several minutes, feeling the air temperature change, smelling the damp, listening to the sounds, when he realized that someone was standing only a short way from him.

He did not move.

After a while, during which he fought to remember details of the language group which he had not used for years, he said, 'I did not see you in the dark.'

'You are the man they took away and returned.' The Indian's voice was calm, matter-of-fact.

'I am.'

If he looked up he could see the sky lighten only slightly. A bat slid silently across the stars.

'You are the man we captured. All those years ago.'

'I am.'

Somewhere there was a snuffling, scuffling noise – a momentary burst from some animal off to their right. Then silence, as if it had simply vanished.

'I am trying to befriend the river again,' Jorge said.

The Indian made a rapid exhalation of air through his teeth.

'I did not see you in the dark,' Jorge repeated.

'They say you are no longer of the river and forest people. They say that when you strip back your foreskin all that is there is white.'

'It is not true,' Jorge responded calmly.

He stood up and they watched the river together. He still could not see who the Indian was.

'Come,' the Indian said suddenly, 'we will see what the white gifts can do for us.'

He switched on the electric torch. Its beam shot out across the earth, turning the grass clumps into green spears. In the weak scatterings of light at the edges of its beam the two men looked at each other.

'They call you Jorge.'

'That is the name I was given.'

'They call me Juan. That is the name I was given.'

He brandished the torch. Its beam swung about. 'See,' Juan said.

They walked to the edge of the river. Thousands of spiders were lined along the river banks, their innumerable eyes glinting in the light like tiny diamond dust. Some had even ventured out on to the water, their bodies invisible as they scuttered along the film, but their eyes bright as distant falling stars.

'Sleeping fish,' Juan said, directing the beam straight down into the water beside the bank. Many fish lay within it, their bodies moving slightly in the current.

He directed the light further out and caught the reflections of yellow, red, and orange that marked the eyes of the fish. 'Night fish,' he went on, 'you can put in the net and take them easily now.'

And Juan slipped into the water, unwinding something from his arm as he did so.

Within a few minutes he had returned, wading up the bank with a net in which silvery fish curled and uncurled as they drowned in the air.

Juan handed the fish to Jorge. He pointed a little further down the bank. Jorge followed him, the net's swinging becoming less pronounced as the fish fell still.

Juan knelt and took from his tunic a cigarette lighter which he flicked into flame. He already had a rudimentary fire set up on the bank. The flame took the dry grass he had placed under the snapped wood. Within a few seconds the fire was blazing on its patch of bare ground.

'You have eaten these,' he said.

'I have eaten these many years ago.'

Juan took each fish and gave it a name. The names came back to Jorge across the years. Each thing had to be named before it was eaten; only then would its spirit be happy. Then he opened their mouths and pierced them lengthwise with long strips of hard wood. The two men sat and grilled the fish above the fire. Now that the fire was established Juan added a different kind of wood. It gave out great heat but little flame, glowing a vivid red and scorching Jorge's hands.

The flesh could be peeled away easily from its brittle fluting of bone. The taste was of hot, burned eel. It made Jorge reel with its strength, as if the past had cut suddenly back into his life. He remembered fishing as a boy; remembered this taste, powerful and direct, the fish pulled from the river and skewered, like this, over fires made from the same wood.

They ate in silence. Around them the spiders gathered in a broad circular band, their eyes catching the firelight so that it looked as if the two men sat by a burning sun surrounded by a universe of stars. But when they threw the bones or fins or guts away, the stars ran together into bright voracious clusters.

When they had finished Jorge's hands smelled of the river and smoke. Oil had run down his chin and he wiped it on the back of his hand. Over to the east a broad area of luminous paleness had appeared between the forest blackness and the night sky. It was dawn.

Juan took him down to the sandbank by the river. In the strengthening light he could see indentations in the grey sand.

'Tracks,' he said.

'Jaguar.'

The jaguar tracks were graceful cup-like markings, each very nearly directly behind the other. Juan dropped to his knees, his hands splayed, and put his nose to them. The sand gave a gritty, quiet sigh.

Juan sniffed sharply, as if he were sniffing mucus up his nose. 'Just before the rise of the sun,' he said. He put his hand to a print. 'Here.'

Jorge knelt and sniffed. There was a smell of freshwater weeds and mud, but overlaying that rose the smell of the jaguar – feline, hot-blooded, heavy.

A little later they came to a pattern of tiny marks as if gulls had trodden the sand. 'Frogs?' he asked, already knowing the answer.

'The kind you cannot eat,' Juan said, 'with eyes that are speckled red.'

And, later, broad, parallel, machine-like repeated patterns where turtles had dragged their bulk up on to the banks.

'Where they took you to,' Juan said, 'were there such tracks? Such creatures?'

'No,' he replied.

'You can tell me what it was like. You will speak the truth.'

'Yes,' Jorge said.

He turned to the river and bent down to the shallows. A flat black-pocked ray slid away in a tiny cloud of sand. Jorge put his hands in the water and washed the fish from them.

He knew that he was being watched for the marks on his wrists.

14

The next day Sophie Parnaby was found stretched out on the ground in her tent. Her body was awkward and awry and she was unable to speak, although her mouth, which had twisted, could make sad and incoherent drooling noises. Her eyes were full of fear.

After this she fell asleep. A disturbed sleep that held no peace for her; instead she suffered on an invisible cross, unconscious and, it seemed, in pain, although she was unable to express it. Peter looked very worried about her and could often be seen in hushed conversation with the other priests. Brother Anthony tilted her head back and poured liquid laced with painkiller down her throat.

They took turns to sit with her. One night, while Toby sat and yawned in the light from the paraffin lamp, Peter joined him and they looked at the still-racked figure beneath the mosquito net.

'If we had built the airstrip', Peter said glumly, 'she could have been taken out. A voyage by boat would kill her.'

'What else can you do?'

'Make sure she does not dehydrate. Try to keep her comfortable. Try to make sure she does not suffer needless pain.'

'Nothing else?'

'All we can do is look after the details. God will decide if she lives or dies.'

Toby nodded off later, waking to the small fury of a moth on the lamp and black-winged beetles crawling on the white shroud of net. Sophie still lay beneath it, breathing lightly. Some breaths rattled in her throat in a viscous gargle.

He had been reading a book. Sophie had dissuaded him from bringing several, telling him that luggage weight and mobility were critical. She had also said that he could find books at the mission, but these had been Bibles, theological tracts, and fundamentalist pamphlets from Bible-belt universities he had never heard of. So he was pleased he'd brought a thick paperback English classic, Richardson's *Pamela*. But already it seemed more worn than it should be. The creases in the spine threatened to break the volume in half, and the print had become fainter where he had rested his hands on the pages. If he raised it to his nostrils it smelled like a book that had been stored a long time, but he had bought it just the day before he had left.

He stared at the book. He remembered something that Sophie had said to him. It was true; he would never have thought of himself as cataloguing the Parnaby library; nor, when he had been living with Lucy, could he have foreseen himself sitting here, somewhere in the South American rain forest, beside this stricken woman. Yet from this very point, if he looked back at his life now, everything seemed predictable, every step obvious. There was indeed some force in the world, some fate, something that he could not name but which somehow provided a direction.

The next day she died.

Father Anthony came and told Toby while he was watching one of the Indians skim across the water in a canoe. He was impressed by the easy grace of the canoeist and had drifted into a reverie of motion and simple, uncomplicated life. When Anthony told him the news he was sufficiently calm to be neither shocked nor distressed by the event.

Jorge found out further details. One of the Indian women had been watching Sophie. She had died quite peacefully, slipping further and further into unconsciousness and then death. The woman had wanted to get one of her men to bite the forehead to see if she really was dead, but Peter had told her that there was no need of such superstitions now.

'They will have to bury her today,' Jorge said. 'She will be first in the cemetry.'

'First?'

'The people buried their dead in the forest. They dug graves that were deep enough for wild pigs not to be able to get at the dead. They threw in their possessions. That was all.'

'And there's a proper graveyard now?'

'At the top of the rise. Just outside the fence. It will be a formal Christian ceremony.'

Toby shook his head. 'I thought that if she died we would somehow go back with her.'

'How, Toby?'

'I don't know. I hadn't thought it out.'

'Think it out now, Toby. Think of the heat. The humidity. They had better get her buried quickly.'

'Will things be as bad as that?'

Jorge smiled. 'It is the way things are. There is nothing to discuss.'

'She should be back among her own people. I wouldn't like to be buried out here.'

'Sophie was very different from you. These are her children. She would want to die among them, as her brother did.'

Toby felt amazed at the speed of events. There was not even time for the loss to sink in; she had to be disposed of, and quickly. As he brooded on this, the sounds of hammering drifted across the camp.

Jorge nodded. 'They have never seen a coffin before,' he said. 'One of the priests is demonstrating how to make one. It will be very simple, but enough.'

A short while later the two of them walked through the camp and up the rise. Some of the women had been given black strips of cloth and had tied them around their arms, necks, and heads. A small child sat in the dust and studied one intently, pulling it between her fingers again and again.

A crowd of Indians had started to dig a hole. They seemed to have begun by using whatever they could lay their hands on, hoes and rakes and machetes, for the ground over a wide area was partly dug, chopped, or otherwise broken. Eventually, when organized by Brother Mark, they had understood that they should concentrate on one fairly small space. Still they all jostled around it, jabbing into the hole while others stood with bare feet, chattering excitedly. The soil was red, the colour of ochre, and dust rose in small reddish clouds.

At first Toby thought it was all a shambles. He couldn't see a grave being dug here; Sophie's burial would be a farce.

'They all want to be part of the ceremony,' Jorge explained. 'They want everyone to be part of the goodbye.'

Brother Mark smiled understandingly at Toby. This smile, which all the priests shared, had begun to irritate him more and more. He imagined them all being taught it. They used it incessantly on him.

'Give them a few moments,' Mark said.

'Will they get anything done?'

'Of course. When they began they did not even know how big a coffin was. They thought it was as big as a tree.'

'That's ridiculous.'

'Really?'

There were several women in the party. One, Serafina, had been noticed by Toby on several occasions as she walked around the camp. He had no way of guessing her age; if she had corresponded to the European image he might have guessed nineteen, but here, he realized, that had little meaning. She could be years younger than that. She had a bob of black hair sheared around the ears and high up on the nape of the neck; the same flattish face and snub nose as her fellows; a slightly protuberant belly of fine-grained skin that shone with health; breasts that stuck straight out with nipples like glistening brown cones. She disturbed him.

He felt guilty about this. He had always thought that people in their natural state, such as this, would bear no erotic charge at all. He believed he would be able to accept them clinically and without voyeurism. And, if he admitted it, he was bolstered in this by his own ethnocentrism. He might not have been able to accept white women in the same conditions.

Now he found that he hungered after some of the women, and this girl in particular. He did not know anything about her, he could not speak her language, he guessed that to her he was a strange and perhaps ugly figure, but when Serafina walked past, or talked to her friends, or sat there grating manioc, he felt disturbed and uncomfortable. He daydreamed impossible scenes of sexual congress, picturing her inviting him into the cool silence of a hut, or shady greenery of the forest.

After a while the Indians fell into a quick, demanding rhythm, leaving the digging to three men with spades. The others stood around the deepening trench, shoring up the growing bank of soil.

Toby was impressed by the way they worked. They never paused, but continued in the same relentlessly steady rhythm, as if they were bending and lifting to a drumbeat. They dug further and further into the ground, refusing to slacken, working themselves deeper and deeper into it. Their back and arms developed a sheen like an oil. Pium darted between them.

Below the surface the ground was damp, and the diggers could lift large wedges of it on their spades. When dumped at the side of the hole, small flint-like pieces of stone could be seen glittering in the sun. The heat made the damp mound steam gently.

When they had finished the three men climbed from a perfectly rectangular grave, sunk as deep as a short man, with sharp, clean sides. The men were stained the colour of iron ore.

One of the diggers was Juan. He and Jorge began to talk. Toby did not understand a word; even the sounds were unlike any language he had ever tried to learn. But he went with them when they walked to the river and Juan stripped naked to wash himself in the shallows. Toby felt unsettlingly envious of his physique, and for a moment or two wished he had spent his life, not among books and museums, but among trees and rivers and wildlife you killed and ate.

'They do not allow nakedness,' Jorge said.

'No,' Juan replied.

Toby tried to look intelligent but neither Jorge nor Juan attempted to say anything to him.

'We do not know what we want or what we need,' Juan said.

'You know where you belong.'

'They cut down our belongings. They burn them. We agree with this. They rob us of our songs, they take away our gods and hide them. We agree with this also. They give us other things in return.'

'Electric flashlights, cigarette lighters, steel axes, spades.'

He had spoken in English but Juan understood him.

'They say you wear the marks of their god. Their god who is now our god. I have seen them on your arms. They say you will carry his power among us.'

'You hear many stories.'

'I do.'

'Some things I never hear.'

Juan climbed from the river. Water coursed down his skin.

'I do not hear your names,' Jorge said.

'You know my name.'

'But I do not know your original name. The priests have christened you all. Have they also robbed you of your names?'

'We use them still. In secret. A man can never be robbed of his name.'

'Perhaps he can.'

'My name is Akorote.' Floodriver.

'Your mother and father?'

'Kreiti and Babrore.' Pighunter, Brightbird.

'Their mothers and fathers?'

'Kremuro, Mangrira, Rauki, Bebkogotu.' Redmoth, Rainybird, Herbroot, Cloud.

'And theirs?'

Juan told him his family tree. It stretched back generations in a litany of the dead. To Toby, it seemed a catalogue of meaningless noises. He was not aware that each name contained within it a characteristic, defining code. Jorge knew this, at the same time realizing that he was not being told the full names. That information was privileged to members of the tribe.

'Sophie's name?' he asked.

Juan did not recognize this.

'The white woman.'

'Eketinu.'

That was what it meant – whitewoman.

'And me? Have they given Jorge a name?'

'They have. The priests told us you would arrive. Most called you by the name they gave, the name you call yourself. Others called you Captive. Now some call you Snakewrist.'

'And Toby?'

'This man?'

'This man.'

'He has no name. We will have to give him a name.'

'He has a name in the country that he comes from.'

'It is no good here. He must have another name.'

'True. You know Miguel?'

'Everyone knows him. How could I not know him?'

'It was Miguel who brought me here.'

'It was Toothedjaws who brought you here.'

'Is that also his name?'

'He has many names.'

'But the man who captured me and brought me here and gave me to Whitewoman – he was Toothedjaws and is now Miguel?

'The priests call him Miguel. We call him Deadface. He still calls himself Toothedjaws.'

Toby had become bored by this lilting, guttural, insistent conversational beat. Impelled by a nagging sense of duty, he went to the wooden church where Sophie's body lay.

He had not been in the church before. It was the first thing the missionaries had built, a substantial wooden shack in traditional, pitched-roof, pioneer style. A large cross of pale fine-grained wood rose from the topmost point of the roof.

There were no windows because they had, as yet, no glass, although Peter had considered bringing glass up the river. Openings had, however, been left in the walls and simple shutters could be fastened over these during rainstorms.

The church had bare wooden walls, although one or two crucifixes hung on them and, on one large panel, someone had begun to carve the ten commandments in Spanish, Portuguese and English. Only part of them had so far been incised, but the rest had been plotted on the panel. Their outlines were visible in pencil. On the floor were rows of benches, and the altar itself was of heavy wood. The pattern Toby had seen on the local pottery was chiselled on its side.

Sophie's rough wooden coffin lay in front of the altar. One of the lid nails had split through the side when it had been hammered home. The coffin was covered in a heap of flowers. They were rain forest flowers, brilliantly coloured and with heavily sweet and pervasive scents. Everything in the building was drab and low-key apart from this bright, striking assemblage of scarlet, emerald, ivory and mustard.

Peter was waiting by the coffin. 'At last you have come here,' he said gently.

'I thought I might take a look at her. I don't want to, but I feel I should.'

'But Toby, you are too late. She is already nailed in.'

'Don't you think that was a little hasty?'

'The Indians understand the corruption of the flesh. They see how quickly it happens. We want them to concentrate on the spiritual side of death. We want them to know that God has reached down and gathered our beloved Sophie up into the sky.'

'I see.'

'Perhaps you, too, could usefully think about this. About the corruption of the body. The immortality of the soul.'

Toby stayed in the church until the rest of the village began to file in and fill up the benches. Then, feeling that the belief in the building was too emotionally raw for his delicate agnosticism, he quietly left.

Jorge was outside.

'You too?' Toby asked.

Jorge walked around the huts. Toby trailed after him. Dogs and fowl and a few pet macaws strayed near their feet and shied away just before they were trodden on. The village was quiet apart from the hymn, powerful but strangely inarticulate, which burst out of the church and filled the bright air. The river, too, was quiet, with all the canoes drawn up on its bank, and its eddies silently flowing through reflections of the sun.

'I thought you would have to be there,' Toby said.

Jorge did not reply.

'I've never been able to understand you much.'

'I do not ask you to understand me.'

They were passing the pile of carved crosses. Almost absent-mindedly Jorge bent and picked up a small one, no bigger than his hand, and began to toy with it.

'I sometimes wonder if I killed her,' he said.

Toby was brought up short by this comment. He decided it was exaggeration. 'I suppose we all have doubts like that.'

'I loved her and I hated her. There is nothing else to say.'

The procession left the church with Sophie's coffin at its head. Everyone followed it up the hill, initially in a long, strung-out line. But, as they climbed, those further down the line spread further and further out, like a widening fan, until finally they resembled the formation of an attacking army. Only the fence stopped them.

They congested around the gates, filtering through only slowly.

The sun was high over the grave. The heap of soil had dried so that its surface was powder, but as the sun reached into the grave its sides continued to give off wisps of steam. Toby thought of fermentation and the smells and noises of Lucy's parents' farm.

Peter gave the address. He said that it was a time for sorrow, but also for rejoicing. He told them that Sophie sat with God and Jesus in the heaven that awaited them all.

The pium zigzagged round Toby's head. He felt one land and slapped it before it bit him. He did not intend the slap to be loud, but it was sharp enough for several heads to turn towards him. Embarrassed, he looked down.

Jorge, who had taken care to stand well away from Toby, felt tears come to his eyes. This extraordinary woman was gone from him now. He had no one.

During the address, which was lengthy, Toby looked up and across the rows of heads and saw, behind them and in front of the village, something which made him think he was seeing things. A man, naked but for a penis sheath, stood on the outskirts of the crowd. He said nothing but stood stock still, a long spear in one hand. Where his face should have been there was a mask of grey clay, with slits for eyes, nostrils, mouth. Black, piercing eyes burned in the expressionless grey mask. He looked like a figure from a ceremony, but took no part in what was going on.

The flies buzzed round Toby. They sounded menacing in his ears, like tiny saws. He could smell the bodies of the tribe, the opened earth, the scent of flowers which he had begun to think were there to drench the sweetness of rapid, shocking decay.

He looked back and saw that the clay-faced figure was still there. It stood unmoving, like a guardian of the tribal past. Only when the first handful of earth struck the coffin did the man turn and trot quickly down the hill. More handfuls were tossed into the grave, and the noise of their impact changed from earth on hollowed wood to earth on earth. The man disappeared into the village.

When he filed past the grave Toby felt that he too should cast down a handful of soil. It was warm and moist and crumbled in his fist. There was almost nothing of the coffin visible now; a broken surface of grainy, lumpy soil and flinty stone covered it apart from the edges. The sun shone on it for the last time.

Jorge, when it was his turn, gently tossed the small crucifix into the grave.

Afterwards, when the Indians were returning, Jorge stopped Toby. They could still hear the slice and slide of the diggers scooping and shovelling the rest of the earth into the grave.

'Did you see him?'

'I don't know,' Toby said doubtfully, 'I thought I might be hallucinating. He didn't seem real.'

Jorge looked at him and for a moment Toby thought he seemed perplexed. Then he turned and walked back to the village.

When they had finished the grave the Indians danced across it, spreading the mound with their bare feet, and then they placed flowers on it. Already the petals had begun to die.

15

It was Juan who acted as go-between. Toby assumed he was visiting the old warrior in the hut where he lived, set apart from the others in its own half-proud, half-stigmatized isolation. Deadface's wife, whom the priests had called Anjelica, had developed a moody tolerance of her husand's particular existence, half hermit, half night-time tracker. She sat outside, her flat breasts flapping as she occupied herself with weaving, or kneading manioc, or plucking a chicken. Sometimes her daughters and their small children would visit her and sit outside too. They hardly ever went into the hut.

In fact Juan met Deadface at night, by the river or at the edge of the forest. In the dark Deadface would be a warrior again, proud, carrying weapons. He stamped the ground and held his palm out, fingers pointing downwards, to show that he spoke the truth, daring Juan to contradict him. He spoke necessary things.

Juan reported what he said to Jorge. He omitted nothing, repeating each phrase as it had been spoken to him. Toothedjaws was one of the greatest warriors who ever lived. He roamed the forest like a silent ghost, his wrath as deadly and swift as the storm. He broke the enemy. He stepped on them and snapped them like a dry twig under the foot.

'Tell him', Jorge said, 'that no one doubts his greatness. That I, of all people, realize his prowess, his potency. That he is so great that only he can tell me what I want to know.'

They waited two days.

Jorge was *his* property, Juan reported; he Toothedjaws, had taken him as a child. How dare he ask such questions of his owner?

'Tell him that he gave me to Eketinu. That now she is dead, I am free.'

They had to wait even longer. Both Jorge and Toby thought that this was the end. Toby even talked of getting the boat to he-did-not-know-where; he brooded about returning to England and trying to take up with Lucy or Rachel again. Anything to give him some stability and a little finance. But Jorge said that, wherever Toby's destiny lay, he knew that *his* was here. Not with this tribe, but with his own people – Javarunu. Toby warned him that he'd seen too much, that no longer could he be the simple savage. Then he saw Serafina passing and daydreamed that this alternative was, perhaps, an acceptable one.

Juan came back. 'He will meet you,' he said.

Jorge spread his hands. 'Where?'

'Tonight. Beside the river. I will take you.' He indicated Toby. 'He says Nameless must come with you.'

'I do not want him to.'

'He says Nameless saw him at Whitewoman's burial and thought he was a ghost. He will prove to Nameless he is not.

It was the same word as *enemy*.

'I do not wish him to go,' Jorge said.

'He must. He will come to no harm. But he cannot make that promise about you. He says you are his property and you ran away.'

Jorge translated for Toby.

'I'll come,' agreed Toby. He had had a sudden and bizarre image of the clay-faced Indian killing Jorge. Could this, he wondered, be shaped to suit his narrative?'

When they went to meet Deadface he was sitting by the river. It was silvered by moonlight. He stood up at their approach, but spoke not a word.

Without the clay mask he had smeared on his face, he looked eerily wounded. The moonlight showed his disfigurement. From the centre of the upper lip to just below the eyes a chasm had opened up, as if the front of his face had been split by the blow of a sword. Although the rest of his skin was smooth and opalescent, the opening in his face absorbed light, like a black mass of scar tissue.

Jorge and he stood facing each other, the years between them tense and dizzying.

Toby and Juan stood away to one side. Toby felt shivery and dislocated; the darkness seemed full of tiny noises. If he strained his eyes the ground seemed to have something moving in it, just beyond the edge of his vision. He wished he had a switch, like the guard of a prison camp, that would drench everything with sharp, inescapable light, and then he wondered if he would be even more scared by what such illumination would reveal.

'I am a fast runner,' Deadface said.

A long time lapsed before Jorge replied.

'The white world is even faster,' he said. 'You caught me, then it caught me. Now it pursues us all and hunts us down.'

'It has not yet hunted down your people.'

'I want you to tell me who my people are.'

'Your people are the Javarunu.'

'Yes.'

'When the gods held the sun in their hands and their feet stamped out the river beds, when they split men like saplings, the father of all the gods created people who were good, strong, intelligent. Now we know he also made people who were white, but he sold those to another god. Then he made the Javarunu. He made them to put evil in the land.'

He turned slightly to the river. Jorge could see even more clearly how the nose had been destroyed, and even the upper lip had been eaten away so that the front of the teeth showed in the gums.

'My father, Karunhote, had his shoulder pierced by a Javarunu arrow. We had to cut him so the blood ran and the poison would not kill him, but still he lay for six days in a fever, and for another thirty days he walked and talked like a man who has been struck hard on the head. My uncle, Meyotu, my father's oldest brother, fell into their ambush when alone in the forest hunting. He was a brave man, strong, and feared nothing, but the birds and monkeys know how he screamed before they let him die. Some say that a god pitied him, and sent a snake so that it could bite him and help him die quickly. My grandfather's sister was taken from us in a raid and although everyone went in pursuit she was never seen again. It is said the warriors raped her then slit her throat and dropped her in a forest pool.'

Deadface carried on telling a series of violent acts; he told of many generations that Jorge's tribe had murdered, kidnapped, maimed and threatened. Then he stopped, they looked at each other, a fish broke surface in the river, and he began again, this time telling of victories. Of how generations had raided the Javarunu, ambushed them, slit their pigs, crushed their skulls, defiled their women, taken their children.

He stroked his forehead with the heel of his hand.

'I am their greatest foe,' he said, 'they know my name and fear me. They hear it spoken and their bowels open, they become like the newborn, ignorant and fearful. The children cling to their mothers' breasts, knowing they will be plucked from them. Hearing that I am near, the women hide in the forest and protect their genitals with their hands.'

'And they will recognize you by the deadness in your face,' Jorge said. He took a step forward and extended his arms, holding them palms upward and then turning them.

'I had heard that you carried the whites' marks. Now I see that it is true.' Deadface spread his fingers in front of his face. 'Just as I carry the marks of the enemy.'

'But I do not belong with the whites.'

'We are both lost men, Snakewrist. We may fight but we can never win. At the moment of passing beyond death, I will awaken to find myself among Javarunu. And you will be among white gods and demons. It would have been better for you if I had broken your skull all those years ago.'

'But you still meet with their warriors.'

'I have heard talk of what you have said. I know what you want.'

Jorge waited.

'Why should I take you back to them?'

'Because they are my people.'

'You are crazy.'

'Because, when you took me, they reached out and marked you.'

'You say this disease is because of you?'

'The Javarunu are taking their revenge for my kidnap. Over the years it has eaten into you. Until you can return me you will always be Deadface.'

Silence. In the distance, it could have been miles away, a noise like a deep breath.

'Take me back. I can leave behind the marks on my arms when

I cross over into death. You need not fear the Javarunu hell. We can save each other.'

Deadface stood silent and did not move. Then he made a noise in the back of his throat as if he was going to spit. And he turned suddenly and sped off into the darkness.

They could hear his bare feet padding softly on the earth, but soon lost sight of his shape as it merged into a black shapeless mound of shrub.

Juan started down the hill.

Toby rubbed his face. Its muscles felt numb. He had the impression of having witnessed something mysterious and brutal.

Jorge never told him the whole truth.

The next day Toby found himself deep within the forest for the first time. He had, it was true, been within its fringes during the early days of their stay. Jorge, who had taken him, had suddenly vanished from sight. Toby realized that he had been so busy looking up into the tree canopy that he had made the elementary error of not keeping his eyes on his guide. Immediately, as in some juvenile nightmare, the forest closed in on him. The trees were crowded and dizzying, the spaces between them as fearsome as an overgrown maze. He had no idea of direction. He was unable to pick out the way he had come; all possible ways looked the same. He tried to keep still, to listen for sounds that fiction had taught him would give a sense of place – the crack of a twig, the rustle of leaves, an explosion of startled birds. There was nothing. Just the silence, the greenery, the gloom. All he could hear was his own breath and his heart thumping faster and faster. Panic rose in his gorge. When Jorge reappeared at his side, as if from nowhere, he wanted to hang on to his arm and never let him go again. Jorge merely glanced at him and then led him safely back towards the village. Toby's fear was so obvious Jorge did not even have to sniff the air to detect it.

This time Toby followed Serafina into the forest. She smiled at him and indicated that she was walking there. Furtively he looked around to see if anyone was watching, but the village was occupied with its own day-to-day affairs. He followed her across the razed ground with thoughts full of energetic couplings.

Serafina walked easily, with a grace that came from knowing the ground on which she walked. She wore a dress of thin printed cotton in obedience to the priests' campaign for all women to cover their bodies fully. Paradoxically this made her even more sensual; her nakedness was now erotic, only a lifted dress away.

In her hand she carried another piece of cloth, rolled up.

Toby walked beside her, changing the rhythm of his steps as he walked through scrub and grass. For the first few minutes he talked about whatever came into his head. She could not understand him but smiled broadly, as if he was being very entertaining. He talked about Lucy and Rachel and the library. Each phrase he used rang hollow. It was as if he was talking about creatures he had imagined, imperfect and unreal.

Once in the forest he kept his eye on her back as she followed a trail that was obviously well known to her. He still felt nervous, believing that she could disappear at any moment and leave him lost.

But the thought of making love to her kept him going. It would be, he believed, an act that would still for him have an underpinning of guilt and sin, but for her would be carefree, easy and natural. He watched the movements of her body and transposed them to an imaginary scene on the forest floor.

Nothing of the kind happened.

After about fifteen minutes they came to a pool that was open to the sunshine. All around it were mosses and heavy, open flowers with vivid leaves of yellow and crimson. Insects burred and buzzed in the air with predatory fury.

Serafina unrolled the cloth in her hand and made it into a sling. Then, with efficient movements, she went among the blooms breaking them off. After only a few minutes she had a heap of them in the cloth.

Toby, in a rush of decision, took a bright yellow flower and placed it behind one of her ears. He did not know if this was clumsy or natural. The flower was unevenly balanced and fell from her ear. She laughed.

On the way back he felt he had missed the moment.

Serafina took all the flowers and heaped them on Sophie's grave. Toby tried to think of Sophie lying under the red soil but was unable to. Then Serafina strode back down the hill into the village, rolling up the cloth as she went.

By the time Jorge had told him he should have trusted his intuition, it was too late. For by then Jorge had been taken inside Deadface's hut, and the last phase of their journey had begun.

This time it was Anjelica who sought out Jorge. She was unhappy and bad-tempered about her husband's command, so she trotted in front of Jorge ignoring his requests for information. When they reached the hut she motioned him inside and then squatted down at the entrance. She put a woven cover over the door to seal off the men. Although every word was audible, she did not hear them. She was weaving a hammock. To her this was more important than anything else.

Deadface sat in the stifling gloom with his front teeth bared by the disease. He had been smoking and a thick fug hung in the hut. His eyes were still sharp and black.

He got Jorge to repeat what he had said about the link between kidnap and disease. Jorge did so, musing as he said it that it might indeed be true. Deadface was impassive as he considered the mechanisms of revenge and salvation.

Then Deadface told him that, even though his people and the Javarunu were enemies, always had been and always would be, this did not prevent them seeing value in the other's work. Nothing violent had happened between the two tribes for years. The reality now was trade.

There was a place in the forest, known only to Deadface and Juan, where exchanges took place. It was only a night away. They expected a trade to be made again shortly.

For years he had gone to this secret place, taking with him goods made by his own people. Now he and Juan took things that the priests had brought – cloth, mirrors, pieces that could be used as body ornaments. Once he had taken some cans of fizzy drink. He had stood in the clearing and demonstrated how to take the top from the can and then, to show that it was safe and good, he had tipped some of the liquid into his own mouth. When he stood to one side the Javarunu advanced gingerly on the cans. At first the drink made them cough and splutter, but soon they were whooping with delight and giggling at this strange taste.

Juan and Deadface returned with a particular kind of honey that his own people could never find, with decorated headdresses, stone axes, bows and arrows, clubs.

Once they had asked him to bring knives and axes made of steel, like the ones he and Juan carried. They did not want to; these people were still Javarunu, untrustworthy and violent.The haggling had gone on for a while. They did not speak each other's language but there were similarities, and long experience of dealing with other people had made both tribes adept at sign language that could carry complex meanings. In the end Deadface accepted that the Javarunu would give him one of their most prized possessions in return for the knives. But he did not know what it was. He knew, though, that it was something to do with magic.

Over a period of weeks he and Juan stole knives and a few axes, and then trekked through the forest to exchange them.

What they got in return, along with the usual plethora of food and weapons and ornamentation, was something neither of them recognized. They passed it from hand to hand, fitted it on their arms, tried it in various positions on their heads.

Only when Juan saw one of the pictures brought by the priests, and stole the book to show it to Deadface, did they realize how the thing was used, but they were still not sure why.

Jorge asked to see the object.

Reverentially, as if he were handling something mysterious and sacred, Deadface passed it over. It was not one, but a pair. The leather had almost perished and the eyepieces were smashed, but Jorge knew straightaway what they were.

Pilot's goggles.

16

There was only one word, and that was *expedition*.

Only that word expressed something of the thrill, the uncertainty and the fear that Toby felt. And if ever life held decisive moments, this was one.

Jorge, of course, had not wanted him to go. Three of them were enough. And this was his concern, and his alone. He even lied to Peter. He told Peter that he had a calling, but said that it was a Christian one. God and Jesus gave him purpose.

It was, he reasoned, partly true. Jorge could find little Christianity in himself – his belief in it had passed as quickly and as passionately as an adolescent's. The scars it had left behind were only physical. Whatever drove him on it was not a sense of mission. It was a need to return, to complete a cycle. He felt he could belong to his own people, rediscover himself in them. And although he sometimes thought that this belief was romantic and irrational, he had nothing left to lose.

Peter, who had been led to believe that the Javarunu were violent and deadly, held Jorge to him in a fatherly embrace. There were tears in his eyes. 'My son,' he said, 'I can see God's will in you. You make me proud.'

Jorge bowed his head.

'But we aren't head-in-the-clouds missionaries, are we? We realize that the enemies of God will use anything, no matter how cruel, to stop the advance of good.'

Jorge didn't understand him.

'That's why you must take this with you.'

It was the gun. The same one he had handled all those years ago when he had spun the chamber and dared it to stop in the killing place. The same model as the one that had been left behind in the Parnaby house in London.

Peter handed it over. It was protected by a waterproof case. When Jorge took it out and checked it, the chamber spun easily and with a sweet mechanical purr.

'I'm sure I won't need it,' he said.

'Please,' Peter insisted, putting his hand on Jorge's arm, 'for me.'

Jorge nodded.

'And of course, you should also take these. We have found them to be of considerable help in all parts of the world.'

They were pamphlets printed on laminated paper to protect them from mildew. In them the stories of God and Christ were told in pictures of stylised simplicity and garish colours. All the characters had a perceptibly Indian cast of feature.

'All over the world?'

'We have different versions for different races. Christ must be made to seem accessible. Immediate.'

'I see. Thank you.'

'Now then, tell me the details of your travel.'

Deadface had only told him in very general terms where the site was, but Jorge still found it politic to distort this further for Peter's benefit.

'And your companion?'

'Have you tried to talk him out of it?'

'I did as you asked.'

'But it didn't work.'

'If you wished, I could forbid him. It would cause me no moral qualms. We would be doing it for his own safety.'

'That would worry me.'

'I ask you; should we do it?'

Jorge considered this for a while. 'No,' he said finally, 'Toby, too feels a call. It would be unwise of anyone to prevent him following it. Even if it leads him to disaster.'

'Do you think he is heading for that?'

'No, although it is possible. I think he is heading for disillusion. Literature has misled him. He does not see that it is a false trail. He expects some kind of culmination. He will not find it.'

'I sometimes think, Jorge, that your beliefs border on the

blasphemous. But I have never been concerned about that. It does not even concern me that your approach to us has been less than honest.'

Jorge considered the marks on his wrists.

'We understand things much more easily, much more deeply than you give us credit for.'

'Yes,' Jorge said.

'I think I know why you are going on this journey. You believe we do not understand this, that we cling to a simple faith in your conversion. But this is not so. We have seen people like you go on journeys before,' Peter tapped the bookshelf. 'Our bibles, our records of the lives of the saints are full of such examples. Somewhere in the forest you will find God. When you do, remember what I said to you today.'

But Jorge tried to brush Peter's remarks out of his mind straight away.

He did not, however, wish Toby to enter the Javarunu territory with him. He had accepted, reluctantly, that Toby would accompany Deadface and Juan and him to the trading place. He had promised that he would try to find out something about Dexter Parnaby, if the goggles turned out to be his and if his memory of his native tongue returned. Toby had got excited and said that Deadface and Juan could surely help. Jorge sighed, Western-like, to show Toby that he was clutching at straws.

'I *know* he's dead,' Toby said, 'there's no doubt in my mind about that. All I want to know, if it was him, is what else did he leave behind?'

Secretly, of course, he was pleased that both Parnabys were dead. It gave his projected biography (in which he had a rediscovered interest) a satisfying wholeness. And evidence of Dexter's death would provide a suitably dramatic finale to the enterprise.

It was also a climax in which he, too, would play a part. An important part. He had begun to weave threads, to tie them together in his mind. Even if the enterprise came to nothing he could make something of it. He could shape a vacuum; the prospective reader would fill it.

Only three of them set off from the village. They stood around, a little self-conscious, while the priests wished them well and the

Indians gazed at them with blank, unreadable faces. Toby was asked several times if his equipment was sound – did he have a medicine kit, a change of clothing, a camera, a tape recorder, a compass in case he got lost, weapons (just in case)? Jorge picked his teeth with the broken stem of a twig. Juan shuffled his feet nervously.

Peter blessed the gifts they were taking, laid his hands on the head of each of them, and asked for everyone to pray for their safety and speedy return. In particular he asked that they should all remember Jorge in their future prayers, and continue to pray that he was well and his mission working. It made Toby feel part of a long tradition of English adventurers, stretching back through Fawcett to Speke and Livingstone and further still, to the Elizabethans.

For a while it seemed as if they would never actually get going, that they were stuck in some bizarre time loop that meant that the prayers never stopped, the goodbyes remained unfinished, the equipment was never fully checked. But then, suddenly, there was nothing left to do.

They shouldered their packs, crossed the razed ground, and entered the forest. When Toby turned to wave, believing that the village would be lined up behind him at the forest edge, he could see nothing. Once more the forest had tricked him. There was nothing but trees.

Deadface was waiting for them after half an hour. Toby was sweating by now, and his pack was heavy. Once or twice it had snagged on low branches.

It was Deadface who led the way. Toby could see his broad bare back ahead of the others. He did not stop to turn round, although once or twice some words passed between them. Toby thought they were maybe keeping to a slow pace because of him.

Within the forest the greens of the foliage were dark, often with a waxen sheen. The leaves were sharp, and yet piled in profusion upon each other. Very little light filtered down to the forest floor, and even the trunks of the trees had a ghostly, insubstantial greyness about them.

Toby felt sweat coating his back where the pack rested. He knew that if he took it off the back of his shirt would be imprinted with its outline. His own breathing had become hoarse; it surged in his throat with a distant rattle. At times he thought that his breathing was the only thing he could hear; the rest was silence.

They passed through grasses that were of shoulder height. Some were seeding, and a whole large patch, a hundred yards or so across, was covered in fine white gauze that hung near the tops of the stems. Above the grasses the trees stretched upwards.Creepers had writhed around many of them. If Toby stopped and craned his neck he could see that, higher still, parasitic flowers had burst into bloom even further up the trunks, and then there was the tree canopy, thick and intersecting, in a still, silent fight for light. He could see very little of the sky.

He could put names to none of these growths. Everything was mysterious to him. He recalled seeing plants in England that had been domesticated, and yet their origins had been quoted as South American. He was sure that none of them would be at home here. Only their larger, tougher, more brilliant cousins could survive.

Nor was he sure about what lay under his feet. It should be ground, he reasoned, but the earth itself was undiscoverable beneath a knotted carpet of roots, small plants, moss, lichen, fungus, suckers, shoots, clumps. Several times he slipped but always managed to regain his footing. Once or twice he realized that he could fall, slip to one side, roll down a hidden hill, and be as lost as if he were a hundred miles away.

After some hours the pace slowed and Deadface and Juan began to search among the tree trunks. The forest was thinner here; they were on rising ground which seemed to have rocks at the surface, and the trees were more widely spaced. There was even a dappling of light and shade on the mossy floor. At last Juan called out and they approached him. He indicated a tree.

Deadface had cut the bark and a thin but steady stream of liquid was pouring from it. He held a bowl to it. As he collected the sap Toby watched him and could not suppress a shudder. It was the first time he had seen him close to and without either night or the clay to disguise the corruption of his face. The flesh had opened into a deep sore that had flimsy strands of healed skin at its sides. The sore had rotted the front part of his face, and Toby wondered, and the thought sent him cold, if the face would just go on rotting until it exposed more and more of the skull, until eventually Deadface could not see, could not talk, could not breathe.

'Drink it without letting the liquid touch your lips,' Jorge said, translating, 'otherwise it will congeal into a rubbery line on your skin.'

Toby shook his head. 'I can't drink that,' he protested.

'Try it.'

'For God's sake, Jorge, what will it do to my insides?'

'Nothing. It will refresh you. I used to drink it as a child. There was a game; you had to drink as much and as quickly as possible without letting it touch the outer skin. If you did, then the line could just be peeled off.'

Seeing the others drink it, Toby decided to try it. He sipped it very carefully, was surprised to find it rich and creamy, and then drank it steadily and without touching his upper lip.

'There you are,' Jorge said approvingly, as if he were encouraging a child.

They began their trek again, and soon the forest closed around them. Toby had the odd, dislocating feeling of sinking into liquid air. All was green and dark; noise was made unreal; they were like explorers of the ocean floor, among huge extravagant growths reaching for the surface. He half-expected to see grey, streamlined fish dart through huge polyps.

He pulled himself together. The jungle was getting to him. Exhaustion was sapping his perceptions; hallucination was seeping in at the edges of his thought.

Toby ached. He longed to ease the pack from his shoulders, to strip himself of his sweaty, uncomfortable clothes. He wanted to sink into easy, comfortable sleep.

Just before nightfall they stopped in a thinner part of the forest where orchids sprouted high up on the pale tree trunks. They ate fruit that Juan lopped from a tall plant with spiky, dangerous-looking leaves. Toby had never seen such fruit before. He handled it uncertainly, not knowing how to open it. Deadface took it from him, hefted it in one hand, cleaved it with a machete. The fruit fell into two equal halves, its insides glistening with yellow juice. Toby ate it with relish. He was very thirsty and the pulpy centre had a satisfying citrus flavour.

They shared some Western food and a flat loaf of manioc bread. Deadface ate with the side of his mouth. Toby gave him a biscuit and he bit it with the molars, as if the front of his mouth gave him discomfort or pain.

Afterwards they slung their hammocks from trees. Jorge tied up Toby's and as he did so he had an animated conversation with Juan. Jorge felt stupid, as if he had no memory of the past. When reminded, he could tell clearly that this was a fool's tree. He took the hammock down and tied it further away between two other trees. Juan said nothing this time.

'What was all that about?' Toby asked.

'Something I should have known.'

'But why did you move the hammock?'

'If I had left it there, red ants would have swarmed across you. Only fools tie their hammocks on such a tree.'

Toby lay awake during the night, listening to the unceasing rhythm of frogs calling in throaty, bubbling, ludicrous cries. Underneath him grasshoppers made dry noises like the striking of matches. And sometimes a night bird rustled and screeched in the foliage near them. If he looked up into the black canopy he could see little sections of stars. Gradually, through the night, their patterns changed as the world turned. He recognized none of them.

Dawn found him tired and sleepless, but the others seemed refreshed. 'Can you go on?' Jorge asked, looking critically at him.

'Of course,' he snapped. Then he said, 'I haven't got much alternative have I?' And then, 'It's what I want. I'll see it through.'

They all went to empty their bowels a few steps away from the trail. Toby was last to go. He took a careful note of his bearings.

The change of diet had made him loose. He was nervous of squatting down in the jungle. At least in the village the priests had set up latrines above a stream (seats or planks in segregated huts). Here there was nothing. He felt uncomfortably close to his own bodily processes.

When he rose, he found, to his horror, that several noiseless, large tar-black beetles had emerged from the undergrowth and were already attacking his excrement with claws.

The party marched for most of the day through thick, oppressive trees. When they stopped to rest and drink, the other three took most of Toby's pack and divided it between them. Toby protested weakly but secretly was glad that this had happened.

The exchange site was at the top of a rise. It was a litter of moss-covered stone with saplings and trees clinging on to it and thrusting up through it. A few thorns looped across the ground.

'Javarunu?' asked Jorge.

'Not yet.'

They ate and then unpacked the exchange gifts. Deadface indicated the limits of the trade area by walking from tree to tree. Then they each took handfuls of the gifts and hung them from the branches. Within an hour the area had begun to resemble a Christmas for pagans, with small crucifixes, mirrors, strands of coloured ribbon, brilliant ornaments hung everywhere.

Then they waited for the Javarunu.

Two days later Toby had begun to think they would never come. He had also begun to feel ill. Every time he urinated his water was hot and unpleasant. Once, just as he was finishing, Juan approached him and sniffed and said something. Toby felt humiliated. Jorge told him that Juan had come to him and said that Nameless was not well.

'He says you should take a certain root and make it into a paste and drink it. That will cure you. He says the root should be near here. He will get it for you if you wish.'

Toby shook his head and said no. He was miserable enough.

That night lightning flashed over another part of the forest. Toby tried to calculate how far away it was but, surprisingly, he could hear no thunder. The light carried on flashing noiselessly as if, somewhere, high tension wires were touching in a gale. But all around was a thick, unnatural quiet.

Next day the storm broke above them. When the thunder crashed it was only a fraction of a second behind the flash. The tree canopy was outlined with aching brilliance, an uncountable web of branches and leaves, and then everything shook as the air around them compressed and snapped. Far away, like a sustained rhythmic drumming, rain fell.

None of them spoke. The little camp had subsided into its own silence.Toby rubbed his hand back and forward across the bristles on his chin and wondered if anything would happen. He was quite prepared to believe that they would be stuck here forever, waiting for an eternity for something that would never happen.

'Javarunu,' Deadface said.

They looked at him.

Toby felt a spark. 'Are they coming?' he asked.

Deadface held up a hand for them to be quiet. They fell silent and strained to see, hear, smell.

Nothing.

'Javarunu,' Deadface said again.

'They're coming, aren't they?' Jorge asked Juan.

'Toothedjaws knows,' he replied.

Toby licked his lips. He tasted salt from his skin.

'Are they coming closer?' he asked Jorge.

Jorge did not answer him.

'Are they?'

Deadface said something.

'They are already here,' Jorge said.

Toby cast a startled glance around him. Nothing could be seen or heard. He hugged himself with his arms, gripping himself tighter.

Gradually, little by little, the Javarunu began to appear, at first only as movements, barely discernible behind the trees, then as eyes which stared at them with unblinkingly direct gazes, and finally as part, then whole, figures who emerged from the greenery and gloom and stood around them in a silent, tightening circle.

17

They were all males. Six adults, and two youths at the edge of puberty. They had broad, strong features and bodies that were hard and smooth, with no excess fat. Their hair was cut in a uniform mushroom-like style, and their faces were brushed with bright red bars of urucu. All of them were naked but for a thin cotton band which passed around the waist and was fastened around the tip of the foreskin. To Toby's eye they seemed symbolically erect, somewhere between menace and playfulness; it took a few minutes before he began to accept that this was merely matter-of-fact.

He was less certain about the weapons they held, for they bristled with bows, arrows, spears. One carried a handful of clubs.

When they stood still he could study them more closely. Immediately he could see what had not been obvious before. Jorge belonged to them. In his stance, his build, the set of his face, he was a Javarunu. Only his clothes and the cut of his hair made him different. Toby could easily imagine him shedding his clothes, painting red across his nose and cheeks, joining his tribe in the circle.

Toby felt exposed and vulnerable. Who would ever know if the four of them were killed here? If, simply, they were speared or clubbed to death, and left to rot? And suddenly Toby felt unfulfilled and unrecorded. He felt he could pass out of history with no fuss, having left no mark. He would simply be a memory that faded with the years, dwindled to nothing. He felt an obscure but potent jealousy for Dexter Parnaby, who had at least left a mystery behind him.

For some time the Javarunu studied them. In particular they

concentrated on Toby and Jorge, walking round them and peering at them, but always keeping their distance.

Toby looked at Jorge. 'Say something,' he said. The silence was profound.

But Jorge was struck dumb. For years he had stewed in uncertainty; he had compromised and lied; he had been devious, unique, praised, ignored; he had been true to what he thought was himself, and broken his own faith; he had remembered, imagined, anticipated, dreamed. Now he was here and the moment seemed curiously unreal. He felt he was ascending through space, the air becoming thinner and thinner, his muscles unable to move. He was certain he was swaying. He thought he would pitch forward in a faint.

Toby had speculated about a tearful meeting, of families reunited after years and years, of recognition passing like a spark across the divide. But Jorge and the Javarunu were cautious of each other. Untrusting, even. They could have been fighters, each trying to sense the other's qualities, each waiting for the opponent to make the first move.

Jorge licked his lips. The Javarunu's reality seemed partial, possibly even illusory. He had conjured up their images for so long that it was difficult for him to accept their actual physical presence. Yet he could see their ribcages move as they breathed, hear the low murmurings they had begun to make to each other. He could even smell them. The smell was clean and comforting, something he had not sensed for years but which was immediately welcoming and reassuring.

Deadface and Juan indicated the trees they had covered with gifts. Then they indicated the Javarunu.

The Javarunu withdrew a short way, and began to unload their weapons on the ground. The wood clattered. Above them lightning flashed.

They stopped, stood up straight, looked at Deadface.

He made a motion with his hand, as if he were throwing something away.

They put more weapons on the pile.

Deadface repeated the motion and said something. The word was guttural.

The two youngest Javarunu went back into the forest and, a minute or so later, returned with a woven bag like a small hammock. From it they pulled some cloth, a few carved pieces of wood and bone, something wrapped in plantain leaves. At each item they stopped, as if expecting Deadface, satisfied, to call a halt to the trade.

Jorge was filled with a sensation he could not name. Bubbles rose to a surface and burst gently into words. The words had shapes and textures of sound; he could remember them but not their meanings. As the Javarunu began to talk he began to search among the words, hunting for their meaning.

And whatever the Javarunu offered, Deadface wanted more.

Their leader tilted the bag until all its contents spilled on the ground. He indicated them with his palm. The ground was covered with necklaces, foodstuffs, brilliant feathers. Then he strode over to the ribbons and bells that had been fastened on the trees, touching them with his hands. The colours trembled, the bells tinkled as if they belonged to open spaces and the wind.

'This is an insult,' Deadface said to Juan.

'What's going on?' Toby asked Jorge.

Jorge held up his hand.

The leader came back, covering the ground between the gifts and their traders in a series of quick, confident strides. He stood right in front of Jorge and put his hand on his face. Jorge flinched, but stood his ground. The leader walked across to Deadface.

'They are trading me,' Jorge said, 'they are not giving me away and they will not let me go. To them I have a value.'

Toby was astonished. Somehow he had never thought that Jorge would become a thing of value, a commodity to be measured in terms of food and ornaments and spears. But that was what their guides were doing.

He took the camera from his bag and began to photograph the meeting. Already he could see them in a book.

'Tell him not to forget to ask about the goggles,' Toby urged. 'I need to know anything we can find out.'

'I think that will have to wait until later.'

'What's wrong?'

Everything seemed to have stopped. The Javarunu stood guard

on the goods they had unloaded; Deadface had drawn a steel knife and had edged closer to Jorge.

'Is he protecting us?' Toby asked. The sense of danger was sharpening itself by the minute.

'He is protecting me. I am valuable. They want me back.'

'And me?'

'I do not think either side finds you valuable, Toby.'

And Toby for the first time saw that he was worthless and in the way. The Javarunu had no interest him beyond a certain curiosity. And to Deadface and Juan he was nothing; they were getting nothing from *him*. He saw, clearly and without sentimentality, that they would as soon kill him as take him back. He was among people who lived with hardship, cruelty and necessity. He had been stupid and romantic to believe anything else. Of all of them, the only person he could remotely trust was Jorge, and every second saw him move further from him and back towards his own people.

They all stood still. But for a few changes of costume, they could have belonged to one of Dexter's photographs.

Obeying some instinct to be tidy in the face of death, Toby closed the camera and slipped it back in his pocket. He squared his shoulders and ran his hands through his hair.

Deadface moved even closer to Jorge. He raised his blade and, with his free hand gesticulating angrily, he addressed the Javarunu in a cascade of guttural and high-pitched words. Even to Toby it was obvious what was being said. He, Deadface, had brought the most precious item of trade the Javarunu had ever been offered. He needed to be paid and paid well for Jorge. And they had better not think that they could reclaim him. He was not to be given away.

The Javarunu seemed to consider this state of affairs for a while, then, still talking among themselves, they withdrew, leaving all their trade items where they were. The tension eased slightly, as if pressure was being relaxed. Deadface let the knife fall away but kept it in his hand. He brushed the cutting edge along his palm.

'They will be back,' Juan said to Jorge.

'Soon?'

'Who can tell?'

Jorge knelt down and checked his pack. The revolver was in there. Unseen by the others, he transferred it to one of the large pockets of his tunic. First he had made sure that it was loaded.

'I thought I was a gift,' Jorge said.

'What's going on?' Toby asked in English. No one answered him.

'You are,' Deadface told Jorge.

'I think you want what you can get for me.'

Juan took a few steps towards where the Javarunu had vanished, peered into the screen of trees, and then came back. On the way he picked up a spear.

'They have a poison we do not know of,' he said. 'They make it with magical spells. If the tip of this spear touches its prey it is certain to die. But it will harm no one who eats it afterwards.'

'How can you ever hope to save your face, Toothedjaws?'

Deadface opened his lips in a horsy, unsettling smile.

'I have told you how the Javarunu charmed your face in revenge. Perhaps now they will take a greater revenge on you.'

'Perhaps,' Deadface said.

'The years with the whites have made you like a man with his head clubbed, Snakewrist,' Juan said.

'You no longer see,' said Deadface.

'You no longer hear.'

Jorge strained his eyes and looked into the forest. There was still no sign of the Javarunu. He wondered if they had gone forever. Despair began to creep through him.

'We have made an honourable trade for what we brought,' Juan went on. 'What we take away is acceptable to us. What the Javarunu take away is acceptable to them.'

Jorge could not understand. 'You are threatening to kill me unless the Javarunu give you more,' he said.

Juan and Deadface paused and then laughed, spitting out the humour in a series of barks.

'You are a fool, Snakewrist,' Deadface said, 'I should have known that you could hold no wisdom.'

'I am speaking the truth,' Jorge replied.

'You cannot see the truth when it lies in front of you. Nameless sees even less.' He pointed at Toby with the knife.

'The Javarunu do not want you, Jorge,' Juan said.

'They will not take you.'

'They say they cannot recognize you.'

'They say you are a stranger. That whatever you are, you are not Javarunu.'

Jorge let go of the revolver. Only when he let it rest in the pocket of his tunic did he realize how tightly he had been gripping it.

'They cannot do that,' he said.

Juan tapped the side of his head. 'Perhaps they will come back,' he said, 'they have not gone far. They are just behind the nearest trees.'

'What can we do?'

'Nothing.'

'We should follow them,' Jorge said.

'No,' answered Deadface, 'we do nothing. We wait.'

They waited.

They stood around.

Toby asked what was going on.

'There is nothing to worry about,' Jorge said, preoccupied.

The Javarunu returned. They came silently out of the forest, all staring at Jorge. Their leader came up to him. He stood his ground. The others began to strip the ribbons and other gifts from the trees.

The leader walked around Jorge. He leaned towards him and sniffed. He reached out, put his fingers in Jorge's hair, gazed into his eyes from a distance of only a few inches, lifted his arm and put the tip of his tongue on it.

The rain began to fall.

At first they could only hear it as thunder in the tree canopy, but soon it had worked its way through the upper foliage and begun to fall in the inner forest. Filtered through the thicknesses of leaves, it was uneven as it fell. At places it descended in thin mists, and parts of the forest looked as if they had been smeared with unfocused light. At others conglomerates of huge drops poured down, as if from hidden spouts. The trunks of the trees coursed with it; their greyness glistened and crawled, as if they held creatures seeking to break free of the bark.

The men stood in their positions in the rain, combatants unable to resolve their conflict yet unwilling to go further. Toby shifted and felt a suction beneath him. He was sure his boots were already wet inside. His collar was soaked and he felt uncomfortable.

The Javarunu gathered themselves and came closer. The rain increased. Their bodies were dappled by it. It dripped from them.

Everything happened quite suddenly.

Toby, appalled, saw Jorge taken into the group of Javarunu. They reached out their hands and drew him in – Toby could not tell if it was as a brother or as a sacrifice. In the middle of a sudden ring of brown arms and bodies and red-painted faces, he turned and looked back. His face was shocked. It could have been pleasure or fear.

'Jorge,' Toby said. Despite everything, his throat was dry.

The Javarunu bore Jorge away. He began to disappear behind the trees, dissolve in the falling rain. Tall plants obscured him. Water coursed down the spines of their leaves.

Toby hesitated. He was gripped by a fear that was both paralysing and furious, as if he were powered by enormous energy that somehow could not pass into the physical world. Vividly, as sharp as any photograph, he saw himself lying dead. Juan and Deadface stood on either side of him. The forest was filled with the beat and roar of the storm.

In panic, he broke.

He hoisted his pack on his back and yelled Jorge's name. Jorge and the Javarunu were smeared figures among blotches of grey and green and gloom. Toby had to run rapidly to stand any chance of catching them. It was not easy to keep them in sight and find his footing.

One of the Indians, he did not know if it was Deadface or Juan, called after him. Possibly they even ran to catch him up.

The rain drummed and hissed. He plunged through curtains and drifts of it. When he slipped and fell to his knees he discovered, to his shock that although he was on a thick mat of roots and creepers the water running between them was already several inches deep.

The Javarunu had vanished. Toby plunged ahead, ran down an incline, and fell as he attempted to climb the other side. He landed on one hand and jarred it. He knew it was painful but could not feel it. As he rose water poured down through the branches and blinded him.

He shook his head and wiped his face with his hands. He could see nothing and hear nothing but the roar of the rain. He looked down. He thought he was standing in a shallow depression but suddenly noticed that the water, instead of collecting round his ankles, slipped away in one direction.

Toby couldn't understand this. He didn't think he was standing on a hill but, with the thickness of the jungle, it was difficult to be sure.

It was an illusion, he thought; the fall had knocked his senses awry.

As if in confirmation, he saw strange, sinuous movements travelling up the bank and out of the depression, against the flow of the water. It took him a few seconds to realize that they were snakes fleeing upward.

He put his hand to his mouth in the classic pose of a puzzled observer.

Then water, foaming and brown, came smashing down the gully with force and weight and dizzying speed. The trees shuddered or tumbled as it hit them. It carried them whirling and rolling with it.

Toby scrambled out of the way and watched the new river rampage past. He was awestruck, horrified. He had been standing there a moment ago. Now the flood scoured it, boiling and seething, scooping out great slices of earth, undermining trees and vegetation, sucking them into it as it wormed its headlong, furious way through the forest.

He sat on a hard tangle of wet roots and watched the river take its course.

The storm had altered the patterns of light so much that nightfall took him by surprise. He found himself, soaked to the skin, in almost total darkness.

Soon afterwards the rain stopped. Toby tried to put up the hammock but could not. He slipped on whatever was underfoot and lost all sense of direction in the dark. The only thing he could find was his pack, and everything in there was sodden and smelled of rot. Finally he made it back to the tree with the hammock half-strung on it. He felt terrified, miserable and achingly thirsty. The storm river, undrinkable, roared in the darkness.

He burrowed among the pack contents but could find nothing

that could help him. He felt blind and hopelessly lost, and within a few minutes he was sobbing bitterly. The spasms made his chest ache as if it had been kicked, and the tears stung his tongue.

The despair exhausted him, and he slid and resurfaced in a sleep that was as black as pitch but ringed by flashes of nightmare. When he woke his head ached violently and his mouth felt as if he had eaten sand.

Everywhere was thick mist. The trees rose up through it in ghostly columns, becoming less and less substantial with height, until finally they dissolved in greyness.

Toby could see the contents of his pack scattered around. He gathered the more important pieces together, but left the laminated sheets of Bible stories where they were. He wondered vaguely why Jorge had given them to him.

He felt wretched.

During the night the flood had exhausted itself, and its channel was empty but for dumped trees and vegetation and shallow pools. Dead butterflies floated forlornly on the pools, their fragile wings already shredding.

Toby slid down to the river bed. A lizard scurried out of his way. He brushed some flies from the surface of the water with the back of his hand and took several small mouthfuls, all the time wondering if this was unwise. The water was muddy and unpleasant, but it made his mouth feel slightly less dry.

Then he climbed back to where he had spent the night, and shouted 'Jorge, *Jorge*,' at the top of his voice. The shout did not carry, but died within the mist and the trees. He doubted if it could be heard more than fifty yards away.

He remembered from somewhere that it is always best to get out of wet clothes, although he wondered if, by sleeping in them, he had already let the damage be done. He stripped and draped them where he thought they would dry quickly.

The mist began to thin.

He had thought that being naked in the jungle would make him feel worse. He found, to his surprise, that the sensation had a kind of natural inevitability about it that was almost comforting, although he felt numb; and part of himself recognized that he was ill and in shock.

His skin looked very white. When he examined it he could find several little marks where insects had fed on him. Despite a thorough search (or a search that he thought was thorough), he could find nothing left on him. No leeches. But his knuckles looked swollen without being bruised.

From nearby came the squawk of some large bird. Toby was dizzy and still tired. He wanted to curl up, forget all this, sleep in safety and dreamy, endless comfort.

He dozed, then slept. Maybe for only a few seconds, perhaps for an hour or so.

And woke.

A face looked at him with black, still eyes. Bars of red were striped across it.

He tried to push the face away, but it bobbed back up in front of him. His mind went back to childhood, to trying to push a bright balloon underwater, the balloon bobbing up time after time.

'Jorge?' he asked.

The face did not move.

It began to rain.

The Indian picked up Toby, who did not know if he should struggle or accept, and hoisted him on his shoulders. The smell of his skin filled Toby's nostrils and the forest moved in a jerky blur. There was strength and speed. He felt he had been taken for a purpose.

It could have been that he was being taken for something which would horrify him. But there was a comfort in his own weakness and the efficient muscularity of the Indian. Whatever was happening, there was no choice. For the first time for many days, Toby was content.

And violently sick. He opened his eyes to find Jorge looking at him. Jorge opened Toby's mouth and someone poured water into it. The water was fresh and sweet but Toby did not know that the touch on his lips was that of the edge of a thick, snapped leaf.

Rain poured down the trees.

When he walked Toby was supported by strong arms. If he walked on his own he would do so without direction, splashing through pools or clambering over mossy tangles of root with the mechanical, exhausted movements of a man in delirium.

Cutter/Wingbeat argued that he should be left, but the others said that a god had given him to them and they were compelled to look after him. Just as, for a time, they would have to look after the one who had been stolen but had been found. Until his mind healed and he became whole again.

The man who had been lost and found looked at them with a face that was half puzzle, half revelation.

It was Jorge who gave Toby some of his clothes. He was wearing less than he had done for years. It was an ordeal of reacquaintance.

The Javarunu gave Toby things to eat and he did not realize they were food. They were unfamiliar in his mouth – slimy or dry as dead bark. Sometimes they wriggled. But sometimes they were sweet and juicy, fruit he could bury his face in and feel it covered with sticky goodness.

Once or twice he threw up, unable to stomach something whose taste, consistency and even shape made him retch. The Javarunu looked at him and pitied him. It did not seem right that a man should be so helpless.

And Toby sank into weary visions of endless jungle. Of labyrinthine passages through gloom, of frogs calling endlessly and echoingly in the rain. One night he lay awake all the time with rattles, screeches, roars pouring into his ears. Those who came to look at him saw his eyes were brilliant with fever.

A vision of Jorge, bare-chested, saying something to him, but although his lips moved his voice came from very far away, like that of a spirit.

Of something fixed, a circle round the sky, children calling and playing on latticeworks of poles.

The scenery had become the same. And women began to appear, their faces held in yellow splints like thorns, and something that resembled a dog came up to him, and a child turned an armadillo over and over, and fire burned in the middle of bare ground that opened into sky. Open sky. He could see clouds, watch the rain fall directly down, smell cooking and hear laughter. The girl bent over him and he felt one of her breasts brush his chest.

The girl made him chew something that was bitter and felt like chewing grass. He experienced a faint, distant ache as she opened up his knuckles with a knife. They had swollen like over ripe fruit.

Dull, detached, he watched as she teased small grey grubs from where they had burrowed beneath the skin. He saw Jorge watching but he said nothing. When she was satisfied that none of the grubs remained, the girl rinsed his knuckles with liquid. A day later they began to throb agonisingly, but a few days after they had begun to heal. The girl made him flex his hand to prove that she had done a good job.

Toby struggled to sit up. He felt drained and helpless, but for the first time conscious enough to appreciate his surroundings.

It was the Javarunu village. He had arrived.

18

The girl's face was round, with eyes that were soft and dark. Plant stems pierced her lower lip and, to further enhance her beauty, a thin sliver of wood had been passed through the flesh between her nostrils. Her waistband, and the small fringed apron of cotton threads that hung on it, was stained red with urucu. So were the bands she had tied around her upper arms. To make herself even more attractive she had tied into her clothes the feathers of macaws and toucans, along with shells and hollowed nuts so that she made a pleasing, jingling sound as she walked.

For weeks she looked after the helpless white man as he swam in and out of delirium. She fed him with bread and fruit and fish, took water to him to drink, washed him when his smell became rank and disturbingly foreign. She helped him take drunkard's steps across the bare earth of the compound, held him in its centre while he looked up at the sun. Clouds were passing across the sky and the sun was a pale yellow disc, but it seemed as if the white man could feel its heat because he stood there without moving until she feared for his reason and led him back to the shade.

For the first few weeks his companion came to see him. The companion knelt down and looked at him and in broken sentences that were strangely shaped he asked if the white man's illness would kill him.

The girl said she did not know.

The companion asked about what he was eating and she told him. Then, after sitting by him a while, the companion would talk to the damaged white man in words that were even more strange, and phrases full of discordant sounds and long unintelligible gabblings.

But as the rainy season drew to its close the companion visited the white man less and less, often walking right past him and ignoring him. It was as if the white man was someone he no longer wished to know or have anything to do with. Instead he spent all his time with Cutter/Wingbeat and Peccary/Root and the other men, testing their skills at spear-throwing or archery, or sitting with bowls of fermented drink, giggling with each other and telling long stories of bravery.

Toby drifted and sank in fever dreams.

His earlier realization of where he was had been washed from him by a new wave of sickness. It unmanned him, took all the strength from his body and all thoughts from his mind. He moved listlessly and helplessly in a world without time. Sometimes, like sunlight through the forest canopy, the sights and smells of what was around him broke through and illuminated his existence.

When he did come to it was usually at night. He woke in his hammock and found himself in darkness but for the fires that were spaced round the village. They were kept up all the time, and glowed with subtle gradations of red throughout the night. Figures sat quietly round them, occasionally fanning them so they glowed more brightly. When the fires died back down he could see the huge and endless wheel of stars slowly turn above them all.

And all night the insects and the frogs and the nightjars called.

Or he would wake to rain pattering on the thatch above his head and dripping from its edge into the muddy compound. The drops sizzled in the fires that were in the open, but one of the Javarunu would throw more wood on it so that it sparked and blazed and hissed in the rain. The droplets resounded on the pots that had been left out of the shelter, they collected in sheets in the centre of the village; sometimes the sky was full of lightning and thunder. But Toby never felt afraid. None of this could harm him. He lay in his bunk, the smoke from the hearths thick in the air all around him, and felt obscurely, irrationally content.

Until one day the fever left him.

Later the girl was to say that she saw it go. It had been fastened on him, a huge invisible creature that was part-leech, part-vampire. It sucked his blood and gave him poison in return. And one day it had had its fill. It rose from him, its invisible wings flapping, and left. Only the girl had eyes to see it as it lifted, gorged with the whiteman's marrow, and flapped away over the trees in its ugly, ungainly fashion.

He was still weak.

'Lie down,' she soothed him, 'don't worry. I am here to look after you.'

He struggled for a little while, but he only had the strength of a child and he collapsed back on to the hammock where he had lain for all those weeks. He looked surprised by his own feebleness.

She sat beside him and told him that he was safe, that his mind had not been his own for most of the rains, that all he had to do was rest and eat and god would make sure he got back his strength.

The fever had gone from his eyes but he still looked helpless.

His companion had gone into the forest, she told him. He was learning how to be a man again. Before long he, too, would be fit enough to learn the same lessons.

Toby struggled to sit up. He felt curiously hollow, as if all richness had been scoured from him. When he put his hand on his body he was shocked at how thin he had grown.

The girl saw him touching himself all over and knew that the sickness had stripped him of his weight. Again, she told him not to worry. She had had difficulty feeding him sometimes. Now he would be able to eat more properly.

'Jorge?'

Did he feel hungry now? Was that what the word meant?

'Jorge.'

She gazed at him for a while. He put his hands up to his face to feel his beard. It was thick. He could not believe he had lain so long.

The girl saw his fingers flutter round his mouth so she brought him some grubs wrapped in a leaf. Although, in his stupor, he had eaten them before, he pushed them away from his mouth. 'There was someone with me,' he said, 'where is he?'

She could not understand a word he said.

Toby looked around the village. It was virtually one huge circular hut surrounding a central area of bare earth. The hut was a complex construction supported by hardwood poles and cross-beams lashed together with liana. Children, their feet tied together for extra grip, played games around the poles, climbing up them with agility but without fear. Above their heads a thick thatch of leaves screened the dwelling areas from rain and sun. About thirty families lived in the village, each keeping their own fire. Most had pets, such as smooth-skinned, almost hairless dogs, many with limps or blind eyes. Macaws, half-plucked, staggered around the enclosure or managed to climb up into the crossbeams. Their scarlet and azure feathers were constantly used as decoration and the birds looked half-amusing and half-tortured.

'My God,' Toby said, suddenly aware that he was stranded here.

The girl offered him the food again. He looked carefully at it. The grubs had been speared by fragments of wood and he thought, absurdly, of kebabs or cocktail sticks. Closing his eyes he took the grubs from the girl and put one in his mouth. As soon as it touched his tongue he wanted to be sick, but he fought the reflex and swallowed it down. The next one he bit. It was unexpectedly dry and, although the taste was unappetizing, he rationalized that the thing was probably high in protein. In this way, with long pauses between each mouthful, he ate many of the grubs. After a while he had a brainwave and fed them back to the girl. At first she refused but, when he insisted, she ate them. He could not tell whether or not she was glad.

The girl's name was Reflection/Leaf. She had a younger sister with only one name. There had been a brother but he had died, quite suddenly, as a young boy. Some said the younger girl should have been killed by the parents, too, for the family needed another man. But the little girl had been their last chance. Now the mother was barren. The little girl, Noisyfrog, was fascinated by the white-skinned invalid and often left off playing with the other children just to watch her sister nurse him.

Now Noisyfrog, seeing that the sickness was gone from this stranger, took the binding from her feet and, leaving her friends clinging to the uprights, ran across the cleared earth. She stood in front of this strange creature, who was the wrong colour, who could not speak but only babble. Some of the children had already said that when god made people he had only half-made this one, and left his mistake in the forest to die. They should never have taken him in.

Toby looked at Noisyfrog and remembered that it had been a

long time since any child had looked at him so seriously and unflinchingly.

Toby got to his feet and walked round the village. Although the eyes of the Javarunu were incurious and never blinked, they watched him all the way.

The village had been constructed so that the inner side of the ring always opened on to the central area of earth. On the outer side, however, the side facing the forest, was a curved, lattice-worked wall of palm leaves and support poles. There were only two entrances through the wall. Inside it the Javarunu cooked, slept, carved, played, celebrated.

One or two dogs barked at Toby, scrawny poultry clucked at his feet, something that looked like a fully bristled pig lay motionless in the dust but for one nervously twitching ear and a mucus-running snout. A troupe of ducklings followed their mother across the compound. Children, women and old men watched him without moving. He could see their gaze following him as they sat beside fires and pots and half-completed blankets. One woman threaded a necklace. He could hear the click of pot on pot as the beads were slid down, one after the other. A raccoon-like animal with a long ringed tail and large night-time eyes hung on to a bunch of plantain stored in the roof. It, too, seemed to watch him as he walked round the circle.

There was no sign of Jorge. Nor, he realized, were there any young men. Still not able to think quickly or clearly, he wondered if some disease had fallen on the village like a curse, leaving only him alive of all the men. After a while he realized that it was much more probable that all, except he, were out hunting. All of them, including Jorge.

When he got back to where he started the girl was waiting for him with hot juice that she raised to his mouth in a clay bowl.

He drank.

It was almost sunset before the warriors returned. Only a narrow crescent was left in sunlight; the rest of the village was in shadow.

A series of jubilant whoops had been heard from the forest, so the villagers began to build up a central fire. The warriors came streaming in from the forest with their weapons held high. Toby strained his eyes to see if Jorge was among them, but he could not pick him out.

The Javarunu gathered around the kill. Toby could not even tell what they had killed, although it appeared to be small. Then he decided that there was more than one kill. The Javarunu circled the fire, fed it extra wood. Their bodies gleamed and were dark against the leaping flames as the sunlight slid upwards off the village.

Toby looked at the girl. Her body had a dark sheen of health. Without a word she stood up and walked towards the chattering circle of Javarunu. In the middle of their guttural and high-pitched cries Toby could hear wood spit and crack, and something sizzle. The smell of burned flesh drifted across the space between them.

Some time later she brought him a thick slice of meat. It was so hot that it burned his fingers, and its fat ran down his skin. But it smelled pungently edible and, although difficult to chew because it was more fibrous than any meat he had ever tasted, he ate it with a determined relish.

This time he forgot to offer any to the girl, but she said nothing.

He looked over to the Indians gathered round the fire and realized that they were the only two outside it. Even the children had joined the feast.

'You should join your friends,' he said to her, knowing he could not be understood.

She looked at him.

'I wouldn't mind,' he continued, feeling like a shipwrecked sailor among a tribe who could never understand him but upon whom he would now have to depend. 'You can get up, walk over there; I wouldn't object at all. You're your own woman.'

The distant fire burned and danced in the black eyes.

Toby began to talk, phrases that halted, that tumbled over each other, that only hinted at sense. Finally, despite all rationalization, he felt foolish and stopped.

'It doesn't matter anyway,' he said, and even those words rang hollow.

He watched the fire through the limbs and torsos. One of the warriors detached himself from the celebration and came over to them. His body was made of firelight and dark. Toby knew instinctively who it was.

'I've been waiting for you,' he said.

Jorge said nothing. His hair, like that of the other warriors, had been cut into a mushroom shape. It was as if a bowl had been upturned on his head and any hair sheared away if it showed at forehead, neck or ears. There were finger-broad streaks of red across his face. He was naked but for the string of cotton round his waist. The tip of his foreskin was tied with it so that his penis pointed upward.

Toby licked his lips. Cooling animal fat congealed on his skin. Jorge looked down at him with immeasurably black eyes.

'I'm getting better,' Toby said.

It was a while before Jorge spoke. 'Yes.'

Uncertainty seized Toby. 'Are you glad?' he asked, and the sudden, hissed urgency of his voice made it sound as if he were summoning some spirit.

Again the delay.

'Yes,' he said.

And he turned on his bare feet and raced back to the feast.

Toby clutched at his head and lay down. He wanted to get up, to spring to his feet and join them all, but his bones felt as weak as sticks and he knew he dared not move.

The camp awoke about dawn. The fires were stirred and rekindled; wood that had lain in piles was divided between the hearths. The morning was cold and the Javarunu draped and wrapped thick blankets around themselves.The dogs sat with parts of yesterday's kill under their paws, cocking wary eyes if anyone came within stealing distance of them.

The men had begun to gather. One or two ate what remained of the feast. They were about to go off into the forest again, but this time in small groups or singly, not in a party.

Jorge came back to see Toby. He carried a bow and several arrows.

'I thought you had deserted me,' Toby said.

'No.'

'Do they know you?'

'They accept me. We begin to know each other.'

'What will happen to me?' Despite himself, he heard his voice crack in mid-sentence.

'When you are well, and can see things clearly, you will be able to live with us.'

'I'm living with you now.'

'You are being supported by us. You contribute nothing.'

'I can contribute lots of things already. Where's the pack?'

'Left behind when we found you. If you are thinking of demonstrating the tape recorder, then forget this. When you were found you were naked as a baby. Even your clothes are mine. You cannot win your way with toys. They are mouldering in the forest. The rats and pigs and ants attack them.'

Toby was silent. He did not know how to react to Jorge's new hardness.

'What's her name?' he asked.

'You woman is called Pripuruk Txukamara.'

The absurdity of all this touched Toby with mild hysteria.

'Christ, Jorge, I can't think of her like that. What does that mean in English?'

'I cannot translate it.'

'Yes you can. I can tell.'

'Part of it means Reflection, like the reflection that is found in a quiet, still pool. The other part means Leaf, like the leaves of a particular tree that grows near such pools.'

'I see.'

'I must go.'

'And me?'

'I have told them your name. They did not have a name for you.'

'My name?' Toby felt stupefied.

'Xavakap.'

Toby looked at him.

'It is the translation of Savage.'

Toby looked across at the girl. She had a blanket drawn up around her face and her eyes peered over the top of it, large and dark.

'And you?' he asked. 'Is this what you wanted?'

'I know what you are thinking, but I have stopped thinking like that. I was meant to come back here. I do not know how or why and that does not concern me.'

'Your family? Your relatives?'

'I have to go.'

'Are all these people related to you?'

'Distantly.'

Toby still did not understand. 'I thought that these people would be your brothers, your sisters. I thought you were going back to your family.'

'My family, if it still survives, is in a village very like this one, somewhere near here. This is a different branch of the same people. A different tribe.'

'My God! Neither of us is safe.'

'I must go. You must act as they would want you to act. There is no need for fear. These are a good people.'

Toby shook his head.

'Goodbye,' Jorge said.

Cutter/Wingbeat strode across the compound, proud and magnificent. He looked neither to right nor left. Jorge ran to catch him up, and the two of them disappeared out of the village.

Reflection/Leaf put some more wood on the fire. It cracked sharply, like a series of shots, but she did not react. The sun appeared quite suddenly, brilliant and with a flood of hot light. The last of the warriors left the village in bright sunshine.

Toby stood up and looked around. He wondered how he would get out of all this.

A short while later Reflection/Leaf took him by the hand and led him from the compound. Only when he was outside did he fully realize the dimensions and complexity of its construction.

The girl took him to the river. Toby did not know there was a river so near, although he realized he should have known. There had never been any shortage of fresh water.

The river was pale brown with the mud it was bearing, although at several places there were rapids that broke in bands of white. A flight of birds, yellow and bright green, flew across the water. Toby watched as the girl stripped herself of everything, apron and ornamentation, and laid them in a tidy arrangement on a bank of hard mud. Soon she was completely naked, her reddish-brown skin shining in the sun. She waded into the shallows, splashed a little, and then beckoned Toby to follow her.

He felt, for a moment, an out-of-place sense of shyness and modesty. But then he reminded himself that the sight of his naked body must have been made familiar to all the Javarunu in the long weeks during which they had nursed him. He took off his clothes and placed them beside the girl's. They looked inappropriate and clumsy next to hers. At first he held his hands together to cover his genitals but this was, he rationalized, totally inapt. Soon he stood near her, the water up to his calves, the currents pushing at his skin.

'Are we all right?' he asked her, realizing the words meant nothing. He knew that they would be safe. It was just that he wanted something to say.

The girl took his hand again and led him further out into the river. The bed shelved only slightly. Toby could feel mud and gravel beneath his soles.

She immersed herself in the water and rose; it streamed from her, coursing down her breasts and the insides of her thighs. Apart from her scalp her body was almost completely hairless, although he could see fine down catch the water and the light.

She opened her other hand. In it she held a smallish, hand-compressed ball of what looked like white fat. He didn't know what it was. She raised it to his nostrils so that he could smell. It was soap.

'Did you get that by trade? Or do you have a way of making it yourselves?'

She grinned at him.

He supposed it was quite easy to make, really. He remembered reading about soap manufacture in the ancient world, but couldn't recall how it was done. He supposed it had been something to do with animal fats – along with something that would be dug up.

Reflection/Leaf rubbed the soap all over herself. She covered her body with whitish smears and bubbles. She never hesitated, and her thoroughness knew no modesty or embarrassment. She soaped her breasts until they seemed to be even firmer, and the nipples stood. She thrust her hand backwards and forwards in her anal cleft, seeming to concentrate on the squelching of water and soap and flesh. She opened her legs and rubbed between them in a motion that was both efficient and sensual, circular, forward and back, up and down. Dribbles of soap dripped from her and were borne away by the river.

Toby felt the beginning of an erection and, feeling foolish, sank lower in the water to disguise himself.

Reflection/Leaf dipped under the water so that all that could be seen was the top of her head, the black hair floating like some huge anemone. She was underwater for several seconds, and then she burst to the surface again, blinking with the river in her eyes, the soap carried away.

She told Toby that he, too, should wash himself, but he did not understand.

He smiled stupidly at her.

'You must clean yourself,' she said, 'you have been ill. You smell. You will stink out the camp. Do all your people smell like you?'

He raised his hands in a gesture that Reflection/Leaf could not understand. He was often doing this. He was a store of meaningless gestures and sounds.

She took hold of him and began to soap him all over. At first he wriggled like a child or dog that wants to get out of the way, but she spoke firmly to him and held him tight and he seemed to understand. When she soaped his hair she was amazed again at how different the texture was to their own. Just as she was intrigued by the different planes of the face, the unusual set of the muscles, the abundant and unsightly body hair.

Some of the other villagers had come down to the river by now, many with their children. The children splashed in the shallows and one or two leaped in from the branches of one of the riverside trees.

When Reflection/Leaf tried to wash the lower part of his body, the sick man squirmed away so that he almost stumbled on the river bed. The water snapped at his clumsiness then surged away from him. He broke away from her with the soap trails stippling his back, and tried to run through the water. The river splashed around him. When he came to the bank he had his hands cupped around his genitals like the figure of the fool in one of their dances. Some of the children and women that were still on the bank saw him and shrieked with laughter. Two of them tore up the stems of a large plant and chased him, trying to whip him playfully with its leaves. The game was so funny they could only run a short distance before doubling up with glee. The savage ran back into the compound, his body ludicrous and unhealthy.

The women waded up to Reflection/Leaf and told her what fun they had all had. When they tried to tell her how funny he had looked words failed them, and instead of describing him they impersonated him. Each of them took their turn in doing this.

It was true, Reflection/Leaf said; the white man was laughable.

She was asked if she still felt he was only part a man.

'Sense has not come to him,' she agreed, 'and he does not know what to do about it.'

But would his sense come back? Would history return to him?

'Yes,' she said. It was certain to come back.

When they reached the village they found the white man huddled like a child before birth. Dust coated his flanks like an outbreak of disease. Some of the women felt sorry for him, so, led by Reflection/Leaf, they took him to the centre of the compound and used all their water to wash him. They tipped it over him from large bowls. They would have to go and get more from the river, that was all.

Soon he was clean again. He stood quietly while they did this. All this time Noisyfrog watched him with solemn eyes.

Afterwards he sat while the life of the village went on around him. He had his head in his hands. Some said he looked sad, others that he was merely stupid. But he seldom looked at Reflection/Leaf. She spent hours in front of him, making up her face and breasts with new patterns of dye, inserting fresh shoots through her lips and nose, knotting new shells into her apron.

Toby felt he knew every square inch of her. She hid nothing from him. He wanted her with a desperation he had never felt before about anyone.

Cutter/Wingbeat touched the tree bark with his fingers. He examined it carefully then stood back and said he was satisfied.

'A poison tree?'

'Yes.' Cutter/Wingbeat was pleased with the way the stranger's language had continued to grow.

'This is the first I have seen.'

'It is the first there is. We used all the others and they died. Young ones are growing but are not yet old enough. Soon the village will move to a richer area, and when it moves back here there will be plenty of poison trees again.'

Badwrist/Shoulder nodded. He understood.

Cutter/Wingbeat selected a piece of bark and made fire by bowing a sharp circular splint in it. The wood blurred as it rotated, and the bark gave off a hot smell. Soon he had a spark, and he let Badwrist/Shoulder feed it while he began to strip away long sections of the poison tree. He had a steel machete; he had bargained it with the enemy. Now it was used to strip the poison bark, but he kept it sharp to cleave an enemy skull.

When they had a good fire they held the poison bark over the flames until its sappy side glistened, then bubbled, with a tacky liquid the colour of red fish tails. Acrid smoke rose from it. Cutter/Wingbeat waited until the liquid was thick enough and then he rotated the arrowheads in it, coating them all over. He sniffed and smiled at Badwrist/Shoulder, and said it was good. 'It is a tree with a strong magic,' he said, 'we must not lose it.' Then he held the arrow tips in the heat of the fire so that poison was baked on to them.

'Now', Cutter/Wingbeat continued, 'I must make things for my father.'

'Your father is dead.'

'For my father,' Cutter/Wingbeat repeated.

He took the pulp from the inside of the bark, scraping it carefully into a large woven sheet. When there was no more pulp he drew the sheet into a bag and handed it to Badwrist/Shoulder. 'Carry that,' he said.

'You give this to your father?'

'We drink it for my father. Not now, but in some months.'

'It will not harm you?'

Cutter/Wingbeat drew his lips back across his teeth. 'It makes us see the truth,' he said. 'In this way we will celebrate his death. From this we will make the holy drink.'

'This is done for all deaths?'

'A man cannot pass into the spirit world without it. A man must make sure that his own father does not become a ghost haunting the place where he died.'

'And if I died?'

'If you die, Badwrist/Shoulder, there will be someone to do this thing for you. Only enemies and demons will be left alone.'

Cutter/Wingbeat studied the arrowheads, turning them and scrutinizing them one by one.

'Did you once do this for a white man?'

Cutter/Wingbeat carried on with his inspection.

'A white man who wore a head-dress of leather over his eyes?'

Cutter/Wingbeat grinned, as if the two of them shared a huge secret.

'The head-dress I traded with the enemy that brought you?'

'Yes.'

'It was before I was born.'

'You know about it.'

'We still tell the story. Perhaps when we grow bored with your unbelievable tales of life in the white world, we will tell it to you. There are many who are old enough to remember.'

'Was he alive?'

'He was rotten when we found him. It was not easy to tell that he had been white. But they knew he must be because he sat in a boat among the trees.'

'The same kind of boat you see crossing the sky?'

'More and more. The tribe was young then. They had seen nothing like it.'

'Did you let him go into the world of spirits?'

Cutter/Wingbeat struck his head with the heel of his hand. 'We do not know what happens to other people's souls. We only know what happens to our own. Javarunu.'

'You left him where you found him.'

'There are some who say his ghost beckons white men from all over the world. That it rises above the trees so that people from afar can see it and watch it beckon them. I have heard it said that the savage answered such a call. He heard the ghost.'

Cutter/Wingbeat shivered suddenly, as if the thought made him momentarily afraid. 'Come,' he said, 'we will return.'

On the way back he shot a monkey. He paused for an age beneath a tree, bow drawn and eyes fixed on the branches. Then he loosed the shaft. The monkey fell through the leaves as its colony screamed and scattered through the canopy. It dropped to the ground, its long orange ruff bright against the floor of rotting wood. It made several convulsive movements, as if it was trying to get up but could not. Its eyes were wide open and gelatinous. Cutter/Wingbeat picked it up and drew the arrow from it. It was still twitching and some blood flowed from the wound. Cutter/Wingbeat made a dismissive face. 'I have eaten fatter ones,' he said.

'Soon', he told Badwrist/Shoulder, 'we will hunt peccary. You must run quickly for peccary. Often the pack will turn on the hunters and they must run up trees or dead ant-hills.'

'How will we find peccary?'

'When they are feeding. Close to, you can hear their teeth grinding together as they tear at everything.'

Before they returned to the village the two struck off the trail to a hollowed tree that Cutter/Wingbeat had been watching. After examining it for a while he sliced into the dead wood with his machete. A cloud of stingless bees rose from it and began to swoop and dart and hover madly around the disturbed hive. Many landed on Cutter/Wingbeat and crawled impotently, hopelessly across him as he plundered the cells of honey, laying it in thick runny wedges on large leaves that he asked Badwrist/Shoulder to tug from nearby plants. The air was full of the rich cloying smell and the rhythmic vibrating hum of the bees. Some of the cells contained small grubs that they took turns in popping into their mouths. When they had finished Cutter/Wingbeat's arms and chest were spotted and trailed with honey. Some bees had become stuck in it, trapped by their own creation. He wiped the honey off with his fingers, making great play of how delicious it was. 'We have had a good day,' he said.

'You are a clever man,' Badwrist/Shoulder said, full of genuine admiration.

'Your friend. Will he do this?'

Badwrist/Shoulder considered. 'He is no friend,' he said finally.

But back at the village the white man hobbled after him, hissing stupidly. 'Jorge,' he cried, 'Jorge', like some bird that can only sing one song.

Such language was becoming strange to Badwrist/Shoulder. He no longer liked to use it. It seemed inappropriate, only partly useful. The Javarunu language, on the other hand, was extraordinarily delicate and full of shades of meaning, catalogues of animal and plant names, classifications of leaves, rainfall, rivers, animal calls, family relationships, stories. To speak English now was difficult, even laborious. It was as if a whole section of his life was dropping away; it had been lived, and now it was of very little use.

'Dexter Parnaby,' hissed the white man.

Badwrist/Shoulder had to think for a moment. 'He is dead,' he replied finally. He held up his hand to his face. The smell of honey was still on it. It was said that there were sixteen different kinds of honey, depending on the kind of bee and the flowers on which it fed. He sniffed. The honey could be classified by colour, texture, smell, taste. He sniffed sharply to fix this particular one in his memory. When he came across the next of the sixteen, he would be able to tell the differences.

'Dead?' the white man, asked stupidly. It was as if he needed to be told everything two or three times.

Badwrist/Shoulder turned away.

'What did he leave behind? He must have left something. They know about him and they had his goggles. I'm sure they must have been his goggles.' He stopped, looked around as if everyone could understand him, and leaned forward. 'What about the last volume of the diary?'

'There is none.'

'There *must* be.'

'Look. See if you can find it. There is none.'

The white man licked his lips. 'Find it for me, Jorge. Please. You can do it. You belong with these people. Find it for me then get me out of here.'

'There is none.'

The white man stood there.

Badwrist/Shoulder forced himself into English again.

'There is nothing here for you. You do not fit. You do not

belong. If I can, I will get you taken back to the priests. But I do not know.'

He walked across the compound leaving the white man behind him. He had lost interest.

19

Savage watched Reflection/Leaf as she wove, gathered papaya and plantain, or went out into the forest to discover caterpillars or frogs that could be eaten. He followed her as faithfully as any dog.

Although he was allowed a place in the communal feasts, he always felt that he was less than welcome. He would sit a short distance away from the others, ignored by them. Reflection/Leaf would help him by indicating when he should lean forward and take something to eat. Sometimes her parents, or more often Noisyfrog, would pick juicy morsels for him and feed him. He could never read their faces. He supposed it was something to do with pride.

Badwrist/Shoulder never spoke to him. Sometimes Savage caught him looking at him, but from now on he saw neither recognition nor sympathy in his eyes.

He had difficulty with the food. It was either too hot or suprisingly cold (and sometimes, in the same mouthful, both.) Its smell varied from a heavy, drowsy fragrance to something that was as earthy and pungent as opened bowels. Its texture could be fine and delicate or gristly, or as wet and grainy as silt. Once Reflection/Leaf had placed into his mouth something from a long wooden tray of steaming manioc and burnt-smelling flesh mixed together like a stew. The thing felt slimy and globular. Convinced that he had been given a monkey's eye, Savage only just managed to get away from where the tribe all squatted round the food. He was violently, helplessly sick. While he hung gasping over the horrible vomit a dog came up and sniffed at it experimentally. The Javarunu talked quickly, agitatedly in penetrating, clashing voices, as if he had just committed a terrible social gaffe and they did not wish to acknowledge it.

But Savage knew that if he wished to keep himself from weakening he would have to force himself to eat food that was strange, unidentifiable, and replusive. He was happy with fruit and with the tubers dug from the cultivated land just outside the village. And he could force himself to eat the grubs that Reflection/Leaf seemed to be a specialist in finding. It did not disturb him that she took him to watch her dig termites from a rotten tree. He knew that, despite their taste, they would provide him with the nutrition to keep going. He even began to understand how they burrowed in the fibrous deadness of the fallen tree; he knew why she picked among them, flicking the older ones out of the way, collecting the pale white grubs together in the centre of a large waxy leaf.

He sat and watched the rotten stump of the tree as several dozen termites crawled around its shattered side. Reflection/Leaf had hacked out the nest site with quick precision. It lay beside her, opened by the machete she had carried with her.

She held up a few wriggling grubs. He took them from her. She motioned for him to place them in his mouth. He held his breath and swallowed them whole, although his gorge rose as they touched it.

She said something to him which he could not understand. He had begun to recognize patterns in the language, but its meaning eluded him.

'I know,' he said wearily. 'I know.'

He suddenly thought that he must sound like someone weary with all the years, knuckling under to a nagging wife. He smiled at this, then laughed, calming himself only when his ribcage began to ache and mucus to run down his nose.

'I know,' he said finally, as if to convince himself of the validity of his laughter.

Reflection/Leaf did not look up, but carried on with her task.

'You know,' he continued, 'I often wonder if the people who knew me think about me. Wonder where I am. I don't even know if news has got to the outside world.'

The pile of food was still growing. It would take several more minutes before the division was complete.

'Before I came here,' he said, and tailed off into silence. He could not bear to hear the sound of his own voice among these hostile, crowding trees. It seemed so pointless.

'Their names would mean nothing to you,' he said. 'And it all seems such a long time ago, anyway.'

A bird called nearby, a soft, cooing noise. It sounded surprisingly English, and for a few seconds he listened to it. Back in England he had never listened to birds.

'I wonder what *they're* doing. Back home. Back where I come from. You wouldn't believe me if I told you. You wouldn't be *able* to.'

Something tiny bit the side of his neck. He hardly noticed it.

'Jorge doesn't wonder at all. He's back. It's as if all his life with us was an aberration. You don't understand a bloody word.'

He dropped to his knees beside her and took the machete from her. She handed it over without complaint but it seemed to him that her eyes were wary.

'Look,' he said.

She went back to sorting out the termites.

He took her arm. '*Look.*'

He was not much good with a machete; it seemed to be oddly balanced and potentially lethal and he was a little scared of it. But after a few minutes he had stacked several leaves into a kind of crude sandwich and then sliced them through. The resulting shapes were, to him, acceptably rectangular. Good enough for recognition, anyway. He bent them across the centre, hearing the greenness bend and tear.

'Look,' he repeated, holding the cropped leaves up to her, 'do you recognize it?'

She said nothing.

He shook the green folded rectangles. 'Someone who once came here had something with him that was like this. If you found him dead it would be with his body. If he was still alive he would carry it with him.'

Still nothing.

'It's a book. Except it wouldn't be made of leaves – '

He stopped as the word struck him.

He shook his head.

'Leaves of paper,' he explained, 'that's what it would be made of.'

He handed the folded leaves to her. She took them and looked at them as if she expected them to do something.

'That's what I work with. That's my life. It's what I want. The book that was left behind. It was a long time ago, but someone will still have it somewhere.'

Reflection/Leaf turned over the lopped greenery. She was puzzled by it.

She took the leaves back to the village and, hesitantly, showed them to the others. She thought that perhaps they held some significance which she was unable to divine. Perhaps there was some magic, hidden but potent, in such a gift?

The others took the leaves, peeled them apart, spread them out on the ground, looked at them. They were just leaves

Reflection/Leaf went to Badwrist/Shoulder and asked him what Savage had meant. Peccary/Root was demonstrating how to carve some figures and Badwrist/Shoulder was watching him. They were patterns that called prey to you in the forest.

At first Badwrist/Shoulder would not answer her, but she clung to him until he said that, in the white man's world, Savage did nothing but collect millions of leaves folded over on each other, and coloured white as crab flesh, and covered with signs that were supposed to hold all the knowledge in the world.

Reflection/Leaf could not believe it. It was all too much to be true. She went back stunned and told her parents. They, in turn, told everyone else. The whole village knew how stupid Savage was.

So now they began to call the white man by a new name. If Toby had expected to be named, he would have dreamed of something fine, romantic, like the names tribes gave to heroes in children's adventure books. He would have been happy with The Blue-Eyed One, or Stranger With the Hair That Is The Colour Of The Sun. It was neither of these. Nor was it poetic or musical. It did, however, express the Javarunu's view of him. It was Idiot.

Idiot because he knew nothing of the forest. Idiot because he was ignorant of their ways. Idiot because, left to his own devices, he would have died within a couple of days. Idiot because he could believe that all the world lay in a leaf, folded, bleached, and marked.

The girl saw how he was being treated, and was ashamed for him and for herself.

The next day she wove him a string to pass about his waist and then she led him into the forest. He stood beside her, uncomplaining. She could not take off the peculiar garments that he wore but she tugged at them until he loosened them and stood naked before her. His body trembled a little. She thought it was with pride. She thought that, at last, he had realized he must be dressed as a warrior before he earned any respect.

But when she lifted up his penis, intending to fasten it upright and pass the cord around his waist, a tremor ran through him and almost before she knew what he had done he had her on the ground among the dead leaves and fungi. She could feel the tip of his penis thrust at her like something blind that searched for shelter. Despite his idiocy he was still male, and she could not refuse him. She opened her legs but even then he was incapable of entering her, and she had to guide him into her body. When she did he thrust at her in spasms like a dying animal. After a few moments he was finished, then he scrambled up, embarrassed and foolish, struggling for his own kind of clothes.

She threw the cotton cord into the bushes and led him back to the village.

20

Rumours among the trees spoke of the world being eaten away at the edges. To Reflection/Leaf this seemed indistinct, beyond imagination, but there were suspicions that it could be real. Peccary/Root confronted Badwrist/Shoulder with the rumour and he looked shifty, as if he knew a great truth and was hiding if from them. They pressed him, but still he was unwilling to say what was happening.

Reflection/Leaf said to her mother that it was the fault of those who had left the airman unburied. It was his spirit that called all the evil in the world to the Javarunu village. It was evil and sickness that had fastened on the idiot and sucked his brains away.

The mother smacked the ground in anger. No, she said, it was Idiot himself who was the cause. All you had to do was look at him. You could see. It was obvious.

By now the idiot had mastered a few words of their tongue. Just enough to let Reflection/Leaf know what he wanted. But, unforgivably, he still showed no interest in becoming a man. He was content to remain an idiot. Even Badwrist/Shoulder was aware of this, and ignored him as much as possible since he, too, could become tainted with scandal.

The idiot was captivated by Reflection/Leaf. He had begun to recognize that his own body must have smelled as strange to her as, at first, hers did to him. And he had begun to be sensitive to its temperature range. How the feel, the smell differed. How when she came splashing and dripping from the river, her skin beaded with droplets, there was an invisible layer of coolness round the thighs. Normally her back held a steady, unchanging warmth, but the water made the temperature dip a little. When she flexed her shoulders the movement of the muscles beneath the skin made tiny rivulets of water trickle down her. He would place a finger in their path and lift it closer to his eyes. There, in the small drop of water, he believed he could see life so small that it hovered at the edge of invisibility.

And she inflamed him. Coupling with her was so easy, so free of guilt, so natural. She neither queried nor resisted him. Forgetting about the ticks and ants and lizards and snakes, he pressed her down among the dead leaves that trembled slightly as he thrust into her. The smells of the earth rose about them, rich and heavy and full of growth and decay. Or they would couple in the dark shade of the village canopy while life went on around the compound. He was delighted that he could teach her new positions. She took to these with the same expressionless vigour that she showed for those postures which, to her, were more normal.

His mind went back to a book he had once discovered in a city attic. He had forgotten what had happened to it, and he spent a few luxuriant daydreams during which he rediscovered it and it made him lots of money. At the same time he tried to recall all its attainable positions. Never before had he had a woman who would go along with any sexual adventure, however absurd.

Afterwards she tried to creep away alone, to ease the humiliation and fear that she felt.

Her cousins took her aside and said that she could no longer submit to such cruelties; the man was mad. No, Reflection/Leaf said, he was as good as a husband. And his mind was still not right. Until that day, she would agree to whatever he wanted.

No one agreed with her. She was placing herself at the very edge of custom and ritual. Many felt she was in danger.

The idiot remained insensitive to such shame; the pleasures of the flesh had numbed his perceptions.

This, he thought, was heightened sensitivity. He could see where the copper became bronze as she smeared herself with a thin film of urucu; he smelled her hair, knowing when she had rubbed it with oil, lifted the shining black strands with his fingers; several times he had insisted on replacing the plant stems that pierced her face, and he would bend down, as careful as a surgeon or a jeweller, passing new clean stems through the tiny holes in the flesh. In return he had let her shave him. It had been a painful operation carried out over several days. It involved soap, a sharp steel knife she had obtained in trade, and tweezers. He did not know whether to weep or laugh. She bent over him, her eyes fixed and unmoving, her hand as steady as any machine. But when she tried to remove his body hair he refused. That was too much.

After a few weeks he wondered if she had become pregnant. It had been a while since he had noticed her staunching the thick flow of menstrual blood. Perhaps it was his imagination that made her breasts appear slightly more swollen. And, in the forest, he believed he could sniff a new, sharper tang when she urinated.

He tried to ask her, but she pretended not to understand him.

The extraordinariness of this did not worry him. It all seemed, on the contrary inevitable. He was convinced that, with a little foresight, his future could have been imagined on that day when he went to Sophie Parnaby's door and Jorge answered it. Afterwards everything had an inevitability that he had only just begun to discern. He supposed he must, at some point, have considered the possibility of either Lucy or Rachel becoming pregnant, but he no longer considered it improbable that a South American Indian could be bearing his child. Furthermore, he had ceased to think of either Lucy or Rachel at all, except in an abstract, detached kind of way, as if they were people he could never meet again. He had begun to think less and less of anyone; even his affection for Reflection/Leaf had less to do with her as a person than as something belonging to part of an interconnected process of cause, effect and symbol.

He had begun to believe in fate. And fate made everything acceptable.

The idiot thought that he was being carried towards a place where everything would be made clear to him. He would understand exactly what had gone on all those years ago, when Dexter Parnaby must have crashed and died somewhere in this area. He would understand why this had come to pass. Just as a diver with bursting lungs searches the ocean floor, he searched the tribe. He knew that, if he persevered, he would eventually be carried back to the surface. And he would carry, not a pearl, but a book. Whether it would be Dexter Parnaby's or his own he was not yet sure.

Idiot believed this despite an uneasy suspicion about the Javarunu's tolerance of him. He had begun to notice the delicate, precise interconnections between kinship groups, behaviour, hunting and gathering, yet he did not see the embarrassment he himself was causing. He was of no value to the Javarunu. They had to feed and protect him because it was their custom with children and the old. But Idiot was neither of these. He had contributed nothing to their group, and was likely to contribute nothing.

To support him Reflection/Leaf gave the tribe food which the idiot was supposed to find and trap. There was no compulsion on her part to do this, but it lessened her guilt at his unmanliness. She joined the men in pounding the drug out of the pulpy heart of a shrub so that it could be poured into a slow green section of the river. After it had been tipped in the fish rose gasping and dancing on the surface, breaking it with their spasms. Reflection/Leaf waded through the green water picking up the fish. The gills gaped apart and their eyes still held their cold fury. The idiot watched her as she collected fish after fish, tossing them, still flapping, on to the bank where they slid and turned and finally died. No emotion showed on her handsome unreadable face.

She even tried to join a hunt for pig, but Peccary/Root, whose name spoke of his greatness as a provider of food, said to her that he would kill her a young pig.

She was in his debt and did not like it.

One day Idiot was trying to talk to another woman. The woman's name was Song/Distantbird. Idiot indicated his own woman and said that she was beautiful. He thought he knew the word but Song/Distantbird could not understand him.

'Beautiful,' he said, in English. But in England she would never be thought of as beautiful. Perhaps her dignity would impress; her looks, never.

'There's nothing to compare her to,' he went on, and suddenly from out of the past, came the phrase. 'A summer's day,' he said, and craned back his head and laughed.

Badwrist/Shoulder had told Peccary/Root about some of the idiot's senseless visions. He called out to the girl, telling her to ask the idiot about the world of the unpeople.

Song/Distantbird looked puzzled.

'That is where he comes from. The lands where people are not people.'

Cutter/Wingbeat placed his foot between his brother and the idiot.

'The idiot cannot talk like a person,' he said. 'He cannot hunt. He cannot fish. He cannot use our tongue. He cannot feed himself or his family. He cannot smell the forest. He will not be able to hear danger when it breathes at his shoulder. He shames his woman by his actions of the beast. He cannot wear urucu. He cannot join the festival. What good is the idiot?'

He spat on the ground and strode away across the clearing. Peccary/Root strode after him.

Reflection/Leaf, who had heard all this, tried again to teach Idiot the ways of the world. She told him the different and varying sounds made by animals and birds. She indicated which fruit were safe to eat. She told him again how to uncover grubs and honey. She said that, if no fish magic was near, then it was easy to spear them. He gazed at the subtle, almost hidden movements of water while she waited and then, swiftly, speared the water. When she lifted out the spear there was a fat twitching fish transfixed upon its juddering point.

'Yes,' he said.

But he was hopeless. He was a man born too soon, a creature alive yet without its necessary senses. Only slowly did he understand things, and then only dimly, as if he peered for ever at the world through a thick mist.

'And this,' he said.

It was urucu.

'We paint our bodies with it,' she replied. 'It is magical.'

'It's the colour of blood,' he said in English, and indicated his arm and body to show that the same colour ran in his veins.

He dipped his finger in the dye. She hissed.

'Idiot,' she said, '*you* cannot wear urucu!'

She taught him how to cross a river.

He imagined crocodile, looked round for their snouts nosing directly to him through the water, and piranha, searched the shallows for their hunting packs. The current pushed at him, tugged. He felt panic rise in him. She held on to him and smiled.

She taught him how to make a shelter. Often the hunters did this if they were far away from the village. He built one and it fell down. He built it again and it fell down again.

She taught him how to shoot with a bow. Watch for the monkey above, she told him, and he squinted into the canopy. Look, she said, there are six kinds of arrowtip; this one you use without a drug. It is for striking the monkey direct. He will fall and bleed a lot. The idiot fired too late, too wide and with too little power. The arrows tumbled back and almost hit him. He would have lost them if it had not been for her.

At none of these was he better than poor, and many times he was so bad that his mere presence would have been a hindrance to any band of men. They all knew this, and they talked openly of his stupidity. He took no notice of their taunts.

When Reflection/Leaf claimed that he was her husband in everything but name Cutter/Wingbeat drew his lips across his teeth. 'Wives do not have husbands that they must feed,' he said.

The idiot sat and played with the children. He watched them stalk lizards across the bare earth, climb the tall support poles, involve themselves in dances and chases and pretend fights. Noisyfrog was his favourite. He spent hours playing with her. He drew things for her on the ground, or pulled funny faces, or sang songs with meaningless words and all the wrong notes.

One of the other women spoke strongly about this. 'Your idiot knows nothing,' she said, striking her head, her heart, 'he does not know that we are *here*. He does not know that this is *now*.'

Peccary/Root pointed at his head. 'All his world is *here*,' he said, adding menacingly, 'He will break us all apart.'

'Don't worry,' Reflection/Leaf's mother told her, 'you will get a proper husband once he has gone.'

'He wants to do what he is not supposed to do,' Song/Distantbird said, 'he will not do what he is supposed to do.'

'They want you to go,' Badwrist/Shoulder told the idiot. His words were thick with strangeness.

'I can't.'

'Soon they will take you. You will be safe.'

'I don't think so.'

Badwrist/Shoulder considered the sky. A high, lazy bird crossed it. He could tell it had eaten by the way it flew. It would be seeking somewhere to sit and digest its meal undisturbed.

'They could kill me, Jorge.'

'You did not understand.'

'I understood everything.' Idiot licked his lips. He paused, waiting for Badwrist/Shoulder to help, but nothing was said.

'Could they take me back?'

'Yes. When they are ready.'

'Not to the trading place. To the mission.'

Badwrist/Shoulder thought about this. 'They are eager to send you back,' he admitted.

Idiot could not help but reply, 'Apart from my woman, here.'

'It would be better for her if you left.'

'Don't you realize?'

'Do not worry. We will look after your child.'

'You all know?'

Badwrist/Shoulder shrugged. It was a sudden European movement. Now it seemed strange and out of place.

'All right,' Idiot said, as if he had been persuaded to leave, against his better judgement. 'All right, I see your point. But I want your word that I can be delivered to safety.'

'I will see what is possible.'

'Your word. If it's worth anything any more.'

'Do not be your own enemy. You are asking us to walk with you among our enemy.'

'And I want the book.'

Badwrist/Shoulder stared at him with eyes that did not blink. Idiot felt a part of himself wither. But he stood his ground.

'You are a fool,' he said finally.

'And one more thing, Jorge,' Idiot emphasized the name.

Badwrist/Shoulder waited.

'The gun.'

Badwrist/Shoulder did not respond.

'I need the revolver, Jorge. You still have it, don't you? That way I'd be certain that I would be all right. It's not yours anyway. I could take it back to where it belongs.'

Badwrist/Shoulder stood still.

Idiot had felt in control; he had felt his old confidence surge through him. But now, like a sudden flood, it had gone. He felt it drain from him. He was dependent and alone once more. 'Or I could give it back to you when we got near the mission,' he added lamely.

Badwrist/Shoulder held the silence for a few seconds. 'A fool,' he said, and walked away among the dogs and pigs and half-plucked macaws.

But a few days later, when Cutter/Wingbeat was bragging about the celebration of his father's death, Badwrist/Shoulder took the opportunity to raise again the subject of the crashed aeroplane.

Peccary/Root talked about the goggles and what they had obtained in trade for them.

'What you do not tell me', Badwrist/Shoulder said, 'is how they were found.'

'I have told you,' Cutter/Wingbeat insisted. 'The man sat dead in the trees. The warriors took his possessions away.'

When he had spoken he glanced aside at Peccary/Root, who was cleaning his teeth with a sharply snapped twig. Peccary/Root considered the point of the toothpick as if it held something worthy of close, steady examination.

'He sat in the trees,' he repeated, 'he was already rotting. Useless things were strewn around him. Whoever had buried him there was a demon or a fool.'

'And this was before you were born.'

'I remember the stories. We still tell them.'

'Someone took the head-dress from his head.'

Cutter/Wingbeat said nothing.

'There are many stories,' Peccary/Root said, and began to probe at the back of his mouth.

'Many.'

'What happened?' Badwrist/Shoulder asked.

'There are many stories,' Peccary/Root repeated.

'Your fathers found the thing in the trees that looked like a boat. Inside was a dead man. They took things from the boat and left the man to rot. That is one story.'

'That is true.'

'And another?'

After a pause, Peccary/Root said, 'They found the thing that looked like a boat. They took things from it.'

'And the man?'

'There was no man.'

'No body? No sign of anyone?'

'This story is also told.'

'Were the things in the plane? Or had they fallen beneath it?'

They both looked at him.

'When it fell out of the sky, it would tear itself into pieces. Things could fall out.'

'Perhaps,' Cutter/Wingbeat admitted.

'There are different stories of how it was found,' Peccary/Root said, 'the ones that found it told different tales.'

'Which is true?'

They both laughed. Peccary/Root reached across and slapped Cutter/Wingbeat's back and Cutter/Wingbeat sniggered and turned to one side. Sometimes Badwrist/Shoulder could be stupid, too.

'They are all true,' Peccary/Root explained.

'But what happened?'

'They *all* happened.'

Badwrist/Shoulder fell silent for a while. The sun broke through the clouds above the village and made the compound hot. Cutter/Wingbeat lay on his back and idly practised some calls. Peccary/Root snapped his toothpick at an acute angle and began to work on the front of his jaw.

'Do you know where this is?'

Badwrist/Shoulder was insistent. It was almost bad manners.

'Of course,' Cutter/Wingbeat said languidly, 'we are not fools.'

'And the things that came out of it?'

'Useless things. They fell to pieces or were worthless or both.'

'Is there anything left?'

'Nothing worth keeping.'

'Who keeps the things which are not worth keeping?'

Cutter/Wingbeat yawned. 'Enough of this,' he said, 'perhaps we will talk about it tomorrow.'

'And perhaps not,' Peccary/Root replied, and giggled.

'Let us talk', Cutter/Wingbeat said, drawing in a deep and important breath, 'about my father.'

'Toby.'

He had not heard his own name for a long time. Now it came to him out of a darkness heavy with wood smoke. It was furred with a strange, laboured pronunciation. He came out of the wistful, indefinite dream and saw the head near him, the moon behind it sharp and bright, the head squat and dark and looking motionless, carved, like stone.

'Jorge,' he said, putting his fingers to his eyes to open them. Something light scurried off his body and fell to the earth. A spider; he hardly noticed them any more.

'You are awake.'

'Almost, almost. Give me a second or so. Jesus.'

The fires glowed red in the hearths round the village. He heard a dog sniff, someone snoring, and the constant ceaseless background noise of frogs.

And words he did not understand.

He put up his hand. 'You're talking Spanish or Portuguese.'

After a pause, the head spoke again. 'My languages are becoming no good. I do not need them.'

'What do you want, Jorge?'

Beside him Reflection/Leaf stirred and woke. She sat up. Her skin was soft and dark where the shade was, but moonlight slid through a gap in the roof and cast a cold line down one breast. Her eyes were fathomless.

'There are only two things. One is what came from the aeroplane.'

'There was something?'

'I do not know what. They say it is without use.'

'Christ! I knew it. I *knew* it. I was right all along.' He looked up at the sky. The moon was so bright that it obscured the stars around it. 'Justified,' he said.

'Perhaps. Only perhaps.'

'Where is it?'

'A man called – ' He stopped, and searched for the English

name. 'The Feather in the Tail', he said, 'and Maker of Head-dresses.'

'Where is he?'

'In this village.'

'But where? Who is he?'

'He is blind in one eye now.'

He'd seen him. An older man, with most of his teeth missing and an eye made glassy by cataracts. His home was almost directly opposite where Idiot lay with Reflection/Leaf.

'Can we get them?'

'It will take me weeks. You must wait.'

'I can't wait.'

'Leave it. I will do what I can. And then you must go.'

'How?'

'They want to be rid of you.'

He turned to Reflection/Leaf. She hung on to his arm possessively. 'They would take me back?'

'You slow everything down. They will be a happier people when you have gone.'

'And the girl. You know I worry about the girl.'

The head hissed. 'She is better without you. We are all better without you.'

He licked his lips. A bat crossed the moon in a nervous, purposeful flutter.

'So I wait?'

'I must be rid of you. You are like a trap around me. I feel you could close on me and we would both be doomed.'

The grip tightened on his arm. 'It's all right,' he said to the girl in English, hoping she would understand him by his soothing tone. '*Christ*,' he said. This would be an adventure that would make his fortune.

'Wait.'

Across the compound Peccary/Root lay on his belly and watched the figure of Badwrist/Shoulder, silver and gloom, move away from the idiot's home and place some more wood on their fire. The fire flared and crackled for a while, and then sank to a red smoulder again.

21

The idiot had never seen the village so active. The women spent days grating manioc and baking it into bread, enough to last for several days of celebrations; men had returned after taking invitations to other villages hidden in the forest (the idiot wondered if Badwrist/Shoulder's near family would attend); the gardens had been almost emptied of what had been grown; new rich honey was stored in jars; eggs had been collected for weeks on end; fish numbering more than the fingers of everyone in the tribe had been caught, split, smoked; the weaving of the village walls and roof had been repaired; the macaws had been plucked again and flapped hopelessly around, their flight crippled. And the domestic pig had been slaughtered. The idiot had heard its terrified, hopeless squeals and felt sorry for it. Now it lay dismembered over a fire, close by the vats of fermenting juice that suddenly seemed to have become a focal point of village life.

Everyone went to welcome the return of Cutter/Wingbeat's father. They stood along the river while he was brought across in a woven sling hung between two poles. Visitors from the other villages waited to enter, their heads covered in bird down and feathers.

The river had become low and clear. Sandy mud drifted in it like a thin mist. The warriors had faces of wood ash and gave high, trembling calls as they crossed the shallows. Some said they could also see the dead man among them, his face and body white, fording the river behind the sling that held his bones. Cutter/Wingbeat, his face a mask of mud and ash, led the way. Where the water splashed him it had washed the ash away, and the natural colour of his skin could be seen.

Alone but for the pets, the idiot crossed the compound. A macaw screeched and waddled out of his way.

Tailfeather/Head-dress's family's part of the hut was the same as all the others – a smouldering fire, a woven blanket stretched up on a frame, some emptily drooping hammocks. Plantains and fruit were stacked on shelves at the back wall.

At first the idiot could see nothing that belonged to the aeroplane – just a collection of bowls, some tools and instruments, the empty shell of an armadillo. He could find nothing of any significance.

He stood there, perplexed and uncertain. He was still at a high pitch of anticipation, but behind it he sensed terrible depths of failure, the end of all his dreams.

And then he noticed, among the clubs and knives, a piece of beaten metal. When he bent to examine it he discovered that it had once had edges, but that now it had been hammered and smoothed as if it had been used as a club for years. He picked it up. A faint tingle of excitement ran through his arm. He tested its weight and its balance. From the plane?

Unable to decide, he put the metal back where he had found it. Was this all there was?

He looked around the area again. He could see nothing unusual at all. The metal was the only clue.

Just as he was hesitating about giving up, not wanting to but feeling he might have to, something about the back wall of the hut caught his eye. There was something odd about it. He had been searching but had only noticed it when his eyes had travelled on. And when he went back to look he could see nothing special about it. But there was *something.* He was sure there was something. Unless his imagination was running too high.

He put his hands on the wall, looking at its broad weave of thatch and wood. And then he saw it.

The book.

It was stuffed behind a wooden crosspiece that supported the wall. Only part of it showed beneath the pole.

Idiot felt faint.

The book had been opened out and placed with its insides flush with the wall, so that he could see only the tops of its outer boards and the spine. It was scuffed until it was almost colourless, but there were still one or two small patches like flaked paint where the original colour remained. It had been red.

Idiot reached out, took the book by its cover, holding it gently but firmly by the edges, and began to ease it up out of the fissure. The pages were hidden by the bulge of thatch, but he could tell there were not many. The book was only thin.

There was a faint, reedy scrape as he lifted it away. Light came spilling in behind it. The book had been used as a cover for a hole. He lifted the book away and turned its inside towards him.

It was empty.

There were no pages in it.

Strength left Idiot and he sat down on the earth to avoid falling. His legs and arms were suddenly, fatally weak. He couldn't think. He turned the book over and over, gazing at the empty covers as if they held some surprise, some secret that he could not fathom.

He looked on the inside of the spine. There was a slight trace of webbing, but most had been wrenched, or eaten, away. There was nothing left. Just a couple of boards connected by a flexible, weakened spine. Just a rectangular thing whose only use was to block a hole. Or be used as a plaything. He imagined the Javarunu children, Noisyfrog among them, running after each other, flapping the book like a toy bird.

The idiot was still sitting there when the Javarunu returned.

Tailfeather/Head-dress gazed at him with his good eye. He had not invited the idiot to visit him and did not want him there. He wished he was away from his hearth. But no matter how he stood, no matter how he cursed him under his breath, the idiot paid no attention. He just sat there, stricken, with Tailfeather/Head-dress's hole-blocker in his hand.

The tribal families entered the village.

They came in a shuffling motion, half march, half dance. Their feathers trembled with the motion of rivers in flood. They cried the body home in long, high, shivering notes and short, coughing barks. Their bodies were covered in patterns of waves, circles, sinuous lines of red, black, grey, orange, blue. They clashed wood together to scare off any evil spirits that might try to sneak in among them.

They filled up the village, standing in a ten-deep circle around the centre of the compound. The idiot came to and saw nothing but decorated heads, backs, buttocks. He smelled the closeness of their bodies. They moved in a steady, easy rhythm. He could feel it through the ground. And he could hear nothing but their edgy, disturbing cries.

The tribes watched as a stack of dry wood was arranged in the very centre of the village. Each family had a piece to add, so that the pile took shape quickly. Then Cutter/Wingbeat, his face the face of mourning, took his father and laid him on the cradle at the top of the pile. He felt his father's presence beside him as he did this.

The body had been lashed high in a tree in a wooden cage so that it was safely out of reach of animals. Nothing could have disturbed him. When the warriors had gone to collect him they first purified themselves in the forest, then recovered his bones. The bones were almost clean. They had been stripped and washed and brought back on their final journey. Their ashes would be buried in the centre of the village.

As Cutter/Wingbeat placed the skull on the cradle, the women began to ladle out drink from the vats.

Cutter/Wingbeat satisfied himself that the bones were properly arranged. Other members of the tribe examined them and agreed. Cutter/Wingbeat felt his father's hand on his shoulder and knew that he was pleased. Then he took fire from where the pig was roasting and put it to the wood.

They passed around the holy drink as the fire rose. The fire crackled, lunged, roared. It threw out such heat that all the tribe shuffled back. The fire distorted everything; if they looked near it all they could see were images that were bent and dancing. The bones blackened and cracked and shuddered in the heat and dark smoke poured upwards from the flames.

The holy drink was rich that year. It flooded their heads with happiness and loss. They thought about those who had gone and whose names could no longer be spoken. They thought of the joys of their own lives, of eating, of childhood, of making love, of making things, of hunting. They filled up with love. They luxuriated in it.

Brothers and sisters, parents and children found each other again. Many had married outside of the village, or into it, and now they rediscovered one another. They clung on to each other around the shoulders, breathing steadily together or laughing. In this way Badwrist/Shoulder discovered his cousin. His cousin would have been scared of him, but the holy drink made him see things truly. They leaned on each other and wept. Badwrist/Shoulder felt reunited, even though he had never met his cousin before. His heart felt bigger, full of blood. He had forgotten about cities, seas, books, libraries, the idiot, everything. Tears ran down his cheeks. Come, the cousin said, join me. But he could not leave Cutter/Wingbeat's village yet. He owed them too much.

The two of them sat together on the ground, their feet hooked round each other, murmuring. They touched foreheads. They were given another bowl of holy drink and shared it between them.

One of the logs burst in a flurry of sharp sparks. Everyone shrieked and fled, giggling as the sparks drifted among them. A child was knocked down and got up wailing with its nose running. A woman picked it up and hugged it between large, wide-nippled breasts.

Someone from the cousin's family came with a pot of dye, put her fingers in it, and began to draw the same pattern on the two men. Noisyfrog ran towards them and watched. She was keen not to miss any part of this extraordinary feast.

Reflection/Leaf broke away and went to the idiot. She held his head in her hands and looked at him. She pitied him and she loved him. He looked back uncomprehendingly, able to sense only the strange, rich smell of the drink.

She left him and he stood up, still carrying what was left of the book. He began to feel that he could sense what was going on.

Reflection/Leaf paused at the edge of the feast, turned and said something. She made a motion with her hand. He understood neither but thought that they might be invitations. He saw Peccary/Root standing close by. His face and chest were splashed with juice, his eyes were heavy and already his belly was distended with all that he had drunk.

Idiot began to recognize that he had made a huge mistake. He had stood apart from these people. He had adopted the role of observer and it had been the wrong thing to do. The secrets of this life would only unfold with involvement. He should have lived as a

Javarunu. Then their way of living, their systems of belief would become obvious to him. Badwrist/Shoulder had done this already. Compared to him, the idiot felt he was far behind.

Idiot shouldered his way into the throng. They parted before him. He went up to a vat of holy drink. He picked up an empty bowl, plunged it into the vat, and took a drink.

The bowl was of the kind that was used only for food. The visitors looked at him in astonishment.

'It's all right,' many told them, 'he is an idiot.'

Cutter/Wingbeat, who stalked round and round the funeral pyre, looked across at the disturbance. He was filled with disgust at the stupidity of the idiot.

Idiot felt the holy drink like a flow of warmth inside him. 'It's good,' he said in English, knowing they could not understand. He raised the bowl and a few drops slopped over the rim. 'Good,' he laughed, knowing they would understand his pleasure. He drank again. It had the texture of curdled milk, but its odour was almost pungent and its strength was surprising and deep.

The idiot walked across to the fire. At its heart he could just see the uncertain, almost spectral outlines of ribs and a skull. He had never seen anything like this before. He would never have thought he would be given the opportunity to watch it. The blaze was so fierce that the air was breathless and filled with the smell of charcoal.

Cutter/Wingbeat came and stood face to face with the idiot. He said nothing but everyone could see his calves quiver with humiliation and rage. He was sweating so that the ash on his skin had begun to pock and flake.

The idiot, who should not have been anywhere near the pyre, made what he thought was a sympathetic face. He was thinking of an English poet who had been burned on a beach in Italy, and was wondering if he could make an allusion to this when he wrote his book.

Cutter/Wingbeat held his hands up to the idiot, with the palms spread. The idiot did not know what this meant. He looked at the hands, looked at his feet and shuffled them, and turned away.

The festival parted before him as he walked across to the pig. He was on the trail of something now. He had begun to realize that truth was entirely subjective. He had always thought of it as a kind of ideal, yet an ideal that was verifiable, measurable. He thought that it existed outside of those who spoke it. But no. Now he could see how appropriate it was that Dexter Parnaby's life should end somewhere in these forests. The leaves of his last diary had become pulp and rotted into a humus from which trees could grow. The same trees that sprouted leaves and were cut down and pulped to make books. The Indians understood such processes. They celebrated decay, death, birth. He had thought Dexter Parnaby's trail had petered out, but now he had come to believe that it had been resolved into a mystery. All his contradictions, all his heroism and his evil, had in the end come to be part of the extraordinary commonplace process that these people celebrated. The idiot had wanted to understand the airman. But understanding was not important. Living was. And here he was, part of a feast that honoured the dead and yet honoured the living. It was all part of the same thing. Good and bad, success and failure, life and death, truth and lies were oppositions which he, from the West, had lived by.

Ridiculous. They were all one. It was false to make such divisions in a climate such as this; it was simply *wrong*. Everyone around him understood these things to much better than he, but now at last he had joined them. He, too, was the same kind of person as they were. He could see the same things.

When they began to divide the pig among themselves he was there. He reached in a hand with the others even though the flesh was so hot that it burned his fingers. He bit it and rolled the meat around his mouth because it was so hot. Fat dribbled down his chin. He swallowed the meat too quickly and felt it slide slowly, painfully down his throat.

And still he hung on to the remains of the book.

He took the meat off the bone and walked through the feast looking for Reflection/Leaf. He found it hard to recognize the villagers. Their faces and bodies were covered with new patterns, their heads obscured by feathers and down and straw; they drank without stopping, gorging themselves until their stomachs bulged. He came face to face with a woman who turned away, and only a few seconds later he realized that it had been Song/Distantbird.

And when he came on small groups of people sitting head to head on the ground in what looked like parodies of copulation, he passed by Badwrist/Shoulder without recognizing him at all.

The idiot was full of confidence and joy. Everything was falling into place. Like Dexter Parnaby, he had searched and found the answer. The imaginary text had taken a shape; he had a conclusion – unexpected, but apt. He stopped by another vat and reached in with his hand. The brown arms of the villagers withdrew from the drink as he reached forward.

He almost tumbled over. He had not thought he would be affected so badly or so quickly. He grinned but the muscles of his face felt numb.

He lifted a handful of drink from the vat. Most of it had run through his fingers by the time he reached his mouth, but he bent his head and sucked the thickening liquid from his palm. He felt drops of it coat his upper lip and chin.

The bonfire crackled again, sparking upwards. He looked back it and saw Cutter/Wingbeat standing against the dancing flames. Reflection/Leaf came out of the crowd and grabbed hold of the idiot's arm. She spoke to him urgently, but her voice sounded far away and he just looked at her. He wanted to say that even though they came from different places, different times, he was still human. Peccary/Root took hold of her by the shoulders and dragged her away. She struggled against him but he was a lot stronger than she was. The idiot looked puzzled.

Soon he came to a part of the village where an old woman stood beside a large wide bowl full of bright red dye. He fell down on his knees beside her. She pushed at his chest but could not move him. He dipped his fingers in the dye. His mind went back years to when he was a child, dipping his fingers in paint. The old woman bared her teeth and chattered a monkey-warning at him, but he took no notice. He began to apply the dye to his chest.

Everyone was embarrassed and hid their faces in shame, the dishonour was so sharp. What made it worse was that they could all tell that the idiot was proud of such clumsy daubs, done without artistry or tradition. Such effrontery as this would enrage a god.

When he had finished he stood up. Like a buffoon. Everyone could see now what an idiot he really was. He walked across the village as if he had created something good and beautiful, but his decorations were so bad, so wrong, that it made everyone turn away from him. He looked as if he belonged to the village and some of the villagers sat down and made themselves small in case a god split the sky with fire and burst the land apart.

By now some of the warriors had begun to couple with chosen women, laying them carefully down, entering into them as they entered into union with god. The idiot had never seen this before. He watched them fascinated. He did not realize that such occasions were the only times when the sexual act was openly performed. Like a fool, he thought it was the effects of the drink. And he thought of Reflection/Leaf, because he had no sense of status or of honour.

He began to hunt around the feast, gazing at couples, bursting into groups of friends, interrupting drinking parties. Cutter/Wing-beat watched him with his face lined with the channel of tears.

When Peccary/Root and Reflection/Leaf were discovered by the idiot she had lain down ready to receive him. The idiot lurched forward, tried to pull Peccary/Root away, and fell in the dust. Reflection/Leaf scrambled away and Peccary/Root gave a great cry of fear.

The feast fell silent. Only the crackle of the flames could be heard.

They all shuffled away from the fallen idiot and watched him. Many shook with fear. All of them were tense, waiting to see what would happen now. They waited to see what he really was.

He stood up, the dust scattered across his lunatic patterns. He was decked out with sacrilege. His eyes glittered with dishonour. They all saw he was a demon, the destroyer of crops, the polluter of fruit. He held the book in front of him like a shield.

The tribes gave a loud cry of recognition and distress. The demon was among them. He spread his hands. Power crackled and spat within him. He could split the tribes apart, explode them from within as lightning shatters a tree. He could summon up forest floods, make evil frogs apear from nowhere, bring fire raging through the trees, invade them with other gods, scatter disease and death. He took their nobility and their honour and tensed himself against it. They could all feel the force of his will. It was huge and terrifying, like nothing they had ever felt before.

The warriors ran towards the demon. He flailed at them but there were enough of them to bring him down.They could feel his body pulse with evil. It burned their hands but they hung on to him.

The warriors took the demon and ran with him to the edge of the compound. He kicked and shouted but they did not dare drop him in case he turned into an animal and ran away. At the edge of the feast they held him face down so that he could not look at the sun.

Villagers swarmed into their own parts of the giant hut and ran with clubs to where the demon was pinned down. They gathered round him and, while others held his hands and feet, they clubbed him many times.

They thought it would take a demon longer to die.

When they were sure he was dead they drew back, scared at what had happened. Cutter/Wingbeat, sobbing, pulled the demon's head back by the hair and sliced his throat apart. Then he threw the knife away because he knew that now it would be poisoned.

He walked across to Badwrist/Shoulder. Badwrist/Shoulder was standing with his cousin. The cousin was holding him up.

Cutter/Wingbeat said nothing, but after a short while he leaned forward and embraced Badwrist/Shoulder. Badwrist/Shoulder shook heavily, a leaf in a storm; Cutter/Wingbeat absorbed his shudders as he would a brother's. He felt them transferred through his own body, felt them safely passed down into the earth.

The ground was polluted so the village had to be destroyed. Before the put it to the fire they collected Cutter/Wingbeat's father's bones so they could be taken in a calabash and buried at the centre of the new village. Then the tribal families said their goodbyes and those who had built the village began to burn it. As the flames ran up the walls and across the roof, Reflection/Leaf and Badwrist/Shoulder went to see the idiot's body. They wanted to make their peace with him, but he was no longer recognizable. From head to toe he was covered in thousands of ants. A few strays were examining the empty book that lay at arm's length away from the body. Badwrist/Shoulder picked up the book and flung it into the heart of the fire. The ants continued to seethe over their find.

After several days' trek through the forest the Javarunu came to a place where the water was sweet, the fruit thick, the poison trees rich in sap. They cleared a large area for the new village and several smaller areas for the gardens. They wanted everything to be finished before the rains. It was built as all the other villages had been built, and as the next one would be. They lashed poles together, covered them with thatch, tested them by standing at their tips and flexing their bodies up and down. Hearths began to glow around the central area and soon a few men could be spared to go out hunting. After ten days the village was settled and secure enough for Cutter/Wingbeat to be able to bury the ashes at its centre.

The rains came.

Before they were over Reflection/Leaf went out into the forest and gave birth to the idiot's child. It was a boy. She killed it by putting a leaf down its throat.

A year or more later, Reflection/Leaf returned on her own to the site of the old village. The forest had already begun to reclaim it. Like all the other sites of abandoned villages, the place had become a thicket of grasses, shrubs, saplings and thorns.

The demon had gone and he was merely an idiot again. His ghost hid behind a tree and would not speak to her, even though she could see it plainly as it peered nervously at her. When she walked towards it the ghost ran away and hid behind another tree, so she left some food for it in the place where it had died. After she had gone it would come nervously out of hiding and eat it in the ungainly, wasteful way of the idiot.

22

Cutter/Wingbeat struck off from the little-used, overgrown trail and Badwrist/Shoulder followed him. They passed under trees heavy with gloom and a screen of head-high plants with open-throated flowers. Pollen spilled from them and thickened the air. Badwrist/Shoulder did not know where he was being taken but followed Cutter/Wingbeat's broad back as it was dappled with sun then plunged into gloom obscured by fronds and shoots and trunks.

After a while they came to a place with smooth-barked trees that had sides knotted where branches had fallen. Creepers rooted in the springy, slippery ground had snaked up them to their very tops. Sunlight penetrated the tree canopy and illuminated the forest in diagonal shafts, as in a cathedral.

Cutter/Wingbeat prowled around the bases of several trees, from time to time glancing upwards. Every now and then he tested the trees by slapping them, fingering the bark, sniffing them, putting his ear to them.

Badwrist/Shoulder watched and said nothing.

Cutter/Wingbeat began to brace himself against the trunks, and hoist himself on to them. He stood on the creepers, his hands balancing his body, his eyes scanning the higher reaches of the forest. The branches were interlaced in impenetrable knots or left sudden, open spaces into thin air.

Finally he decided which tree was best and began to climb it, rhythmically and steadily, his machete hanging at his side.

Badwrist/Shoulder followed him, testing his balance and strength on the securely fastened helix of a creeper. The higher he climbed the more exposed he felt. When he paused for breath and looked down the perspectives were dizzying. The tree he was climbing narrowed away from him as if, top-heavy, it would fall;

the ground seemed both to recede and advance like some optical puzzle.

They moved upwards through a patch of sunlight that was hot on the skin. Marauding spiders ran out of their way. All along the trunk were tiny holes drilled by insects, and at one place there was a series of sharp incisions, made by teeth or claws.

Eventually they stopped. It was in a thicket of branches that were difficult to climb through but which gave a sense of protection and security. The trees had assumed new shapes here, as if dozens of galls had sent the branches off into crazy directions. Badwrist/Shoulder felt he was in a bewitched area. He rubbed his feet on the bark to get rid of the sweat. When he looked down the ground could only just be seen, an amorphous, characterless blend of grey and green and brown.

Cutter/Wingbeat edged himself against the trunk and wedged himself in. He was going to spend some time there. When Badwrist/Shoulder looked at him he pointed outwards.

The object had bent the trees and torn them and sent them into strange directions. Now it lay supported and harnessed in a cradle on intertwined branches. Foliage shielded it and flowers bloomed on its mossy, fungal surface.

Badwrist/Shoulder had a lightness within his ribcage; his brain felt as if it were dizzily coming to its senses for the first time. The place was heavy with magic. It tingled among the leaves.

It was quite easy to reach the main body of the plane. The trees which held it aloft had thickened over the years so that the branches were broad enough to support him without difficulty. The plane was even fastened, like the victim of a serpent, by a creeper which looped around it before heading upwards along the branch of another tree.

Badwrist/Shoulder edged forward. The cage of branches must have trembled ever so slightly, because he noticed the leaves give a tiny shudder. Soon he was beside the wreck.

Now that he had moved into the aircraft's presence he was no longer afraid of the height. They seemed suspended somewhere between earth and sky. The noise of the high-flying insects was rhythmic and heavy as a scent.

He brushed a section of the wing with the back of his hand and large, thin cakes of moss fell away. Underneath them the wing seemed delicate, as brittle as paper, but when he pressed on it with his fingers they did not go through; instead he felt resilience still in the body.

He moved along the flying edge of the wing. Halfway along the impact had snapped it. Plants had rooted in the fracture and marked it by a line of bright blue flowers.

Around the nose there were gaps in the branch support, and Badwrist/Shoulder had to move carefully. Beneath the lattice-work he could make out the ground, indistinct and without detail. The nose was bulbous, shapeless. At its base it was split apart.

Part of the fuselage was missing. If he knelt slowly on the branches he could lean along the underside of the plane and place his hand into it. As soon as he did so he disturbed a colony of tree rats, which burst squealing out of the hole and scattered furiously along the radiating branches, vanishing into the foilage. Their sudden appearance shocked him and he lay still for a while, prostrate beneath the mouldering body of the plane. Cutter/Wingbeat watched him but came no nearer.

There was no sign of life when he thrust his hand into the hole again. Just the touch of rot and, when he sniffed his fingers, the faraway, buried smell of metal and oil.

To get to the top of the plane he had to edge his way like a mountaineer past thick leaves that sprouted like a shrub in the joint of body and wing. Once past this he was able to step gingerly on to the wing itself. He was surprised when it took his weight. He had feared he could plunge straight through it.

He stood in a patch of hot sunlight for a moment, then edged his way on to the broken back of the plane.

The cockpit was closed.

He had expected it to be gouged apart and shattered, but instead of that the perspex shell was complete, although mould made it opaque.

Badwrist/Shoulder eased himself into a better position and scraped some of the dirt from the cockpit. The rotted wood was as crumbly as soil and showered down on either side of the fuselage. Still the cockpit was covered on the inside by moisture and endless specks of green, like algae. He could not see into it at all.

He took hold of the canopy. It did not feel as if it had been opened for a very long time.

At first it would not move, but he put all his strength behind it and the cockpit began to open. The moss squelched and the metal made a low, trembling groan. His arms ached with the strain and it felt as if his head would burst. The cockpit edged open, little by little. When it would move no further he craned himself up and looked inside it.

The entire cockpit, from side to side and down as far as he could see, was full of white mushroom-like fungus. It sprouted from everywhere, from the sides, from the panel, the seat, the controls. There was nothing but ghostly stalks and heads and a smell of damp and thick decay. Nothing but fungus.

Badwrist/Shoulder plunged his hands into the mass. He felt the stalks snap weakly around him. He swept his hand from side to side, searching for anything that might remain of the pilot. The fungus broke and tumbled, some of it loosing spore clouds. It fell and clogged the cockpit further. After only a few swings of his arm so many stalks had been snapped, so many fungus heads tumbled, that the enclosed space was an impenetrable mass of them. Their whiteness was eerily bright, as if it would, at night, throw off a phosphorescent glow.

He withdrew his arm. It felt cool and damp. Where the ropes had scored his wrists there was a wet mottling of greenish powder. He felt tainted.

Cutter/Wingbeat asked him nothing when he returned. Together they climbed down the tree.

When they were back on the ground Badwrist/Shoulder looked up into the branches. Cutter/Wingbeat motioned him to a particular place. Sunlight and darkness dappled his skin. He pointed upwards.

The sun was directly above the plane, delineating it in its web of branches. It was in the shape of a crucifix.

Badwrist/Shoulder stood in the shade of the cross for a while, and then moved away.

Before they left, Cutter/Wingbeat placed some food in a little bowl at the foot of one of the trees.

23

The rumours have been speaking loudly. The tribe are uneasy as they move through the forest to the site of another new village. They half-expect to meet the monsters with steel teeth that consume everything.

Cautious, a little frightened, they halt. Some say there is a smell in the air. The same smell, the older ones say, that the aeroplane gave. They stand sniffing the air, tasting it.

Three of them go forward. Badwrist/Shoulder spends some time with a strange metal thing that he spins and clicks and whirrs.

After some time they meet men with light skin, moustaches and steel carapaces across their heads, as if they are part-armadillo. They stand among mud and smashed wood. Behind them yellow monsters crouch and stumble across rows of snapped-off trees. The monsters roar and give off thin, throat-tightening smoke. The whole place reeks of them.

Badwrist/Shoulder hangs back but Cutter/Wingbeat and Peccary/Root go forward, half-appalled, half-amazed at such power and newness. For a while they stand face to face with the whites. Each group is fascinated by, and wary of, the other. All the Javarunu senses have been thrown awry and are working strangely. Here they can see the world cast off its old skin and take on a new, disturbing shape.

And suddenly there is a scuffle. Hands reach out, bodies collide, a machete is raised in the air, there is a terrifying bang and smoke.

Badwrist/Shoulder, well away from all the others, raises the gun and fires. He alone makes it back to the tribe.

The bodies of Cutter/Wingbeat and Peccary/Root are emasculated and bulldozed into a ditch. The companions of the dead white man want to bury him under a cross, so they drive him back along a muddy track. On either side of the track, for mile after mile, huge pyres of felled trees blaze and smoulder. There is a pall of smoke covering the entire sky. Thick flakes of soot fall from the air like black snow, covering everything.

Some of the tribe say that there are riches to be found among the whites, that they have control of things the Javarunu have never even dreamed of.

Only a short time later, a matter of months, Song/Distantbird is dead. A disease the tribe has never seen before makes her shiver, be sick, lose control of her bowels. She dies after three days. The tribe cannot understand it and none of their medicines work. Nor can they save the others who fall ill with the same mysterious sickness.

A few more months after this and Reflection/Leaf has become a beggar. She haunts a township of plastic and corrugated iron, with a gutter running through its middle which carries sewage and motor oil. When it rains the soil is stripped away so the channel always widens. Transistors fill the air with tinny distant music. Reflection/Leaf ransacks the plastic bags of rubbish that the whites throw out. Or she begs food from them when they sit outside with their bottles and cigars. Sometimes they feel sorry for her and give her scraps, but often they throw things at her and spit on her. She never flinches.

Noisyfrog sells herself for cigarettes, fizzy drinks, sugared food, and raw spirits. She has a one-room shack of boards with a tin roof. It stands to one side of the town. Sometimes, on paydays, the men queue outside, swaying with drink and joking with each other. She wonders if they all came here because they saw, from their own land, the figure of the dead airman beckon them from above the trees.

Every two or three months Brother Mark comes to see them. It takes a long time to get to them, he says, but he expects this might improve when proper roads are put in and the land begins to be farmed. Reflection/Leaf will have nothing to do with him but the younger members of what used to be the Javarunu do what he asks them to do. They kneel with their hands clasped and their mouths open and he puts strange food on their tongues. Noisyfrog is among them.

Sometimes Noisyfrog dreams of Badwrist/Shoulder. It is said that he went further into the forest. Some say he will return one day and walk through the wastelands, and that where he treads the trees will spring up again, the birds and animals return, the air become sweet, the streams fresh.

She lies under a heavy, pale thrusting body and dreams that he will come back and make everything all right.

Life closes behind Sophie, Toby, Jorge. After Sophie's death the church receives the house she left to it. There is a little brass plaque on the door now, and from the outside that seems the only change. But Becky has left. They did not want her to stay. She has married a new boyfriend, not told him about Jorge, and gone.

Now further telephone lines and a telex have been installed. And, as befits an international organization, they have computerized records and plans. A map on the wall shows that the church is active in almost all the poorer countries of the world. Several officials, two wardens, and many overnight visitors stop at the house.

Most of the library has been crated. Some of it has been sold. The bookseller Toby met at his interview has bought most of the travel and children's books, and made a handsome profit from reselling them. Their places on the shelves have been taken up by gospel commentaries and manuals on conversion.

Dexter's diaries and Toby's notes on his life have been put together in the same box and stored indefinitely in the attic. No one is interested in them now.

After his disappearance Lucy forgives Toby, cannot forget him, wonders if somehow he will return, but realizes he was just a part of her life, not all of it.

Just a chapter.

She finds someone, they go out to exhibitions and the theatre, but they do not live with each other. Nevertheless, they wonder if marriage, and children, will work.

And Lucy seeks out Rachel. She feels she needs to see her, just once.

Rachel has already written one novel, a thin work about academic self-doubt and amibition. Now, unexpectedly, she has produced a thick, intense, visionary book. Lucy find out that she is signing copies at a large bookshop. She stands there with her copy in her hand.

They exchange cautious glances, and ask about each other's health, what they are doing now, and whatever happened to Toby. Then they part, never to see each other again.

Lucy sits at home and opens the new novel.

Immediately she can see that Rachel has used, or stolen, things that Toby must have told her about the Parnabys and Jorge. But everything has been changed round, and the central characters are two women who may in fact be the same woman. One inhabits a world of literary and academic infighting at a new English university, the other lives in a tribal world of tight social structure, bizarre ritual and sympathetic magic somewhere in the South American rain forest.

Lucy does not like it. She reads the reviews; to some critics it is a powerful merger of European naturalism and Latin American fabulism, but Lucy finds it unappealingly erudite. She might have expected Rachel to produce something that was constructed in accordance with a mechanistic theory.

But she keeps hearing about the book. It becomes a cult, then a boom. Many readers take it more than seriously; others incorporate its images into works of their own; students refer to it in theses; the fashionable carry it around with them; the film rights are sold.

Such is the book's fame that one or two people even try to find its hallucinatory magic land. They never get there. They sit in shanty towns, their tattered copies in their hands, for ever waiting for the way to clear. Around them, remorselessly, the destruction of the Indian continues.